A DRAGON'S CHAINS

BOOK ONE OF THE REMEMBERED WAR

ROBERT VANE

To the Lvoff family, friends in the storm.

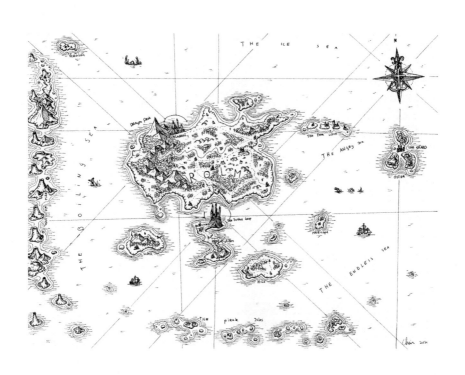

ONE

I wanted to eat a human.

Not just any human, of course. One of the plump ones with a bulging belly. A lord would be the best. They came frequently to visit the king's city of Eladrell, wearing colorful clothing and shiny metal trinkets. My fellow dragons and I carried many of these oversized humans on our backs, helping them cross the sea from their keeps on the scattered islands of the kingdom, so they could appear before the king to rub their knees and hands on his polished marble floor (which then had to be cleaned by other, skinnier humans).

During their visits, these lords feasted on the best that the royal larder had to offer: baby lambs from the plains of Harcourt, huge kingfish pulled each day from the Thunder Straits, and roasted goats from the Northern Range. They drank cup after cup of dark ale until they belched out foul wind arising from their bellies as if it were dragon fire.

Rich, delicious, exquisite ale.

The Keepers who lived with us on DragonPeak never shared their ale. Even our ryders withheld that secret pleasure drink from our bottomless stomachs. But two moons ago, I got lucky. A stray barrel had fallen off the back of a supply wagon, shattering on the winding cobblestone pathway outside Lord Big Gut's keep (that might not have been the lord's actual name), while I was waiting for my ryder to return with the lord himself. The wagon driver hadn't stopped. I, helpfully, cleaned up the mess with my massive tongue. None of the lord's human servants had bothered to thank me for ensuring that Lord Big Gut's pathway was dry.

One barrel was all it had taken for me to understand why humans spent so much time drinking from their cups each day. After I'd finished every last drop (and chewed the broken wooden barrel into pulp) my belly sang and my head swirled.

The return flight with Lord Big Gut on my back was a hazy memory. As I lay on the rocky ground of my cave on DragonPeak, I remembered only two things clearly: one was the sharp commands of Jona, my ryder, echoing in my head as I tried to keep steady in the unusual winds that had been shaking the sky that afternoon, and the other was Lord Big Gut puking onto Jona's feet the moment he slid out of the saddle that had secured him to my back during the flight. I had rolled away from the stink, lying on my back, trying to determine why the sky still shook even though I was on land. My ryder thought me mad, or at least sick. He was wrong on both counts.

For weeks before that night, the human voices that echoed in my head had been fading, but after my binge of ale, the unwanted clamor was finally silenced. My mind hadn't been addled by the fine drink—it had been cleared. Despite the binding rune carved onto my chest, no human commanded me. That morning, I vowed I would never go back to what I had been almost since birth: a slave dragon. Somehow, I had been set free.

Today was not as fine a day as that one had been.

Foremost among my complaints: there was no ale. I missed it. Next, I had a human on my back rather than in my mouth. Even if he had been in my mouth, all that metal armor would've made him a lousy meal, and I doubted this particular human was worth eating anyway. He was my ryder, Jona. He knew as much about fine dining as a fish did about flying. Despite having access to the privileges of a dragon ryder, instead of tasty meat, Jona often ate strange protrusions that grew from the ground—the tiny green stalks that looked like stunted trees and misshapen brown orbs that resembled giant goat crap that human farmers dug out of the dirt (the humans called them potatoes). To top it all off, Jona often stank of the sour aroma of pommice fruit, which he constantly ate even though its bitter flesh made even hungry chickens waddle away in terror. I suspected that Jona would taste no better than chicken feathers. Not that I wanted to eat those, either.

In addition to not being my lunch, Jona also yelled at me to do things, none of which I particularly wanted to do. He often did that. He thought he was my master. He wasn't—not since that day of my great ale celebration—but Jona didn't know what had happened to me and I couldn't let him find out. That would mean my death, or worse. Jona was a dragon ryder sworn to King Mendakas, and all the king's dragons were slaves. Except me.

Jona's penetrating voice screeched at me. "Bayloo, dive!"

Humans called me Bayloo. I knew it wasn't my real name because it sounded so strange to me. I had to stretch my jaw to say it properly. Humans didn't think about the trouble they caused when they named us. Of course, there were plenty of noises dragons could make that humans couldn't have uttered if their lives depended on it. For example: our roar. Humans sounded ridiculous when they tried. A human roar was less fearsome than a dragon's fart.

Still, I had to keep playing my part. There had been a raid on the Kingdom of Rolm—an attack on the humans' precious grain stores—and Jona and I had been sent by King Mendakas to find and destroy the interlopers.

I dipped my head, tilted my wings, and dove just as Jona ordered, heading toward the rolling waves of the Oren Sea beneath me. I'd made steeper dives, but the wind was picking up, and I wanted to keep things smooth. Jona never appreciated how considerate I was of his well-being. Even though a dragon saddle included sturdy leather straps, humans—even specially conditioned dragon ryders—tended to overestimate their own ability to remain seated and conscious during attack dives.

I couldn't see Jona as we flew, but I knew his face as well as I knew the look of any human—he had a pair of tiny eyes with gray centers that never changed color, a squashed nose that only made noise when he was sick, and a mouth with teeth so small he had to eat asparagus, potatoes, and pommice fruit because he couldn't chew bones. A bit of black fur grew on his head and he seemed to think the length and direction of the fur's growth mattered. He fussed over his hair like a mother hen tending chicks. Like all humans, he lacked a tail and couldn't breathe anything but a bit of stinky air (not that every creature needs to breathe fire to be worthy). He was condescending to me and my kind and believed himself far more capable in battle than was merited, but at least he wasn't cruel to me or other dragons. That hadn't been the case with my other ryders.

The runes that had been sculpted onto Jona's chest, in a pattern that resembled my own markings, made him my ryder—the human who commanded me. At least they had until recently. When Jona spoke, his voice echoed inside my head, which was particularly horrible because he also had the annoying habit of speaking every instruction as if it were the decisive action in a great war. The runes on each of our bodies created a link between us. I'd never known life without a human in my thoughts. Like all slave dragons, I'd been carved during the first moon of life. Three moons was the longest time that the malicious Sculptors could put control-runes on a dragon. After that, our scales were too hard, our will too strong, and bad things happened to Sculptors who tried to control mature dragons. Humans could be carved at any time because they were soft (or perhaps because they weren't being enslaved by the runes). Jona was my fifth ryder, but he was the first that I didn't need to obey.

"The lead ship is our target!"

It was another brilliant tactical decision by my ryder; there were only two ships. Still, I kept my opinions closely guarded. Even if that hadn't been essential for my own safety, I would've done it to avoid hurting Jona's feelings. I realized he meant well. He just didn't realize that I knew more about fighting than he did.

Humans get excited in battle; they behave as if they have a major role in the actual fighting, as if they were able to fly or do something useful like that. The two-legged beasts could barely manage to travel from one island to another within their own kingdom without us, much less destroy anything. This engagement was no different.

A pair of warships plied the rolling waters beneath me. From my perspective in the clouds, the vessels appeared as tiny specks on the vastness of the sea. As I plunged through the air, the targets grew larger and I could make out more details. Both were twin mast vessels, forty oars to each ship. They flew no flag. That could've meant they were raiders with no allegiance to any kingdom, but I've seen more than my share of raiders, and these ships didn't have the look. Their hulls were too well cared for, their decks too orderly. Each also had a shiny rotating ballista mounted on its foredeck. Even the pirate king, Halfhand, didn't have such weapons; these ships had been built by skilled shipwrights, their ballistae made in large ship-yard forges. Definitely not pirate ships.

Once I got us close, even Jona's tiny human eyes spotted the dangerous weapons. "Bayloo, take out the rear vessel instead. Come at them low and from behind. Their own sails will shield our approach."

Again, Jona thought he was helping me with this advice, but the lead ship had already spotted me and fired its first arc-bolt. I banked left. Jona grabbed one of the hard spikes on my mane to steady himself. I hated when he did that, but I understood—I ripped through the sky at tremendous speed while the closest thing Jona had to wings were two hairless ears that protruded from his skull. At this range, I doubted if one of those arc-bolts could've pierced my scales, but there was always the possibility of a lucky (or unlucky, from my perspec-tive) shot finding its way into one of the gaps in my armor. Even if it hit my well-protected belly, those things hurt.

The projectile missed me by the length of two dragon tails. I came out of my turn fast and angry; if the ships' captains hadn't realized their peril the moment my shadow first passed over them, they did now. Oars splashed frantically as the vessels attempted to put space between each other, hoping that at least one would escape. I resumed my dive, swerving as I plunged. The more distant of the two ships had its own ballista poised but held its fire. It wanted me closer. Wish granted.

I turned again, circling around the first of the imposter-raiders. Bowmen lined the deck in neat, disciplined lines. I didn't care about them or their puny little stick hurlers.

Jona chimed in with another of his astute observations. "Beware their arrows!"

He might as well have commanded the archers to fire. As he spoke, dozens of projectiles flew at me. I twisted my belly toward the fusillade of prickly sticks, beating my wings with as much force as I could muster. The gusts of wind my effort generated disrupted the trajectory of the arrows hurtling toward me. Most missed, dropping into the ocean. The few that reached me barely tickled my scales.

"The ballista is the threat, not the archers," I told Jona, speaking with my mind through our rune-link rather than my mouth. Since my ale-awakening, I'd tried to avoid using the link as much as possible. I sensed certain emotions from Jona when he spoke to me using the magic of the rune-link and I worried the reverse might be the case as well.

Jona shifted in his saddle. I'd been flying humans around long enough to recognize his purpose—he was pulling himself to his feet to stand in the stirrups and fire his bow. A moment later, Jona loosed an arrow. It moved through the sky with the speed of a diving hawk, its path straight and true. The projectile's tip passed through the ballista trigger-man's neck. Jona had already launched a second shot before the first had even struck. That arrow took out the second ballista operator. Humans weren't always useless, just most of the time. I had no complaints about Jona's archery. Those little fingers were adept at plucking their clever little contraptions, even if they lacked the strength of a dragon's claw-tipped digits.

Without the threat of the ballista's arc-bolts to hold me at bay, the ship didn't have much of a chance. I circled around my floating prey, flexing my claws in anticipation. I gave my wings a modest flap as I went in for the kill. My ideal attack speed matched that of a diving owl—fast but not too fast. A few of the crew jumped overboard before I even got there. I was flattered by their fear. I hadn't even roared.

I sank the claws of my forelegs into the wooden hull of the ship. I could've squeezed and crushed parts of the upper deck into a collection of toothpicks, but that wouldn't sink the ship. I would've had to circle all the way around again and make a second attack on the vessel, during which time I'd be a target for the other ship's ballista. Not to mention that I didn't feel like flying in unnecessary circles listening to Jona make obvious comments. Instead, I dug my claws deeper, gripping the hull. Then I beat my wings—hard. The ship jerked violently as I yanked one side upwards. Or at least, I tried to yank it. The ship was heavier than I'd anticipated—its cargo hold must've been full, or the crew were particularly plump. For a quick moment I felt myself dropping toward the deck. I beat my wings hard enough to create a squall of wind. The sea trembled violently; water flew into the sky. Finally, the vessel yielded to my strength. I tipped the ship onto its side, its keel coming out of the water like a hooked fish. The remaining crew spilled into the waves. I could've plucked a couple of big humans out of the water for tasting, but that would've given the game away to Jona. Slave dragons didn't feast on humans due to a reasonable fear of starting bad habits. Fine.

I soared upward, spinning as I went, tucking my wings in close to my body after each heave to make myself a smaller target. I needn't have bothered. The remaining ship had gone into a full flee-for-our-lives operation. Its first tactic was trying to hide. A distinctive yellow smoke emitted by billow-stones rose into the air on the eastern horizon. The rising smog was thick and acrid enough to burn a dragon's lungs when inhaled. Big, beautiful dragon eyes like mine were particularly sensitive to its effect. The fleeing ship turned directly into the wind, hoping to escape behind the rapidly expanding smoke wall.

"Perhaps we should let them go," Jona said, speaking more to himself than me. "Let them crawl away with a bit of the grain in their holds. They paid a heavy price in blood for whatever booty they managed to steal in this raid."

I decided to answer honestly, glad not to use our rune-link. "Raiders wouldn't have billow-stones or ballistae on their ships."

Had I shown too much independent thought?

Jona didn't notice. "Yes, they are almost certainly King Galt's men. They row hard, moving east, in the general direction of their home in Oster."

"I'm faster, and I do not fear their yellow smoke." That's what a slave dragon would've said. I had no idea why I said it. Old habits faded slowly. Why did I care if the Osterans managed to sulk off with a bit of King Mendakas' precious grain in their hold? I wasn't even sure why the humans cared so much about that stuff. I knew they made bread out of it—which tasted slightly better than asparagus and potatoes—but it still wasn't meat or ale. Certainly, it wasn't worth getting killed over.

"They'll be past the outer atolls soon, into the open sea. The Osterans may have other ships out there, their best four mast warships."

I didn't see his point.

Just stay out of it, I reminded myself. *There are worse things than flying back to Eladrell before dark.* The Keepers would have goat scraps for me to eat. It would be mostly bones, of course, because the humans took the best parts for themselves, but still better than being hit with an arc-bolt. I was about to turn back toward Eladrell when Jona opened his little mouth again.

"Those Osteran ships might even have furies aboard. You're not a fire-breather, so I don't want to risk a solo confrontation against a fleet at sea."

Oh. That.

Both of my hearts began pumping fiery blood through me. I'd heard similar words all my life. I was the only ash dragon who couldn't breathe fire. Always that was thrown at me, as if I was somehow less than the others. Now, even Jona joined the chorus of doubters. I turned my head in the direction of the fleeing vessel. "I can see the other ship. They're alone, no other fleet in sight," I said.

I lied. I couldn't see the fleeing ship, or anything else, but Jona didn't know that. Dragons have far better sight than humans, and slave dragons can't lie. It turned out I could lie, and apparently, I was good at it.

Pretending that Jona's silence was the same as his approval, I flew toward the smoke shield. I never would've done that with any other ryder even if I could've, but Jona was a gentler sort of human. I thought I could get away with it. I flew as if I cared about the Osterans stealing my king's grain. While I couldn't spit flames out of my mouth, I was faster than my brethren. My wingspan was wider than almost any other dragon—nearly as wide as the highest spire in Eladrell was tall. I could outfly any dragon, even mighty Traxis. My claws were sharper, my digits more versatile, and my eyesight superior to theirs, particularly at night. Also, my farts smelled better than theirs. The other dragons could keep their fire. I didn't need it.

I punctured the perimeter of the curtain of yellow smoke with a burst of speed. I could barely see within the cloud—the dense fumes made my eyes a stinging mess. That wasn't the worst of it, however. Usually, I didn't need to see to fly—if I'd been to a place once, I could find it again. But billow-stone smog fouled my directional abilities. I had no idea where I was going, despite my speed. However, I still had an excellent plan: wait for the humans to panic.

Jona was probably correct that whoever had planned this raid on Rolm would have considered the possibility of being pursued by one of King Mendakas' dragons. There was also a decent chance that Jona was right about those Osteran ships waiting out at sea and having furies aboard. A part of me acknowledged that it was rather decent of him to give any consideration to the danger furies posed to me—none of my other ryders would've done that.

Dragons hated furies—the creatures had been bred specifically by Oster to kill us. Once released, the deadly bug-like fliers flew faster than arc-bolts. If a fury caught a dragon, they latched onto our scales and bored through our armor until they reached our soft flesh. Then they used their poison stingers. I'd once heard a ryder describe furies as massive killer bees, except that the bug-hybrids lacked the important benefit of producing honey (which humans also never shared with dragons).

I guessed the captain of the fleeing ship would sail for what he believed to be the protection of the Osteran navy. So, where would King Galt's ships anchor themselves?

The most direct route between Rolm and Oster would be to sail southeast. However, those waters were filled with rocky shoals where colonies of nearly invisible ghastrays made their home. Better to bathe in dragon fire than sail into a pod of ghastrays. Any sensible ship's captain would avoid those waters. I reasoned a better place to anchor a fleet would be in the open sea east of Rolm's outer isles. Pretending I could see the fleeing ship, that's where I headed—flying in the opposite direction of the dropping sun.

I dove down near the water, flying close enough that my claws could've scraped the waves if I'd stretched them. I could barely see, but that wasn't necessary. Those holes on the side of my head allowed me to hear far more than human ears ever could, and they didn't stick out like the silly side sails attached to humans. All I had to do was glide and listen for the sound of oars being rowed by frightened sailors. It took about ten beats of my hearts before I found them.

Their swift little ship had covered more sea than I had expected. I adjusted my course based on the sounds of splashing oars. A wiser captain would've taken a different course so he could use his sails, sacrificing speed for stealth. Like I said, count on humans to panic.

When I swooped out of the billow-stone-generated cloud, I was so close to the ship I could see the terrified expressions on the crew's little faces. I hadn't realized human eyes could get that big. They were all so stunned they stopped rowing. My experience destroying the previous ship made me wary of trying to flip this one over. Also, its ballista was poised and ready. I saw no fury cages on deck, so I made the machine my priority. On my first pass, I extended my claws as far as I could and tore the ballista off the deck. I accidentally grabbed the man trying to fire it as well. He screamed as I dropped him and his machine into the sea. I made an arcing loop back toward the ship. A portion of the vessel's crew was already jumping in the water. Given my size, they probably assumed I was a fire-breather. Only a few intrepid archers readied themselves to meet my next pass.

Jona eventually noticed the arrows. "Beware the arrows."

I flew in low, this time smashing my foreleg's claws into the side of the ship. I also tore the top off the mast. That was the end for the ship and its crew, unless another vessel sailed into the area to rescue them. They were taking on water and had lost their sail. I could've left it at that. I *should've* left it at that, but instead, I made one more pass, intending to make an even larger hole in the ship's hull. A fire-breather wouldn't have allowed the ship to survive; I didn't intend to either.

I swooped down. There was no one left on deck to oppose me; the surviving sailors were all splashing in the ominous green water. With all the noise they were making, they better hope there wasn't a leviathan nearby. I hit the ship again, this time dragging the claws of my hind legs through the wood of its hull. The timbers shattered. I flew upward, satisfied with my work.

"Arc-bolt!" Jona shouted.

I banked, twisting my body in an effort to change my course and avoid the projectile. I hadn't seen it—the damn thing had not come from the fleeing vessel but rather had been fired by some other ship hiding in the billow-stone haze. Not all humans are stupid; some are cunning. The bolt clipped my tail. It hurt, but it could've been worse. I'd been sloppy. A volley of arrows followed the arc-bolt. I turned again, avoiding about half of the incoming wave of projectiles. The rest bounced off the scale armor of my back and tail. I still didn't know the location of the enemy ship or if there was more than one. I beat my wings with purpose, heading straight up toward the clouds. Ten powerful flaps put me high enough to be out of range of any arc-bolts. Even furies couldn't fly as high as I could.

Once back in comparative safety above the clouds, I waited for Jona to tell me to return home. We'd accomplished our mission. There was no point in attacking the Osteran navy through clouds of billow smoke. That was what he should've told me. But he didn't speak.

"Jona?"

No answer.

I tried the rune-link. Still nothing.

Uh-oh.

TWO

I flew for home.

Once I'd crossed back into the safety of Rolman waters, I twisted my neck around to get a better look at Jona. He had an arrow sticking out of him. The tip had found the gap between his helm and chest plate and lodged itself into the soft flesh beneath. Blood covered Jona's neck and chest; his eyes were shut. Only the leather saddle straps kept him from falling off my back. The sound of his labored breath told me he lived, for now. I turned my attention back to the sky ahead, pushing myself for speed. If the winds cooperated, I could be back at Eladrell—home of the best healers in Rolm—by sunset.

Racing against the fading day, I cut through the sky, something akin to panic surging through me. Jona irked me like a stubborn fly constantly buzzing around my nostrils, but I didn't want him to die. To my surprise, the worry was a throbbing ache in my hearts. I wondered if I should care about a human or not. I had my doubts. *Is my concern for Jona caused by our link or is it really me?*

I kept pushing for ever more speed. Whether my worry for my ryder was a legacy of the magic runes that bonded us, the result was that I did little but fret about Jona as the sea rolled beneath me, my mind consumed by his welfare. I had lost ryders before, so I knew the horror of the death of one linked to me. But as the easternmost island of what had once been the Free Cities of Toth came into view, a singular thought crept into my head, stealthy and dark: *Why should I care about a human?*

I pushed the notion away, but the idea was persistent. My blood heated as this forbidden feeling tickled the inside of my head. This was something a slave could not even consider ... yet, I could.

I contemplated the race that had enslaved me, shackling me with invisible chains so terrible that I had not even suspected the horror that had been done to me and my kind. These humans could not fly, they could barely see, and they grew hair from their noses and ears. I could kill any man with the flick of my tail. Yet because of their magic, the humans dominated us. Was that right?

I didn't think so.

Human voices have echoed inside my head from the time of my earliest memories. Almost every meal was brought to me by human Keepers on DragonPeak. I listened to them speak, laugh, and argue year after year from the confines of my cave. I knew humans better than I knew my own kind. Some humans—my ryders—were almost extensions of myself. With a newly free mind, I considered these two-legged creatures. I found them lacking.

Four ryders had preceded Jona, each coming to an untimely end (none were my fault). Hadrial had been first. He taught me Avian, the language that we used to communicate with our human masters because their common tongue was impossible for dragon mouths to mimic. The memory of his brutal mind was like a searing hot branding iron that had imprinted itself inside me. To Hadrial, I was a hound to be trained, to be taught obedience, to be used and to be sacrificed when necessary. My inability to breathe fire had been a slight to him, one for which he had never forgiven me. He'd died in the flames of a dragon's breath on the high peaks of the island of

Veralon, the island from which all my brethren were stolen, while trying to take a hatchling from its mother's nest. Only now did I appreciate the justice in the manner of his death.

Two other ryders followed Hadrial over the next two years: Geron and Ladrel. Geron was careless with a harpoon during a fight with a large leviathan. I was told that Ladrel had died in an alley in Eladrell during a dispute over weighted dice. Who knew those little number cubes could be so dangerous? Both men had been equal parts cruel and condescending.

Next was Karthus. The man had lived for battle. I was a slave to his commands, but over the years, through the link that eroded my will, his purpose had become mine as well: to kill. I could still hear his favorite words echo in my mind: "I give the mercy of death."

He said it every time we fought.

Together, Karthus and I won some great victories. In my eighth year, we helped smash the Free Cities of Toth, bringing their shattered remnants into the domain of Rolm. Karthus had laughed at the screams as each of the three cities burned, speaking his favorite words as I, his instrument, circled overhead. Five years after that, we had fought the mighty nation of Ulibon and its so-called Highstar, conquering that land in a vicious campaign that had cost the lives of no less than six of my fellow ash dragons, and twice that number of smaller horned dragons (who can't breathe fire either). Karthus had cursed the dragon deaths, but mourned none of them. He finally met his end in the first of the Hunger Wars with Oster, fighting against its new king, Gillian Galt, and the mighty beasts that had been bred in the dark depths of the Pits of Gargen. Oster's lethal furies were new then, and we hadn't been ready. It had been a costly defeat, but the world was a better place without Karthus.

After those ryders came Jona. He was a better man than Karthus or any of the rest, although I hadn't realized that until very recently. Often, he would visit me in my cave on DragonPeak, bringing me large smoked kingfish from the Thunder Straits. Why had he done that? He didn't need to win my affection—I was a slave. The runes ensured my obedience; indeed, they made me want to please my master above all else. Jona also spent far more time talking to me than any ryder before him. As I ate his fish, he would ask me strange questions about my memories as a hatchling and if I remembered my mother (I had no memory of any of these things). The Keepers on DragonPeak had whispered about the idiocy of Jona wasting his gold on expensive fish to give to a dragon. I hadn't thought it unusual at the time because an enslaved dragon did not question the actions of his master. Only once my mind became free could I recognize the oddity of Jona's behavior toward me, particularly when compared to those who had preceded him. I huffed to myself as I flew, struggling with unfamiliar emotions. I wanted to save this human. It wasn't the rune-link that drove my concern. Jona was a decent human.

My brethren and I didn't deserve to be slaves. The ryders were part of that, even if it was the Keepers who stole the hatchlings and the Sculptors who did the actual carving. Yet, somehow, Jona was different than the others. Had it been Karthus or any other ryder strapped into my saddle right now, I would have let them die. With Jona, I couldn't do it. I knew him in a way I hadn't known the others. With my mind secretly free, the link between us allowed me to glimpse what was in his mind. I had shared his emotions. I realized Jona cared about me... and it was not just that regard that set him apart. There was even more to him that I still didn't understand. I reached out to Jona as I flew, trying to push into his mind through our link, to find answers I should've sought weeks ago. I could sense nothing. His mind was somewhere else.

I dreaded returning to Eladrell, but I didn't change my course. If I had been wounded in battle, and Jona had the opportunity to save me, I knew he would have done it. I had deceived him so I could pursue those Osteran ships. If I had been paying attention to my mission instead of trying to act like I was better than a fire-breather, I would've seen those arrows in time to avoid them. I was responsible for his injuries. If he died, it was I who had killed him. I didn't know if dragons were supposed to have a conscience, but it seemed that I did.

Freedom wasn't all ale and goats.

THREE

The Kingdom of Rolm passed beneath me.

King Mendakas' domain consisted of three greater islands, including the conquered land masses that had once been the kingdoms of Aramath and Ulibon, as well as perhaps a hundred smaller islands, although most of these were tiny land specks that were little more than atolls. Harcourt, the great island that was home to Rolm's capital city of Eladrell, was the largest land mass in the known world, bigger than all the isles of Oster put together. That's where I headed. I crossed the east coast of Harcourt, with its rocky, scarred mountains that had been ravaged for the metal ore hidden in their depths ages ago. Some of the peaks were now healed enough for patches of weed and grass to sprout, attracting delicious, white-coated mountain goats. I hungered, and it took considerable self-control to avoid diverting for a quick meal. Jona didn't have time for such diversions.

Quickly, the mountains gave way to the lush lands at the heart of Harcourt, where Rolman farmers grew their foul-tasting crops in the dark soil. As the twilight deepened, I finally gazed upon the spires of Eladrell in the distance. I flew still faster, and the city drew near, as did its stink. Eladrell was the greatest collection of humans in the known world, unrivaled anywhere else in Rolm or Oster. Its streets teemed with humans packed so tight they rubbed against each other as they made their way between homes, shops, and taverns. Near the center of the city was the great Temple of the Sculptors, a soaring pyramid capped by a golden apex that glowed like a lit beacon as night began to fall. As I looked upon the nest of the slave-masters, I vowed that there would come a day when I returned to that place, and I would offer them the same mercy as my former ryder Karthus had offered his foes (death).

Overlooking the sprawling masses of Eladrell like a vigilant mother was DragonPeak, a lonely mountain rising up against the coast, its steep western face dotted by dragon caves intersected by narrow paths of man-carved steps. There were easily a hundred caves, but most were empty. Nestled against the peak was King Mendakas' citadel, a fortress of thick stone walls built around a central keep capped by five spires of varying heights arranged in a manner that gave the castle its name: the Fist.

Normally, when I returned from a mission, I landed at Dragon-Peak. That was where our Keepers, and sometimes even our ryders, resided. The Keepers usually kept a nice supply of meaty treats there as well. However, the king's healers weren't on the mountain, and it was a long journey to the dragon caves from Eladrell for a human on foot. Waiting for a healer on DragonPeak would probably mean Jona would die and I would've wasted my chance to escape Rolm for nothing. So, I needed to land closer to the healers—inside the city of Eladrell itself.

For twenty-three years, humans have forced me to serve them. They captured me before I was ready to fight, stealing me as a hatch-ling from a nest on Veralon made by a mother I never knew. They took all of us that way—usually before a single moon had passed. Stealing babies wasn't fair at all, and neither was this world. A lesson to me from the humans that I intended to remember.

Jona's injury gave me the opportunity to indulge in terrifying a particularly large number of humans without subjecting my actions to undue scrutiny. Indeed, I was going to both be a hero and get to scare the humans. If everything went well, Jona would get healed and I'd get fed a fat sheep.

I began my descent, wary, as all creatures must be when flying above the skies of Eladrell. Here, the wind and air behave like no place else. A combination of DragonPeak and the warm waters of the Boiling Sea to the west conjured unpredictable weather patterns, as well as one other unique phenomenon: the lift-stream. I didn't completely understand it, but some ryder I didn't remember had once claimed that the strange confluence of wind and warmth was caused by air being forced through the caves of DragonPeak from the waters to the west. Whatever the truth, the result was that a steady gust of warm, light air flowed upward just outside the city. It allowed for easy flights and low-hanging clouds. The problem was that just above those clouds, colder air from the north caused the formation of dangerous crystalized ice that could rip even a dragon's wings. For this reason, or maybe because of the dragons that lived nearby, no other creature dared frequent the skies above Eladrell. But I had lived with the lift-stream my whole life, and it posed little danger to a skilled flier like me.

The citizens of Eladrell were accustomed to dragons. They saw us fly to and from the nearby mountain on a regular basis. Still, we usually avoided flying over the city because the lift-stream could cause unpredictable shifts in the wind there. Also, the humans disliked having a giant winged creature blot out the sun over their city on a regular basis.

I ignored the unspoken rule about flying over Eladrell. It was an emergency, after all.

I came in low, my tail shifting from side to side, wary of unexpected wind shear. The skies felt calm. I spread my wings into their full, glorious span. I figured I'd probably only get to fly into the city like this once, so I might as well make the most of the opportunity.

My passage kicked up sand from the streets; my shadow stretched long as the sun's light faded on the western horizon. Even the jaded residents of Eladrell turned their heads upward as I swept over their homes. I heard the shrieks of children—some frightened, others delighted—as I passed. A group of sailors gathered around a barrel on the harborside raised their cups skyward at me, as well they should've—my kind frequently drove off the leviathans that harassed Rolm's sailing fleet, in addition to keeping the ghastray swarms away from Rolm's shores. Their praise pleased me, although I would've preferred to share their drink.

The best place to land in Eladrell without crushing a building was the city's central plaza—the Grandquell. The expansive public space was the location of the greatest market in all of Rolm each Lastday, but at all other times it was a gathering place for the citizenry of the city. It was also flat, paved with stone, and close to both the Fist and the districts of the city with the largest homes, but not too close to the Temple of the Sculptors. The presence of coin-rich humans in that portion of the city meant there would also be healers nearby.

I didn't want to kill anyone else today, so I was careful to hover above the Grandquell, beating my wings long enough for the space to clear below me before I landed. That happened quickly—humans moved promptly when motivated. I set down gently on the pavement. My tail bumped into a marble statue of some human with a crown on his head and a sword in his hand standing beside a pet wolf who was constantly spitting water out of his mouth into a reflecting pool below. I heard a cracking sound, but the statue didn't fall. It would've been better if it had; it looked ridiculous. wolves couldn't breathe water from their mouths and the human had been carved all wrong, with big parts in the wrong places.

Jona was still breathing. I'd gotten him back to his own kind, but now I needed a healer to help him. The digits of my forelegs were nimble enough that I could've plucked Jona off his saddle, but I didn't see the point in risking that.

"Come forth!" I roared out, loud enough that even the people in the Fist must've heard me. "My ryder is in need of aid!"

The few humans who remained in the Grandquell ran away instead of coming to me as I asked, despite my having spoken in my clearest Avian. The people of Eladrell couldn't even follow basic directions.

I really didn't see why my landing caused such a ruckus. It had been many years since a dragon had gone berserk—indeed it had been decades since a dragon had gone on an actual killing spree in Eladrell, and that was the humans' own fault. The Sculptors should have known better than to try to carve runes of control on a dragon after its third moon. The only other dragon I knew of who had turned on his masters had been old Jaxis during the war with Oster, and the circumstances had been very different. The humans were really over-reacting to my unexpected arrival.

I behaved with complete courtesy. I even smiled with my mouth in the human fashion as I looked around the Grandquell for someone to help Jona, my teeth gleaming (a dragon's true smile was made with our eyes—we used our teeth for more important things like eating and killing). Still, no healer came forth. I wondered if coming to the city had been a mistake.

Finally, I spotted one of my brethren flying down from the mountain. I stared hard until I recognized her—Jemila. She was a horned dragon, not more than half my size, but she carried three humans on her back. Even though they were a smaller sub-species, horned drag-ons' thick wings allowed them to carry almost as much weight as a larger ash dragon, so the humans often used them for transportation. My sister (as I called her; we weren't really related as far as I knew) set down next to me, glancing around the Grandquell with unsettled eyes.

"I bring our masters," she announced, unnecessarily. Shortly after my mind had been freed, I'd realized that the control-runes made dragons into conversational dullards; we were so focused on our human masters, we rarely had anything remotely interesting to say to each other.

"My ryder is injured. He needs a healer."

There were two Keepers among the arrivals, along with Jemila's ryder, a human whose name I had forgotten. I rarely spoke to horned dragons. I certainly had no interest in her ryder.

The two Keepers climbed onto my back to examine Jona, while the ryder ran off, hopefully to fetch a real healer. The Keepers unstrapped Jona from his saddle and began to lower him to the ground. I thought they should've waited for the healer before moving him, but that wasn't something a slave dragon would've said. Dragons didn't tell humans what they should be doing, even though it would've improved things considerably if we did. Once they'd laid Jona onto the hard cobblestone ground, the arrow still stuck in his chest, they turned their attention to me.

Of the two Keepers, one was considerably older than the other. I knew this because humans' skin wrinkles as they age. Also, the old ones often lose the fur on the top of their heads but compensate by growing more out of their nose and ears. This keeps the cold air from getting inside their heads in winter, thus reducing the need for a furry head.

The old, hairy-nosed one stood close to my head and held up two fingers on his hand, which was a signal that he should have my attention. I forced myself to raise my neck and regard him like an obedient slave.

"Bayloo, who did this to your ryder?"

Dragons weren't expected to give elaborate answers. Most humans wanted to think our intellect was inferior to theirs. They were wrong, but I kept up the charade of being an idiot. "The enemy."

I figured even a grouchy old Keeper would have a hard time finding much fault with that answer, but this one wasn't easily satisfied. I tried to remember his name. He spent most of his time with the horned dragons. I was relatively sure the other humans called him Jakobo.

"How did your ryder get shot by arrows?"

Let the idiot game commence!

"The enemy used longbows."

I smiled with my teeth. I sensed the Keeper's impatience, so I broadened my fake grin even further, showing close to all eighty of my magnificent teeth. Jakobo's frown deepened.

"Where were the archers with these longbows?"

"On a hidden ship."

"Hidden?"

I closed my eyes, as if struggling to answer his question. "We sunk the two raiders who had stolen from the king. But they had billow-stone smoke. Within the smoke hid another ship."

As much as I disliked speaking Avian, I could've done a much better job than these fragmented answers. Not to brag, but I was rather eloquent compared to my fellow dragons. But I'd never spoken to this Keeper, and he wouldn't know my abilities. He was probably used to dragons who could barely talk. Horned dragons were considerably less intelligent than ash dragons.

"Your ryder chose to pursue ships equipped with billow-stones even though you were alone?"

This was getting more complicated than I'd anticipated. "Thieves. They took the king's grain. They didn't escape us."

Jakobo grunted unhappily. "Jona will have much to answer for. If he lives." The Keeper glanced at my fallen ryder's bloody body. "We don't have so many dragons remaining that we can afford such rash decisions. Every ash dragon is precious, even the misfits."

I snorted with annoyance—rather loudly. I shouldn't have done that. The Keeper's eyes narrowed. I put on my best dumb-obedient face. I learned that look from the dogs who live on DragonPeak—I opened my mouth slightly and breathed heavily. I didn't wag my tail. Humans don't like the odor of my breath, and in the past few moons I'd discovered that heavy breathing helped end undesirable conversations (by which I mean every conversation with a human). The Keeper made a sour grimace as he turned his head toward new arrivals.

Striding toward me was a woman attired in the ivory robe of a human healer, along with the ryder who'd fetched her. The healer wore her cloud-colored hair in a braided tail behind her head. She made big eyes at me but began to run when she caught sight of Jona's bloody body spread on the paved ground of the Grandquell.

"Who moved this man here?" I was familiar with the tone of human annoyance and that's how this woman sounded. I kept my mouth shut, but it would've been satisfying to tell her that I hadn't wanted him moved. Keepers know less than they think they do about everything, including healing and dragons.

Neither of the Keepers confessed. I wasn't surprised.

The healer got to work. She removed Jona's armor, cutting the straps with a dangerous knife she wielded with a soldier's proficiency. After a cursory examination of the wound, she took a vial of reddish liquid from her satchel, punctured the wax seal, and poured the entirety of the contents around the protruding arrow. Without pausing, she placed both hands on the shaft and yanked it out. Jona convulsed, his body spasming even as his eyes remained closed. My tail smacked against the cobblestones, breaking several. The healer didn't take her eyes off Jona. Another vial came out of her satchel, this one containing a thick, clear substance that looked like sap. She poured three drops on Jona's lips. I liked the poise of this healer. I'd not seen her before. The healers sent to DragonPeak were generally of the very old hair-in-ears-and-nose variety of human.

The healer continued to work until the next group of humans arrived. The man in the lead wore the black ring mail of a dragon ryder. Hair the color of rust covered much of his face and head, with two pearly black eyes shining behind his bangs. I recognized him: Aleman Brindisi, First Sword of the king. He was also the ryder of Traxis. Whenever King Mendakas went to war, it was Brindisi at the vanguard of the fighting. I'd seen the man put an arrow into the eye of an Osteran griffin from two hundred yards away while in flight. Brindisi knew how to kill. He also got other humans and dragons killed.

Brindisi barely glanced at Jona as he strode through the cautiously growing crowd occupying the center of the Grandquell. Instead, he fixed his attention on the Keepers. Brindisi growled like an angry hound. "The king demands to know why there are two dragons squatting in the great plaza of his capital."

Heat flowed to Jakobo's face. "This ryder was injured in battle. His desperate dragon brought him here."

Brindisi arched a brow. "Into the Grandquell?"

"It's a flat, open landing area. There aren't healers on the mountain. After all these years as a ryder, you should know that the beasts are capable of independent thought on occasion." I didn't like the way Jakobo said that. My independent thought was to bite off his smug head.

Brindisi grunted as he looked at me. "Some dragons maybe. Traxis isn't known for his intelligence."

I was offended on my dragon brother's behalf. This human had been Traxis' ryder for over fifteen years. While it was true that Traxis had slipped in the past years, he had won no small number of victories for his human. Brindisi owed him respect.

Jakobo was wise enough not to engage in a disagreement with a man such as Brindisi. I wasn't the only one who knew about the ryder's propensity for killing. Instead, the Keeper shifted the subject. "The dragon said that they were pursuing the raiders who attacked old Toth. The escaping ships had billow-stone aboard. Jona took an arrow in the engagement."

Brindisi scoffed. "Those ships that raided Toth were no more raiders than I am a ballerina. They were sent by Oster, and I tire of Galt spitting in our faces. Something must be done to end these raids."

Tough words from a human who couldn't even fly.

"Two of their ships were sunk." The Keeper raised his chin with pride, as if he'd had anything to do with my work. "They cannot match our dragons."

"Famine makes Oster desperate. The raids will continue until we send enough of their ships to the bottom of the sea and they realize they cannot feed their people by sending ships to raid for grain. Only then will King Galt come in force." To my ears, Brindisi didn't sound alarmed at the prospect of another war with Oster. Quite the opposite—he relished it.

Jakobo didn't share the enthusiasm. "The dragons are so few, the griffins many. Each of our losses is irreplaceable."

If Brindisi heard the Keeper, he gave no acknowledgement of it. Instead, he strolled up to me. He reached out a hand and placed it flat onto my side, rubbing my scales as if I were a puppy. I wasn't his pet, but I forced myself to keep still. Pretending to be a slave grated on me, although I also knew defying Brindisi would be a mistake. I'd seen other men do that in battle. It didn't turn out well for them. No, if I was going to fight Brindisi, I best ensure I kill him quickly.

He turned abruptly. "Healer, what is the condition of the dragon's ryder?"

The woman looked up at Brindisi only once she'd finished wrapping Jona's wound. "His injuries are serious. Too much blood has leaked out. It was fortunate the dragon brought him here so quickly." Those words made me feel a lot better about myself than they should have. "I think he has a chance."

Brindisi made a guttural sound of skepticism from deep in his throat. "You are not among the king's healers. What is your name?"

The woman stood slowly, her hand bloody but her head held high. She was nearly as tall as Brindisi. "Aurora of the Menders Guild, at your service."

"Why are you here and not one of the usual healers?"

"I was nearby. A man was in urgent need." She shrugged. "And it seems the king's soldiers move faster than his healers."

Brindisi grimaced. "The king's steward will arrange payment for your services. The royal healers will see to this man now."

"I will stay until they arrive," Aurora informed him. "No fee is necessary."

Brindisi kept his sour expression but didn't challenge her. He turned back to me. I cringed at the prospect of Brindisi touching me again, but he kept his fleshy hands to himself. Instead, he fixed me with a hard, appraising stare, moving his gaze from my head to my tail, then back again. The spikes of my mane stood up with my discomfort. Brindisi stepped closer, speaking in an ugly whisper that only I could hear.

"Now I must decide what to do with you."

FOUR

I got chicken scraps for dinner.

Not even the whole chicken. Just some torn bones with a bit of meat still sticking to the ends. Apparently, sinking two ships and getting my ryder back to Eladrell fast enough to save his life (possibly) didn't merit an improvement in rations. I sniffed unhappily at the meal the Keepers had deposited inside my cave before they closed and locked the gate behind them. Chicken was the vegetable of meats. The scrawny little creatures' flesh tasted like their dirty, bitter feathers, while the bones were a slimy, marrow-less disgrace that splintered in my mouth. The humans must've been angry with me. Or meat was getting too valuable.

I'd heard several Keepers grumbling about how much food we dragons ate while humans didn't have enough. Those sentiments surprised me. I understood famine. I'd lived through the Long Summer when the ghastray swarms ravaged the fishing waters of Rolm. I'd done my part during that terrible summer—the supreme sacrifice of eating potatoes for two of my daily meals.

Things weren't that desperate now. On the rich land of central

Harcourt, crops and livestock thrived. The waters around the conquered nation of Ulibon should've offered the opportunity for better fishing. Stinting on dragon food was stupid. Dragons were the source of Rolm's power. Without us, it wouldn't just be Oster that would be a threat, but pirates and sea monsters, as well as the mysterious Mizu raiders who appeared periodically in their strange ships from the other side of the Wall of Fire. The Keepers might think we ate too much, but there would be less to go around, if not for us.

Lack of decent food wasn't my only complaint. The day that followed my dramatic landing in the Grandquell had been worse than dull. No one came to tell me about Jona's condition. With no ryder, I was mostly left locked up in my cave (the steel gates were supposedly for our protection). The long stretch of isolation left me plenty of time to think, something slave dragons don't do. Or at least I couldn't remember doing much of it before I became free. With my newfound ability to focus my thoughts on anything I desired, my mind decided to spend a good part of the endless day worrying about things I could do nothing about.

I fretted about Jona. Aurora, the healer woman, seemed to have helped him, but even she wasn't sure if he'd live or not. I'd sacrificed a rare opportunity to fly away, and I wanted it to mean something. If I had to pretend to be a slave and I had to have a ryder, it would be best that it was Jona. If he died, I decided that I would have to flee. I wasn't going to risk being bonded to still another human. I had no idea what the re-bonding process would do to my newly freed mind.

My other worry was the possibility of war.

The chicken bones were just one more indication of the troubled times. A dozen fishing boats had been lost over the past moons. The dragons who had been sent out to investigate found shattered wreckages or nothing at all. Hungry leviathans were generally believed to be responsible, though the massive creatures didn't leave much behind when they attacked. Fish was becoming as scarce as animal flesh. Even if the situation was not yet as severe as during the Long Summer, empty bellies were always dangerous. The last great famine had led to the first of the Hunger Wars with Oster. King Mendakas' injured pride at his defeat had caused a second, smaller war several years later. The losses had been terrible, including the horrible death of my dragon brother Jaxis. I didn't want to fight Oster again. The humans' war had nothing to do with me or mine.

This was a fresh thought.

Dragons were used by our masters as tools of war. The minds of men like Karthus made us crave battle. Freed from that human pollution, I understood the folly of fighting Oster, at least for my kind. The beasts of Oster were the most formidable enemies Rolm had ever faced, as demonstrated by the continued independence of that land. I feared no griffin, no war wolf, no fury, nor any other of the diabolical creatures that the Pale Wrights of Oster bred in their dark pits, but dragons gained nothing from fighting those creatures. In a conflict, my kind would die and gain nothing. Humans bred like rabbits, with the stink of their teeming masses rising from the packed houses of Eladrell, but too many dragon caves were empty. In my two decades as a slave, far more dragons had died than arrived on DragonPeak. I had been the last ash dragon taken from Veralon. Rarely, if ever, had I heard a human speak of that. No one cared for the future of my race.

Perhaps that was a duty that fell to me.

That notion echoed in my head as the sun moved across the sky. I didn't like how it felt in there. It was a responsibility, a burden. I had no idea how to help my fellow dragons.

Eventually, night fell on DragonPeak. I still could think of no place for a free dragon in this world. I also didn't know if Jona lived or not. I reached out to him through our link but found only a numb void. Alone, that told me nothing. I had felt the same nothingness as I carried him back to Eladrell. I paced about my inadequate cave, unwilling to sleep. For the first time in my life, I realized that this was not my home—it was a cage. I didn't like being imprisoned. I was a dragon, meant for the sky. The humans had done that to me, and all my kind. I snarled at the thought.

With anger in my blood, I stared at the only exit. As far as I knew, no dragon had ever tried to break the gate. The steel bars appeared dauntingly thick, even if they were old. A human-sized door had been built into the larger gate, so the Keepers could enter and exit without lifting the opening wide enough for a dragon to escape. I sniffed the gate, probing gently with a claw. There was no rust, no obvious weakness. The mechanism that lifted the gate was far out of my reach. It wasn't worth the risk trying to knock out the bars tonight. Eventually, the Keepers would come to let me out to fly or stretch my wings in the sun. That would be my opportunity to escape, if I decided to do that. But first, I needed to know what happened to Jona.

The night ended and a new day came. I'd slept little and awoke agitated, my tail flailing into the stone wall of my cave. This space was oppressive. Hearing human footsteps on the stairs leading toward my cave was a relief. My hearts beat with anticipation, which annoyed me because I shouldn't be so anxious, but I wasn't used to spending long days in my cave contemplating freedom and warfare— so much thinking hurt.

The short and squat form of a familiar Keeper arrived at the gate of my cave dressed in the dusty red tunic of his kind, a sour frown on his face. The man's name was Kelum. As Keepers went, he wasn't the worst—Kelum was lazy but usually not cruel. He held up a thick metal dragon collar with a metal link chain attached. He stared at me expectantly.

Suppressing a snort, I shuffled obediently to the front of my cave, lowering my neck so he could secure the metal collar around my neck.

They treat us like dogs.

There wasn't any reason for the collar and chain. Even though they weren't our ryders, slave dragons almost always obeyed the spoken commands of the Keepers, even if we had no fondness for their kind. The instinct to obey had been imprinted in us by our first linked humans when we were still little more than hatchlings. Only in instances of extreme fear or danger would a Keeper's command be insufficient. The collar clicked shut around my neck. Its hard edges rubbed against my scales. Without the rune-link to cloud my mind, I realized I could snap the chain of the collar if I tried. It couldn't hold me or my brethren—the device was about superiority, nothing else. I'd been blind to the humiliation before this moment.

Kelum placed a worn metal key in the large gate's lock, then pushed it open. With a yank on my chain, he urged me out of the cave. The links of my leash dragged behind him as we made our way along the ledge outside my cave. Far below was Eladrell and the mighty walls of the Fist. I followed the Keeper, annoyed at every clink of the metal chain. I kept my eyes low, lest Kelum see the anger in them. Why did the dogs who wore these things act so happy? Perhaps because dogs can lick themselves in places dragons cannot, so they are simply happier creatures by nature.

"Bayloo, to the Shelf," Kelum said, confident in being obeyed, as if I couldn't swallow him in a single bite. At least we would be going someplace easy to depart from, if I chose.

We ascended along one of the pathways that had been carved in the mountainside by the toil of men in ages past. It had been made wide enough for a dragon—barely. But even if I slipped, I could just fly back to the peak. It was the Keepers who had to be careful.

The path led upward, spiraling around the width of the peak. Along the way, we passed the caves of several of my brethren. The first was that of my lithe sister, Narsis, whose scales were an elegant shade of gold. As we passed, she lifted her long neck high enough that we might see her eyes glowing in greeting from the darkness of her cave, although I think the greeting was more for the human Keeper than I. Kelum ignored her, but I offered a low trill of my tongue and throat, a sound too soft for human ears, but a call every dragon knew —it was how we found each other when we flew in formation, letting each other know our positions, and that none of us were alone. It wasn't something I would've done before I found my own will inside of me, but it wasn't obviously rebellious either.

Narsis flashed caring eyes at me, a hint of gentleness I hadn't bothered to see in her previously. I paused to regard my sister, but Kelum yanked on my chain. "On with you."

Narsis showed no sign of being concerned at my treatment. I didn't blame her. Two moons ago I'd been like Narsis. I wouldn't have cared either.

We passed the home-prison of Traxis next, the eldest and largest among us, save for the king's own dragon, Triton. Traxis lay back in the furthest reaches of his den, his bulk resting against the wall. Human eyes couldn't have pierced the black void separating us, but I had no trouble gazing upon my massive brother. Even though his scales had frayed at their edges, there was no mistaking the majesty of Traxis. Or his power. In the battle for Ulibon, his fire had melted the stone of the Highstar's tower. On that day, there was no creature in Rolm mightier than Traxis. He was not the same now. Time was a worthy adversary.

Traxis offered no greeting, but when our eyes met, a surge of amber came into his gaze, which he allowed to dim only gradually, expressing his sympathy for my injured ryder in the dragon way. This sort of display was rare among my kind, but the peril to a ryder was a concern all slave dragons understood, even more so than when one of our kind fell. As I passed Traxis' cave-prison, I remembered watching his egg-brother, Jaxis, die horribly in Oster, years ago. No dragon had mourned that death, although it had been uniquely horrible, and few among us even knew the full terrible truth of it.

I thanked Traxis for his concern with a sharp flash of my own eye. Kelum remained oblivious to our exchange. Humans cared only for themselves, if that.

After another steep climb, we came to the so-called Shelf, an outcropping of rock on the north side of DragonPeak. It extended the length of three dragons with a surface pounded and scarred by the treading of my kin over decades. The Shelf also afforded a magnificent view of the Thunder Straits. It was here that hatchlings, newly maimed by the Sculptors' control-runes, were sent to their first flight. Kelum hooked my chain on a line of iron spikes that had been driven into the mountain just for this purpose. I could've snapped the chain anytime I wanted, and the Keepers knew it, yet they persisted in degrading us. I wondered at the origins of these rituals. Perhaps the first Keepers had realized that even if a dragon had an inkling of free will inside, the chains and locked gates and humiliation would keep our true self suppressed.

"Stretch your wings, or they will stiffen," Kelum told me. "Breathe the mountain air. I'll return before the sun leaves the sky." Kelum held up a stern finger. It reminded me of a pale asparagus. "Do not leave the ground upon which you stand. No flying." He waddled off down another path, glancing back over his shoulder as if he expected to catch me hovering over the edge like some errant child.

One other dragon shared the Shelf with me, a lesser horned beast the humans had named Crema. Her scales were the color of an oyster's pearl, smooth and elegant. She was the youngest dragon on the mountain, her twisting horns not yet half of the full adult length they would one day achieve. Crema took note of me, but offered no greeting, keeping to herself on the far side of the rocky expanse, a long trough of water separating us.

A stiff wind pushed across the Shelf. On it was the smell of sea, but also something foul—the odor of a death tide. At least that's what sailors called it. I knew of no better term. It was a layer of muck that sometimes came to the shores of Rolm, killing marine creatures in its path. Even leviathans weren't safe from its poison. Any who dared to eat the flesh of dead creatures caught in the tide would sicken. The odor tainted the fine view. It also overwhelmed any other smells carried on the air, leading me to the belief that I was alone on the Shelf with only my lesser cousin. I was wrong.

I walked over to the water trough, the sound of the metal chains grating in my head. I savored the sensation of the cool liquid as it ran down my throat into my belly. I kept a careful eye on Crema as I drank, but she paid me no mind, her attention focused on the horizon. I wondered what slave dragons thought about during these moments. I had been on the Shelf for countless afternoons, yet I could barely recall anything about those visits before my mind awoke. The Sculptors' runes had stripped me of even my own memories.

I studied the carved symbols of magic on Crema's chest. The inscriptions were similar to my own—a series of five interlocked circles contained within a greater circle, with a series of intricate symbols that combined to resemble a pair of spread wings in the center. There was an unmistakable message in the pattern, a message that was just beyond the edge of my understanding. Crema's markings were smaller than mine, with one less circle. Still, they were equally hideous.

The wind shifted and so did the scent in the air. I raised my head as I heard the footsteps of a human. I pretended to share Crema's interest in the horizon. Oh, how blue! And big! Did I mention blue already? What in the Abyss was Crema staring at for so long?

The human stepped onto the Shelf from a little-used path above the outcropping. I knew the way she'd come. It led to nowhere except a small, isolated ledge from which the humans tried to speak to their gods above in Haven, occasionally leaving offerings of flowers, animals, or other trinkets. I'd also seen Keepers peeing from the same locale on occasion, presumably to appease some god of the sea below. Human deities had strange preferences.

I recognized the human—a female. They were rare enough among the denizens of DragonPeak that I knew her name: Bethy Rann, the ryder of Crema. Only three human females had successfully triumphed during the Rite and won the opportunity to become a ryder of a newly arrived hatchling. Of those, only Rann still drew breath.

She wore a longbow on her back and a curved blade at her side. Even the most fearsome of other ryders—men like Brindisi and Del Quickblade—respected Rann's accuracy with that bow. A few even called her Longshot, both because of her aim and how unlikely it was that she was still alive. I had trouble understanding human naming conventions. By their logic, if Rann was Longshot, then Kelum the Keeper should've been called Short Annoyance and my sister Adriel's ryder should've been known as Garlic Stink. That would've made more sense, but humans rarely made sense.

Rann had the look of a dragon about her, with a wonderfully longish nose (at least by human standards), dark olive skin, and eyes the color of the sun, not unlike those of an ash dragon. Her movements were catlike, sparse and quick.

Crema shifted her attention to her newly-arrived ryder, her eyes flickering with an azure glow that was the equivalent of a smile for my kind. To my surprise, Rann seemed to understand the expression —her own lips stretched on her face. Few people on DragonPeak recognized a dragon's smile. Of course, Crema's gesture meant nothing because it wasn't given freely. I was the only dragon that could bestow a true smile, and there wasn't any human worthy of it, Bethy Rann included.

She laid a hand on Crema's neck. "Sorry I kept you waiting. The Sisters in Haven must have their due." Rann gazed out toward the north. "We travel to Greater Toth Isle tomorrow to fetch some fat lord with business in Eladrell."

The horned dragon dipped her head obediently, as if this information pleased her. As if she had any choice about where she would fly. Rann pulled a pair of pommice fruits from her pocket and fed them to Crema, whose eyes glowed with satisfaction at the sour treat.

That was just gross. I had thought only Jona enjoyed those things.

The fruit made me think of my ryder, how his flesh stank of the pungent odor of that fruit. The single sample Jona had given to me after becoming my ryder had made my tail curl and my bowels move so fast that the Keepers had forbade him from ever offering pommice fruit to me again.

While Crema delighted in her foul treat, Rann took her hand from the smaller dragon and gazed at me. The whites of her eyes were polluted by thin lines of hot red, as if she was upset or angry (it was hard to tell with human eyes). I pretended to be newly fascinated by a wispy cloud passing overhead that resembled a chicken's beak, but Rann didn't relent. The stare she directed at me had force—cold and dark, in stark contrast to the kinder look that she had laid upon her own dragon. I didn't understand why any human would be more pleased by an adolescent horned dragon than a fine specimen of adult prowess like me. Not that I cared about human opinions.

Rann wasn't satisfied merely staring at me. She walked toward me, her jaw tight. I had to be a respectful dragon and grant my undivided attention to her, of course, so I tore myself away from the sky, craning my neck down to look at her (which we weren't supposed to do because humans were our masters). Rann's forehead crinkled as her eyes scoured my face as if searching for something.

"Bayloo, to heel." Her command reminded me of a whetstone rubbing a sword. The spikes of my mane stood higher. I hoped she didn't notice.

I forced myself to obey, lowering my neck so that the bottom of my lower jaw rested on the ground, which also put my eyes beneath those of the human who addressed me. The rest of my body pressed against the stone of the Shelf. Even hounds sat upright when called to attention, but dragons weren't even left that dignity.

"Are you cursed, Bayloo?" Rann's voice grated as she said it.

"Cursed, honorable ryder?"

"Your ryders fall like leaves at the onset of winter. No other dragon has had so many die. Not even Traxis, who has lived your lifetime several times over."

Oh. That.

It wouldn't have been proper of me to tell Rann that those deaths weren't my fault. Also, depending on what had happened to Jona, one of them might end up being my fault. I offered stupid slave platitudes in place of truth, hoping that this conversation ended quickly. "I served as best I am able, Master."

"But one human is much the same as another?" Rann's tone was raw, but slowly heating with anger. Her ignorance stung me. I had forsaken a flight to join my brethren on Veralon so that I might carry Jona back among his kind, to save his life. I'd made a mistake with the ships, but I'd also sacrificed to try to set it right. I wanted to growl the truth to this human. It took all my newfound will to restrain myself.

"To fail in service hurts us. We wish only to honor our masters." I managed to keep my tone respectful, barely. I could grovel only so much.

"Service," Rann spat, her temper seemingly growing hotter. "Honoring your masters. Is that really all you felt for your ryders, Bayloo?"

Since my awakening, I'd had several encounters with strange humans, but this was the champion of them all. Did this human, to whom I'd never spoken more than a word or two before this day, somehow suspect me of being a killer?

My hearts thundered as I weighed the risks this strange ryder posed to me. A surging current of hot blood ran up my neck to my head. I ached to speak the truth, to tell her what they called service was slavery. But that moment of satisfaction surely would bring about the end of the real me. I struggled to keep the crimson shade of anger from seeping into my eyes. That could be the end of me. "What else would you have me do, Master?"

Rann's eyes widened. Despite my steady voice, Rann might've noticed the crimson entering my gaze. The fur on top of her eyes (which seems to serve no useful purpose in combating cold, unlike human ear hair) rose up on her face. "You are angry?" she asked. "So am I. You are supposed to keep your ryders alive, Bayloo. But five are dead."

My hearts hit the inside of my chest.

Five?

I forgot myself, forgot how a dragon was supposed to speak to a human.

"Is he dead?"

Rann reacted as if I'd struck her. She took a step back, staring at me through a narrow slit of barely open eyes. Her lips twitched. I thought she was outraged at my tone, at the emotion surging in my eyes, but that wasn't it. Rann was surprised by something else. "They didn't even tell you." Her words contained more bitterness than any pommice fruit. Rann shook her head. "You killed another of us. Jona is dead."

FIVE

The night tormented me.

That wasn't very dragon-like. After drinking and eating, sleeping ranked as my favorite activity. But unwelcome images came unbidden into my head whenever I closed my eyes. I stirred restlessly, my hearts feeling like rocks as Jona's fate haunted me.

I'd killed him. Not directly, of course. But my vanity and my carelessness had ended him. One of my first acts as a free dragon had been to get a person killed. How very human of me.

I resented the torment that haunted me. Humans enslaved us. Jona was part of that. I owed him nothing. But the night grew long, and I could not put the troubling sensations aside. Guilt ailed me without causing physical pain. I'd never experienced anything like it before—I'd have preferred straight agony. I knew how to deal with that. This rattling of my mind and body was far more relentless. I hated it.

As Rann had cruelly pointed out, I had seen the deaths of four other ryders before Jona. After each, I'd eaten a full dinner and slept soundly. Perhaps that was because my ryders before Jona had been different men—those others were creatures of contempt and fury who thought themselves masters of a mere beast. The more I thought of Jona, of his lopsided grin, of his sour stink, of the fish he had brought me deep in the night, the more the wound inside me festered. I couldn't avenge him because I was his true killer.

Rann's anger on the Shelf had been fresh. She must've learned of the death of her fellow ryder just before she'd spoken to me. For some reason she had been particularly upset about Jona's death. I found that strange. No one had been angry after the death of my other ryders. I was responsible for Jona's death, but Bethy Rann couldn't know that. Why was she so upset?

I had seen human warriors weep at the side of their comrades fallen in battle. At such moments, I'd been relieved that my kind didn't have leaky eyes. I suspected Bethy Rann's emotions had been deeper than that, though. Were she and Jona mates?

That might explain Rann's behavior, but I had rarely seen them together. Jona had never mentioned a mate, nor had I ever sensed that he possessed any special regard for Bethy Rann through our link. I wasn't aware of any mated pairs among the ryders, but I also hadn't bothered to pay much attention to such things. Perhaps Jona had been more to Rann than a fallen comrade. If so, it made her even more dangerous to me. She might seek revenge if Jona had been her mate.

I already suspected that Rann had noticed my un-dragonlike reactions to her provocation: my flash of anger and my direct question about Jona's fate. Bethy Rann wasn't just the voice of my guilt, she might also expose what I had become. She was like chicken feathers mixed into a bowl of vegetables—trouble.

Once Rann realized that I hadn't even been told of my ryder's death, much of her temper had faded. She'd stared off into the sky like some slave dragon. Eventually, she'd been ready to question me further, but Kelum had returned to fetch me before she could resume her interrogation. It had been one of the only times I'd been relieved to see a Keeper. He brought me back to my cave, leaving me with another disappointing meal of chicken bones.

I considered fleeing DragonPeak as I walked down the mountain with Kelum to my cave-prison. Even with my neck wrapped in a collar and chain, I could have broken free. I could have flown off ... to somewhere. Why hadn't I done it?

My excuse to myself was that my fellow dragon, Cornethius, had been brought to the Shelf by his ryder. He would've come after me almost immediately. Even though I was faster, where would I go? If King Mendakas knew what I was, he'd have all his dragons hunt me. He couldn't risk a freed slave on the loose. One free dragon could lead to others. Mendakas wouldn't risk letting Oster believe such a thing was possible.

It would've been a risky time to escape anyway, in the daylight, my chain held by a Keeper. I told myself that it was better to wait until I could slip away unnoticed. All that was true. But as I lay in my cave alone with my thoughts, I knew the real reason I stayed: I wasn't quite ready to believe Jona was dead.

My last thoughts turned to my old ryder before I finally closed my eyes to rest. To whisper an apology. Dragons had no gods. We did not speak to the unseen. We didn't believe in Haven or the Sisters who supposedly dwelled there. Still, I think Jona had believed in some higher power. For his sake, I hoped he had made it to the Haven the humans talked about and was having a fine meal there, including pommice fruit if it suited him.

The Keepers came for me at first light. For a fleeting moment I dared to hope that Rann had been mistaken, and that Jona would be with the arrivals. He wasn't.

In place of my ryder, one of my least favorite humans appeared on the ledge outside my cave: Lisaam Payne, the Chief Keeper. He resembled a dry stick given life; his thin lips wrapped around his teeth in a bitter pucker. Payne reeked of decay, and maybe chicken livers. By the look of him, he could've been as old as Traxis, but even the grumpy old dragon was kinder. It was Lisaam Payne who had insisted that dragons be saddled with their heads on the ground and that we lay our necks flat when speaking to humans. He enjoyed being the master, calling us beasts or dragons, but never by our names (and even those were made up by humans). Seeing Payne outside my cave made me unhappy. His companion made me even more so.

Beside the walking collection of flesh-covered bones that was Lisaam Payne stood a human boy stretched into the body of a man. That human looked as if he had been dressed up by a vain mother to resemble a warrior: a pair of eyes as blue as the clear winter sky dominated an unblemished face framed by golden curled hair, but that was the least of his finery. He wore scaled armor in the style of ryders, but enameled with a tint that matched his pretty eyes. Three rings of gold, each studded with sapphires, cluttered the fingers of the hand nearest to a sword pommel studded with similar gems.

"Bring him out, Payne." There was nothing boyish about the voice, which reeked of the expectation of obedience. I waited for the foul-tempered Payne to rebuke the command, but the old stick merely grimaced as he unlocked the gate to my cave with a golden Keeper's key.

I realized then who had come to visit me, even though I had never before laid eyes on Payne's companion. I had heard the ryders speak of King Mendakas' second son, Dayne—the so-called Sapphire Prince—and never kindly (but always very softly). Indeed, I'd once heard my fellow dragon Lothar's ryder say that the boy's mother had shoved several of the glittering stones up her son's ass to convince everyone that even his crap was precious.

"Onto the ledge outside, dragon," Payne ordered.

I tucked in my wings and obeyed, my tail twitching.

The prince stood with a rigid back outside my cave, his eyes hungry, his fingers dancing about. The sparkle of the sapphires drew my gaze to the prince's hand. Like everything the boy had, the rings had supposedly been given to him by his mother, Queen Florin. Dayne wore a ring for each of the great islands of Rolm. I heard that Prince Horace, Dayne's older brother by way of the king's first wife, received no gifts from his stepmother. But neither of the royal sons' issues had mattered a lick of a chicken's backside to me before this moment.

"A great beast," Dayne said with his jeweled hand on his chin. "That beautiful mane sets it apart from the others. Truly a mount fit for royalty. It will serve nicely."

I was an "it" to him? Deep inside me, my hate for this human bubbled hot.

This prince could've at least learned my gender. I would've enjoyed showing him—this little boy thought three little gems were impressive. He hadn't seen anything yet.

"Jona was the beast's fifth ryder, my lord. The Sculptors advise that it would be wise to call for a Rite, to let the Sisters of Haven above choose a new ryder to be bonded to him."

Dayne's lips puckered like a babe given sour milk. "The Rite is to choose new ryders to train with a hatchling."

"The Rite and the Tell is for all dragon ryders." Payne struggled to keep his tone respectful. "Every ryder must climb to the top of Arrow Peak, outracing all contenders, retrieving a bone of the ancient dragon that lies there, thereby defeating the other, less worthy suitors under the gaze of Haven. Even then, the victor has only completed the Rite of Bonding by surviving the consumption of dragon bone essence. Only in this way are they judged worthy of linking with a dragon, thereby bringing a deadly menace prone to slaughter into service of humanity. The final step is the Tell—the binding pledge of loyalty to Rolm and its monarch."

Dayne waved his jewels at the Keeper as if he were a pesky fly. "Spare me your talk and your excuses, Payne. I've been onto your precious Arrow Mountain, where the wind is so hard and cold it blows the skin off a man's bones. I breathed the thin air of the peak without a care. I plucked a bone from that picked-over skeleton of the long dead creature that sits on the plateau—part of its leg, I think. The queen's own personal seer, Jaresh, oversaw the preparation of the brew which I drank. There can be no doubt of my loyalty, of course. My Tell is my blood. I've done more than the Rite. Do you now need to hear what I dreamed before I pissed and crapped the essence from my body?"

Payne's face became the same shade as snow.

Prince Dayne paid the Keeper no further attention. He looked at me with shining eyes. "I am chosen. This is my dragon. This was the arrangement."

Payne's breath became laden with unease as he shifted his weight between his feet. "A hatchling, my prince... the arrangement was for the next hatchling. You were to win the Rite fairly, not make your own... pilgrimage—"

Dayne cut him off. "There hasn't been a new hatchling in years. Every one of your expeditions to Veralon that my mother supported has failed. The female dragons are all gone; soon the rest may be as well. Our patience is exhausted. I have the blessing of the Sisters. I survived drinking the dragon bone brew—the foul taste and the stomach pain. I'm as blessed by Haven as any ryder. Even more so, for I'm the blood of the king. What I haven't had is dragon." A snake-like tongue slipped out of Dayne's mouth and wet his lips. "But now I do."

Payne gazed up at me, then back at the prince. I didn't doubt that he regretted whatever bargain he had made with this arrogant prince and his mother, but the restlessness in his eyes and the speed of his heart's beat told me that he also feared something. Not this over-dressed, overgrown boy, certainly. More likely his mother, the queen, who was by all accounts as formidable as her husband.

"It would be unprecedented for someone who has not competed in a Rite to be named a ryder of a dragon, much less an adult creature, an ash dragon—"

"You are wrong," Dayne nearly shouted. "It is not without prece-dent. I know history. During the Hunger Wars, and the conquest of Ulibon, fallen ryders were immediately replaced, carved in camp by the Sculptors. Another war with Oster threatens. They raid our farms, harry our ships. As ever, they seek to steal what belongs to my family. Do not try to evade my point, Lisaam Payne, or you shall regret it."

Payne blinked several times, his sour expression betraying unease. "This is not my decision alone," Payne said finally, his voice dropping to a near whisper. "I will speak to the Seers who advise the king on these matters. I will tell them that... I believe no Rite is necessary, and there is urgency to linking this dragon. This will leave you as the only person who has survived a Rite ... of some kind ... who is not already linked with a dragon. The rest is up to you and your mother. Are we agreed?"

The prince wasn't even listening anymore. He was staring at me, an ugly smile on his face.

SIX

I was cursed.

Five ryders dead. Now, the Sapphire Prince conspired with Lisaam Payne to become my sixth. If he tried, he would likely become the first ryder that I had intentionally murdered.

It was hard to accept that the Sculptors would bond me to a human fool whose primary attribute was being the current queen's eldest hatchling. He wasn't even the true heir to Rolm under human law—Dayne's stepbrother had that distinction, as he was the older sibling. Alone once again in my cave, my blood boiled hot enough that I expected I could've breathed fire if I'd tried. This royal pup and his mother seemed to have bargained with Lisaam Payne for me, as if I were an oxen to be bought and sold at the market.

I stalked about the tiny confines of my cave, snorting and whipping my tail about. No ryder would have been acceptable, but this selection was humiliating. The Rite to choose a new ryder was supposedly ordained by the human gods—the Sisters of Haven. Ryders had to demonstrate uncanny stamina, as well as the ability to perform at high altitudes by scaling the highest peak in Rolm. The winner was considered the elite of the kingdom, but even that wasn't enough. Dragon flesh is deadly to humans if consumed, so digesting the poisonous essence of that poor dead dragon on Arrow Peak supposedly demonstrated the favor of the Sisters of Haven for the winner of the Rite. Apparently, none of that actually mattered. Nothing was sacred to humans—even the things they themselves had declared to be sacred in the first place. How had such a species risen to dominate dragons?

After a few turns more in my tiny cave, I settled back down on the ground. I sucked wind in through my throat, struggling to calm myself. Smashing the walls of my cave would just get me discovered and re-enslaved or killed. I comforted myself with the notion that being bonded to one human wouldn't be that different than any other. I would still be me. Or would I?

I didn't fully understand how I had become free. I remembered the day with the broken ale barrel vividly. That was when I realized what had happened to me. But the shackles on my mind had started to unlatch earlier than that. I just hadn't noticed what was happening before the Great Ale Day. Having been awakened, I found it difficult to accept that any new ryder could dominate me. I was no hatchling with soft scales and a weak mind. But I couldn't be sure. It would be better to leave now. I knew with certainty that Jona was dead. There was no reason to remain here, even if I still didn't know where else to go. I would escape at the next opportunity. Unfortunately, the Keepers didn't cooperate with my plan.

After the prince left, I was kept in my cave, the gate locked, food pushed through the bars. Each approach of footsteps made me think that the Sculptors had arrived, but each time it was just the Keepers coming to feed me. I distracted myself by looking out at the sky, watching my brothers and sisters fly, soaring on the warm air of the lift-stream, dancing in the clouds. I envied their flight, but not the burdens of the humans on their back or shackles on their mind.

Just before nightfall, I spied a sight I'd not seen in nearly a year: my brother Triton, flying westward, back from the far coast and who knew where else. On his back flew his illustrious ryder, King

Mendakas himself, a speck of a hairy human next to the massive bulk of Triton. Indeed, no other dragon equaled the king's mount in size. Triton's head alone was equal to nearly two of mine. His breath was the deadliest of all the dragons, a flame so hot it was tinged white. Some called him the last balefire dragon—drawing on an ancient legend that in the early days of this world, my kind had once breathed a magical fire that could unmake anything it touched, even mountains or the sea itself.

Alongside Triton flew the beautiful and mighty Lothar, his cobalt scales glowing in the fading western sunset. I wondered from where they came. What had been important enough for the king himself to take the flight? Dozens of important islands lay to the east, as well as the enemy kingdom, Oster.

The king landed at the Fist rather than DragonPeak. Darkness fell across the now empty sky. The Keepers brought me a disgrace of a meal consisting of poorly plucked raven, which soured my mood further (and my stomach as well). I examined the bars of my cage again. There was no chance of escaping quietly. The starlit sky mocked me, tantalizingly close, but impossible to reach without a Keeper coming to open the cave gate with their metal key.

As I gazed into the sheet of stars on their black field, another omen appeared, this one ill according to humans and their superstitions. Rima, the so-called Scarred Eye of the Sky, appeared, her dark, pockmarked form illuminated in blue-tinged starlight as she moved rapidly across the sky, outpacing the moon. Unlike the sun and moon, Rima appeared seemingly at random intervals. The human Seers claimed Rima was sent by Wrath, overlord of the Abyss, to watch for souls to bring into his dark domain. Some humans went weak-kneed at the very sight of Rima, crossing their hearts with shaking fingers. I gazed at the object for the first time with free eyes.

I understood how she had gotten her legend—Rima had the shape of a slightly crushed human eye with ugly cracks running all along her surface. One of its ends had a jagged edge which reminded me of a chewed goat bone. I suspected that the human Seers had no more idea what Rima meant than I did, although I had to agree that it looked like something that belonged to the Abyss rather than the sky. Almost as quickly as it appeared, the apparition vanished, as if swallowed by the night. I'd heard many explanations of this strange behavior, but the most sensible one was that the object was often present, but only visible when a certain combination of star and moonlight struck its strange surface.

I didn't sleep. I knew the humans would come in the morning, and I was anxious. As it turned out, they didn't even wait that long. In the depths of night, men came. That was a bad sign. The only human who had ever visited me so late had been Jona.

By their footfalls, I guessed five humans came for me. That was too many to be anything other than what I dreaded. If I had to, I could kill five humans easily enough. One of them would be a Sculptor, but I could think of no reason they wouldn't die like other men if I ripped their heads off.

I didn't get the chance.

The humans entered my cave one after the other through the smaller Keepers' entrance through which humans but not dragons could enter, bringing their burning torches inside my space. Prince Dayne was not among them, but that brought me no comfort. The first to enter were the same Keepers I'd encountered on Grandquell—Jakobo and his younger companion whose name I still didn't know. Although I disliked Keepers, the pair were the least unwelcome of my visitors.

Behind them strode a pair of Sculptors, their faces concealed by masks of enamel. The face coverings were painted to demark their respective ranks in the Order of Sculptors—crimson for the Arch-Sculptor, ivory for the acolyte. The face covering revealed only their eyes, with tiny slits for their nostrils and mouths. The faces behind the masks must have been hideous indeed if they believed the covering improved their appearances. The acolyte carried an iron box cradled in both hands. That box contained trouble for me. The final entrant to my prison cave was the worst surprise: Aleman Brindisi.

Seeing him again was about as welcome as seeing goat bones after they made the long journey through my bowels. The ryder wore an arrogant smirk of satisfaction, but that wasn't what drew my attention —his disgusting human nipples did (yes, male humans have nipples). The man was bare-chested, his front side emblazoned with rune-scars of a ryder. Why was he here, bare and ugly? Why was Brindisi here rather than Dayne?

My stomach suddenly felt as if I'd eaten stones for dinner rather than chicken bones. I'd made a fool's mistake. Prince Dayne had been outmaneuvered.

Brindisi's face split into a hungry smile as he gazed at me. "He shall do nicely." Brindisi rubbed his chest, as if his calloused palms should rub away the runes there. "He is a third of Traxis' age. Strong, fit. I shall have him."

My stomach churned unhappily.

Did Brindisi truly intend to become my ryder?

My first instinct was idiotic outrage that Brindisi would abandon Traxis. Disgust surged through me. Yes, the great dragon was old, but he had carried Brindisi to victory in countless battles. My elder dragon-brother was owed more than such treatment. But those were the residual thoughts of a slave dragon. Did it really matter who rode Traxis? My great brother's mind was trapped and addled by the control-runes. He wouldn't care.

My next thought was about my own situation.

Prince Dayne repulsed me with his arrogant ignorance. All his talk of deserving a dragon, as if I were another ring for his fingers, made my scales shake. But I had been arrogant as well. I had been outraged at being presented with an unworthy ryder like Dayne. I'd had chicken feathers in my head. Dayne was a fool, but his inexperience and pretensions would've made him easy to manipulate. Brindisi was an altogether different matter. He'd been bonded to Traxis for decades; he knew dragons, and he was a warrior born and bred. The man had killed more humans than I had.

Goat guts. I should have taken my chances flying from the Shelf yesterday.

Ten human eyes stared at me in the blank, colorless manner of humans. Brindisi spoke first, his voice harsh. "Let us be quick about it, Sculptor. Time grows short. It would be best to have this over with before the boy-prince awakens and cries to his mother."

Jakobo frowned like Brindisi had stolen his dinner. "You go too far in mocking Prince Dayne."

The warrior snorted. "You have nothing to fear from the pretty Prince of Sapphires. He'll whine but do little else."

Jakobo's unhappy expression didn't change. "His mother is formidable." In a softer voice, he added, "And vengeful."

"Do not fear the woman," Brindisi assured the Keeper. "This is the king's wish, as I have told you. I spoke to him as soon as he returned this evening. He is not blind to his second son's limits. He still favors Horace as heir despite the older boy's mishap. What he has seen in Dayne troubles him more than an angry wife. War with Oster is once again upon us, and we cannot afford to waste a dragon with a hapless ryder."

The young Keeper's eyes had become steadily wider as the others spoke. "We are to take the blame for defying the queen?"

Brindisi shrugged with a carelessness that seemed to surprise the other humans. "Her ire will fall upon me. She will suspect I acted at the king's orders, but that is my burden. Tonight, we solve two of King Mendakas' problems: we keep his dragons in fighting conditions for the coming war with Oster, and we keep him from having to endure the full might of his wife's outrage."

"The latter is a noble undertaking indeed." Jakobo's lips twisted down further. "But will he protect us from Queen Florin's wrath?"

Brindisi growled with impatience. "You have worked with these great beasts all your life. You know them, you know those who ride them. Every ryder is chosen under the gaze of Haven, each of us the legitimate champion of a Rite. Would you see some boy who was carried to the top of the highest peak by his mother's minions and drank some soup laden with chicken bones become a ryder of a dragon?"

Both Keepers bobbed their head in agreement at this. Jakobo spoke for both of them. "The boy is unworthy."

It seemed as though the humans had convinced themselves they served a higher purpose in the depth of the night. I wondered if Brindisi would have been so anxious to be righteous if he hadn't been hungry for a new dragon to ride.

I kept my jaw clenched but my eyes clear. These humans would notice if I behaved oddly.

Brindisi walked closer to me. "Then let us begin. Otherwise, this morning might well end with the little Prince of Sapphires falling off a dragon."

"Who shall become ryder to Traxis?" Jakobo asked. I wanted to know that as well.

Brindisi shook his head, full of regret, as if he cared about the dragon's fate. "Traxis weakens. His sight fails him, his wings are unsteady. He tries to hide it, but I can feel it through our link." He gazed down as his chest with a dour grimace. "Traxis is still remarkably strong, but even that will fade. He has perhaps a year or two before he needs be put down, maybe less. Let one of the horned dragon ryders claim him if they wish, but I must have one of the greater dragons, and there are no others but Bayloo."

"Might we offer Traxis to Prince Dayne?" suggested the younger Keeper.

Jakobo looked upon his fellow Keeper with outrage, but it was Brindisi who answered. "The prince wouldn't take him. Dayne knows Traxis' time grows short. Once linked to an ash dragon, it is rare for a ryder to have another chance to claim a different dragon. Then there is the matter of the boy's pride, and that of his mother. They feast on grievances and do not accept scraps."

It pained me to hear Traxis' ryder speak of him so. Was it even true? Traxis didn't exactly confide in me, and he was indeed old. But there was no doubting his strength. I chose to think that Brindisi underestimated my brother.

"Enough talk," Brindisi said. "Sculptor, it is time to do what you must."

The man in the crimson mask walked the length of my body. He wore a toga that matched his mask along with black gloves on his hands that together concealed almost all of his form. He moved slowly, his breathing labored. When the Sculptor finally spoke, his voice reminded me of the crackling of a fire. "All must leave, save Brindisi."

Jakobo frowned but didn't argue. The Sculptors permitted none to witness their work. Obediently, the two Keepers departed, locking the gate of my cage behind them.

The Sculptor listened to their departing footsteps before turning back to me. There was something dreadful in the man's voice. "Bayloo, hear my words and obey: roll onto your side, so that the runes of power face toward Brindisi and I."

The force of the Sculptor's command hit me like a great fist inside my head. A chill ran through my bones. I wasn't sure if I could have resisted the order, and I didn't try. Even if I could have killed these humans, the gate of the cave was closed and locked. I couldn't get out of here. This travesty was going to happen. I would be forced to match my mind against Brindisi. Not having any other choice, I assumed the instructed position, turning awkwardly on the stone floor of my cave, those hideous circles and slashes carved into the scales of my chest protruding as if I were proud of them.

"Head down, shut your eyes," the Sculptor commanded. "You are not to open your eyes until I expressly allow it."

Not even dragons were permitted to witness the carving. Hatchlings had hoods placed over their heads, but for already carved slave dragons, that wasn't necessary. Or, that's what the Sculptors believed.

I lowered my snout to the floor as I'd been commanded, relieved that my shut eyes concealed the black hate that filled them. The

Sculptors were the true slavers of my race. They alone held the power of the control-runes. These were the enemy that I had to kill.

"You must wear this as well, Brindisi," the ArchSculptor said. Even without looking I knew he handed the ryder a blindfold. The Sculptors were so jealous of their secrets, it made me increasingly curious. Was their power so delicate that a bit of forbidden knowledge could threaten them?

"Really, Sculptor?" Brindisi huffed mockingly. "You think I don't know what you do? I know of the Flux; I know of your carvings."

The Sculptors both hissed like angry serpents in a choir. "Hold your tongue," said the senior. His chest, with its single heart, thumped hard enough that I could hear it. "You follow the rules or there shall be no carving this night."

"As you say, Sculptor," Brindisi said, a hint of mockery in his tone, as he placed the black cloth over his eyes.

There was a satisfied grunt from the Sculptor. "We begin with you, Brindisi. Are you ready?"

"I am."

A scoff of skepticism followed Brindisi's assurance. "It is rare to break the link between a living dragon and ryder. Only after a ryder's death is a dragon re-bonded. Here we must break the bond, and it is strong. There shall be pain." The Sculptor said the last with relish.

"I do not fear your cuts."

"Ah, but worse than pain shall be the emptiness you shall feel," the Sculptor promised. "Your mind dominated another for decades. It will feel like losing an arm. Even more, it shall be like losing a part of yourself, at least until the new bond is formed."

"Enough with your talk. Move your hands, not your mouth."

The Sculptor blew an annoyed breath through his mask. "Get on your knees, Brindisi."

I heard him comply. The sounds also told me the Sculptors focused their attention on Brindisi rather than me. I cracked open a slit of my left eye, an opening so narrow that I doubted a human would realize I could take in all the sight I needed through the gap. I watched what no other dragon had ever seen.

The Sculptor removed his gloves, revealing a pair of burnt, scaly hands that resembled the flesh of a molting lizard but for the black inked runes painted onto them. He motioned for his acolyte to approach. Using a key concealed on a chain around his neck, the ArchSculptor unlocked the metal box held by his assistant. From it the Sculptor first withdrew a stylus of carved bone inlaid with enchanted golden runes. Its gleaming tip pulsed, as if a heart pumped within the bone shaft. The Sculptor examined his instrument in the torchlight, a faint exhale of pleasure escaping his lips.

"Bring forth the Flux."

The acolyte reached inside the box and withdrew a small device, forged of gold and covered with strange writings. It resembled an ink pot, similar to those that I'd seen the Keepers use when recording their supply tallies. The ArchSculptor flicked his thumb to open its top and dipped the stylus into the container. When he withdrew it, the pulsing bone tip had disappeared, replaced by a void of black. The Flux went back into the golden box, and the acolyte backed away.

The Sculptor studied the great rune carved into the center of Brindisi's chest as he whispered unintelligible sounds that could've been mistaken for the wind's howl. He touched the stylus to Brindisi's chest. A spark flew into the air, as if he'd struck flint rather than flesh. Brindisi's jaw bulged, but he kept his teeth locked together. More sparks flashed as the Sculptor traced the pattern of the existing rune. Brindisi's body trembled, but still he made no sound. When the Sculptor finished his work, Brindisi's chest was an angry slate of red flesh. The rune that had been there had been erased but for a single remaining symbol near the center.

This was something I had not thought possible. Ryders sometimes died, and dragons were re-bonded, but that was usually to a new ryder who had won a Rite, not to an existing ryder. In the rare case where a ryder outlived his dragon (humans being rather fragile creatures), that ryder usually left DragonPeak. Only during the great wars with Ulibon or Oster had there been an opportunity for a dragonless ryder to be re-bonded to an available dragon. As a slave, I'd never given any thought to the process of how a ryder was joined to a new dragon. Only the Sculptors knew those secrets. I was so enthralled with what I had witnessed that I didn't anticipate that the Sculptor would turn his attention to me.

The masked figure moved with surprising alacrity, shifting his gaze from Brindisi's chest to mine. I clamped my eye shut again, my hearts surging in my chest. If humans could hear like dragons, I'd have been discovered, but those useless skin-wings protruding from their skulls were so clogged with hair and wax, they barely functioned.

"Bayloo, you are to keep absolutely still," he commanded, his harsh whisper echoing like a piercing roar inside me.

Up until that moment, I'd believed I was a free being, that the chains that held me were broken forever. But, as I lay there at the mercy of this masked human, I realized a terrible truth: my mind was free, but the power of the runes that once bound me had not been destroyed. My prison could be re-forged, and this man had the power to do it.

My blood turned so cold I might have been frozen. I wasn't entirely sure if it was due to fear or some power that the Sculptor possessed. He wasn't linked to me, but when he spoke, I could feel his will inside of me as I could with a ryder. Even with my eyes shut, I could sense his motions and feel the heat of his flesh.

The Sculptor brought his grim instrument so close to my chest I thought he intended to press it to the runes on my body as he had with Brindisi, but he stopped a finger's length from touching me. Instead, he waved the stylus over the symbols in a series of circles that I think mimicked the inscriptions carved into me. While he worked, he whispered; his voice was so low no human could've heard him, but I did. The words were not from a language I knew, but they fit together, nonetheless, like pieces of a child's puzzle; the sound of each word resembled the initial sound of the next, the tones rising, falling, and repeating in a pattern, like some terrible song conjured from the darkness of the Abyss. The carvings on my chest heated, with the crossed claws at the center, so hot they felt like fire. The beats of my hearts became erratic, leaving me dizzy. For a brief, fleeting moment, I glimpsed something indescribable—another reality beneath this one, a deeper world of brilliant, interlocking patterns of light. It was as if all of the cave, all of the humans, and even I were weavings within a great quilt which had been sewn together with a pulsing thread that linked all of existence together. It was grand, it was perfect. Then it was gone.

The Sculptor had turned away from me.

To be free of that human's attention was equal to the relief of passing a jagged dagger through my bowels (that had only happened once, but that was plenty). The chilling song still echoed in my head. As awful as the Sculptor's magic had felt, I was elated: I was still me. Whatever he had done, I had survived. So far.

I dared to crack open an eye once again. The Sculptor's back was toward me.

"Bring it," he said to his acolyte.

Again, the Sculptor withdrew the ink pot—the Flux, as Brindisi had called it—coating the bone stylus in its impenetrable blackness. Once he was satisfied with the tip of his instrument, the Sculptor started carving Brindisi's flesh.

Flashes of light ignited each time the stylus contacted skin. I've heard the toughest of ryders hollering in pain as they were joined to their dragons, their cries so piercing that other men cringed. Jona had cried out too. But not Brindisi. Through it all, his jaw remained hard, even as sweat dripped down his forehead. Still, I knew Brindisi was in agony, and this pleased me. Until I felt the link.

If my mind was a cave, having a new ryder bonded to me was like a tunnel being dug through the walls. It started as an itching vibration, a premonition of dread, before turning to something more tangible; a steady drumbeat of pain followed, growing until the sensation became akin to having the shrill cry of an angry seagull squawking in my ear. The physical discomfort ended only when the mental passage was complete, and a tunnel had been carved into my mind. Brindisi was on the other side of the new link that had been formed by the Sculptor. But it wasn't the same as my previous link. The bridge to me had been formed, but my own runes no longer enslaved my mind. For now, I hid my strength from my new ryder.

"It is done," the Sculptor pronounced, pleased with himself. He returned the stylus to its container, holding the lid closed until the lock clicked. The acolyte scurried away, his purpose complete.

Brindisi unleashed a howl of satisfaction as he opened his eyes, the sound more wolf than human. A shiver ran through me, although it wasn't the noise that shook me. Rather his utter delight in having a new dragon to control surged through the link between us and through to me. *Such power!* I fought to keep myself from spreading my wings in a triumphant celebration that matched Brindisi's own delirious satisfaction.

"Rise, dragon." My new ryder's voice echoed through my cave and in my head. The power of that command—and the steely will behind it—struck me harder than a ballista's arc-bolt. I'd become accustomed to Jona, whose desires were motivated by reason rather than force. This human before me was not him.

Before this moment, I had never feared any of my ryders. Perhaps as a hatchling taken from his mother, I had been scared of Hadrigal at first, but I didn't recall that. Now, with my mind clear and free, I experienced true fear of the man to whom I was joined. The beats of my twin hearts rang in my head. In my precious days of freedom, I'd come to believe that Jona could not command me. I'd believed that being self-aware and resisting his will meant I was free forever. That was foolishness on my part. Brindisi showed me otherwise.

Not even the terrifying force of the Sculptor's commands matched the will of this human. Brindisi's desires leaked through from his side of the link that bound us like water through a sieve. Through the magical bond, he showed me his thirst for blood, his hunger for power. There was no bend in this human. He did not desire friendship or a partner. He only wanted obedience. I was an animal, his to command. I wondered what he could sense from me, and it added to my fear.

Brindisi's eyes bored into me. As tiny as he was, he had a dragon's stare. He ordered me to move. I did, rolling onto my feet while telling myself it was my choice, part of my deception, not because I had to obey. Yet a chilling voice inside me wondered if a slave who thought he obeyed freely was any less a slave.

"Keepers, open this gate."

Footsteps answered Brindisi's call. Jakobo put his key into the lock and my prison door opened.

Brindisi was anxious to play with his new pet. "Outside, Bayloo."

My ryder led me into the open air, through the gate to see the distant horizon just as the dawn came. I met my new master meekly. Brindisi's chin rose and fell in satisfaction as he examined me in the light of the new day, much as a cook might admire a newly slaughtered lamb before roasting.

"He may not be as large as Traxis, but I sense his vigor, his youth." The manacles of will tightened about me, and I dreaded that I might disappear in that moment. Mercifully, Jakobo spoke, and the intensity of my ryder's hold on me lessened.

"He is a fine beast. Agile in the air. He is among the cleverest of his kind."

Brindisi nodded. "If only he could breathe fire, he would be even more formidable."

If I hadn't hated my new ryder before that moment, I did after his words. Always with the fire thing. Why not bind me with chains and piss in my eye?

Jakobo shrugged without concern. "His first ryder may have damaged him in some way, or perhaps his affliction is somehow related to the scarcity of new dragons. His defect may have been a sign of what would come. Bayloo was the last great ash dragon recovered. All the beasts that were to follow him were smaller and weaker. The dragons dwindle, and times grow desperate."

Annoyance surged through Brindisi, but it wasn't directed at me. "That is your concern, Keeper. Make no excuses for your own failings. I'm here to win the king's battles."

"To do that, we need dragons."

"What would you have me do, Keeper?" Brindisi's shadow loomed over Jakobo. "Must I go to Veralon and sire a new clutch of beasts?"

I was careful not to snort, but I would've traded a barrel of ale to see Brindisi give that a try.

The Keeper's lips twitched with a retort, but he held his tongue in check. Instead, he forced his version of a human smile onto his face, making it look like a cracked tree branch. "We are not yet facing such a need, I hope. But coins are needed, another expedition to Veralon to explore—"

Brindisi waved him away. "Bring your petitions to the king."

"But you have his ear, as we all know. After this, he should owe you a favor."

The warrior showed his teeth. "Careful, old man. Careful. The king owes no one." He turned his back on the Keeper, focusing again on only me. The strength of his will surged through the runes inscribed on my body. If I could've spit fire, I would've sprayed it upon my breast, where the hideous runes were inscribed. "A fine, powerful beast."

I spread my wings, perhaps because I wished it, perhaps because Brindisi did. The sky had brightened as the humans spoke. Soon, it became a welcoming shade of blue, the horizon clear. My thoughts turned to escape: I could fly away from this place ... or could I? Something held me in place. Brindisi's will was not only a means of control —it was a tether. He did not want me gone, so I could not go. I considered fighting, to make my struggle at that moment, but I hesitated. I might not break free. And if I flew, other ryders on dragons would pursue me. I doubted myself.

"A saddle!" Brindisi's voice echoed up the peak. "Keepers! Haul your lazy bottoms from your bed and bring me a saddle."

As Brindisi shouted, the dark presence of the Sculptor emerged from my cave. "The runes are complete, but you should let the link flow for a time before you fly, Brindisi." His voice was no less terrible without the echo of the cave. "Let your new carving have a night to heal before you press fabric or metal onto yourself."

Brindisi waved the words away as he waited impatiently for a Keeper to come to fix me with a saddle. His chest throbbed, and even with the chill of the heights, Brindisi paid the wind and temperature no mind.

The Sculptor and his acolyte said no more. They melted away down a narrow pathway, their locked chest clutched tightly. As the Sculptors departed, Kelum appeared with a dragon saddle. Brindisi sucked in the wind with ugly zeal.

He intends to ride me now.

"Bayloo, to heel."

The words traveled through me like someone rang a bell inside my head, the command shaking me. I couldn't lie to myself this time. I had no choice. Or perhaps I was a coward. I lay flat on the ground.

The Keeper strapped the giant saddle onto me with deft hands. My new ryder climbed onto my back.

When Brindisi ordered it, I flew.

SEVEN

Prince Dayne raged.

No one had to tell him Brindisi had become my ryder rather than him. He saw it in the sky above his royal suite when he awoke. Brindisi made sure of that. He had me do a circuit of the tower, not once but three times that first morning, until the outline of a curly-haired figure appeared behind a window of stained glass. Dayne's mouth dropped as he watched, the realization of what had happened coming slowly and painfully. Finally, the prince released the piercing cry of a spoiled (human) toddler. Only then did Brindisi order me to fly eastward.

"Better he finds out this way," Brindisi said, more to himself than me. "We likely saved a servant's head. Prince Dayne must learn that the greatest prizes must be won in battle. They cannot be stolen."

I hated my new ryder, but he had a passion to fly. He knew the winds as well as any human, he kept a tight seat, and he feared nothing. His business with Prince Dayne concluded, we set off over the skies of Rolm. I flew past the rising air of the lift-stream, making a course along the length of the island of Harcourt all the way to Arrow

Peak in the west, then back again. Brindisi wanted to test my speed and I showed it to him. He laughed with mad delight as I soared along the underside of the clouds, then plunged downward like a falcon seeking prey. At one point, we flew so close to the water of the Thunder Straits that a cresting wave splashed onto my belly. The wind gusted at my back, propelling us to greater speeds. In the moment, I forgot everything except the glory of flight and the song of the wind until it was time to head back to DragonPeak, to my cave with the locked gate. The door shut, reminding me that I was a slave again.

Or at least it felt that way. For the next few days, I flew when Brindisi climbed on my back; I went where he directed me. Every moment I was out of my cave, he was with me, his will holding me. To assuage myself, I snuck the occasional glance in the direction of Veralon whenever I could, but that was all. I ate, I obeyed. At night, when I might have at least made the effort to shatter the bars of my cave, I did nothing but stare. I told myself I was merely biding my time, waiting for the right opportunity, but I was really waiting for someone to come to tell me what to do. I still had a slave's mentality. My greatest fear, the one that inevitably found me in the depth of the nights, was that I might be losing myself.

The more time I spent obeying Brindisi, the more I became accustomed to his commands. Each day, my own thoughts became more addled. A fog marshalled at the edge of my consciousness and I struggled to hold it at bay. I wondered how long I could keep up this fight or if I would even know when it was too late for me. It was like no other battle I had ever fought; instead of facing an enemy of flesh and blood, it was my own mind that threatened me. Or perhaps it was just my imagination.

I both dreaded and anticipated each morning when Brindisi came. The dread was easy to understand because Brindisi was a terrifying human. Through the link between us leaked an inkling of the man who was now my ryder. He had a singular focus, which he pursued without fear or doubt. At the moment, he desired to make me an extension of himself, a weapon to be used against his enemies. I should've cringed at this, raged against it, but it was not that simple. My mind may have somehow pried itself free of the rune-prison, but Brindisi had shown me that my liberation remained incomplete. When he was on my back, his focus was my own. His direction flowed to my mind. I turned, I dove, and I wanted to impress him. I had no worries, no cares. I merely did as I was bid. I should've been more ashamed of the comfort I took from that feeling.

For three days and nights, Brindisi was my constant companion (mercifully, he'd resumed wearing his dark scale armor over his chest runes after that first, horrible bare skin morning). Sometimes, in the evening, when I was free from the intensity of Brindisi's will, I vainly listened for any sign of Jona, even though I knew he was dead. During the long nights, I wondered if he had truly died of his injuries or if Brindisi had killed him so that he might claim me. I kept a wary eye out for Bethy Rann or her horned dragon Crema, but the smaller dragons were kept lower on the peak, and Brindisi kept me flying about for much of the daylight hours.

On the fourth night following that dark evening when Brindisi claimed me, footsteps approached in the darkness. A single man climbing from below. I knew it wasn't Jona—even if he were alive, the cadence of his steps was different. This man climbed along the narrow, rocky paths of DragonPeak without caution or even fear. The figure that appeared at my gate was none other than Prince Dayne.

He wore no finery on this visit, no rings or enameled mail, just a simple tunic. He carried a lantern in one hand. By its flickering light, I saw that the prince's lips were turned down and a crease ran across his forehead.

"Come here so that I can see you, dragon."

I snorted my displeasure. It was an indulgence to show defiance, but this boy knew too little of my kind to suspect such disrespect. I pulled myself over to the gate, moving sluggishly. Let the little prince wait for me.

When I had come close enough for Dayne's satisfaction, he spoke through the bars. "I came here to make a promise." He looked at me expectantly. I stared back, doing my best to seem as vacant of thought as this young human. His frown deepened. "Do you wish to know what that promise is?"

The little human didn't speak Avian very well, so I deliberately answered him in that language, even though I can also speak the common tongue of Rolm better than any other dragon. "If that is your desire, Master." I snorted again as I spoke the human honorific.

I didn't know if Dayne understood me. He just assumed I'd said whatever he wanted, I supposed. I imagine he'd done a lot of that in his life. "You were stolen from me. No one steals from me. I have sacrificed to claim you. So, the promise I make now, under Haven and before you as well, is that you shall be mine one day, dragon. *Mine*. Together, we shall be a force in the sky like this kingdom has never seen. When I rule Rolm, it shall be I who chooses the ryders, and we shall win conquests the likes of which neither my brother nor even my father ever dreamed."

I thought it more likely the chickens would become the new occupants of DragonPeak. Still, I moved my head ever so slightly downward, as if acknowledging the gravity of the prince's promise. I was tempted to release the gas in my bowels at that solemn moment while the prince's pledge hung in the air, but that would've been a waste of some fine flatulence, as well as a unique opportunity. I needed to escape from this place. I had no allies or friends or even confidants in Eladrell. But I had a mind, and I needed to start using it. My plan required a fool, and he had delivered himself to me.

I flashed my eyes at Dayne. I can't do sapphire, but I managed my darkest shade of amber. I put on a display of my finest Rolman speech. "Destiny."

Dayne's eyes bulged as a malevolent grin split his face. "Aye, destiny. You feel it too, dragon. Excellent." He looked about suddenly with suspicion, as if worried about the unexpected success of his late-night jaunt. "Tell no one of this. Tell no one."

I wondered how a slave dragon would respond to a command from one human to lie to another. A dragon couldn't lie to its ryder, but I wasn't sure about the rest. For me, lying was easy. I bestowed my version of a human nod, flashing my eyes, as if I understood.

The prince left me, still wearing his wicked grin. I had no idea what he planned, but I had little doubt that it would not be pleasing to Brindisi, and that could only help me. I slept soon afterwards, believing that I'd finally hit upon the first stirrings of a plan to free myself from my new ryder. My satisfaction lasted only until the morning.

Brindisi arrived at first light, as was his custom, but I knew immediately something was different. Usually, he carried my saddle with him and wore armor only over his chest. On this morning, metal scales covered all of his body, while his quiver bulged with fletched arrows. At first, I feared he had somehow learned of my scheming with the silly prince, but when the Keepers arrived with additional supplies, I knew this had nothing to do with Dayne. The humans filled the saddle's flaps with skins of water, dried meat, and fruit (but no ale). Brindisi wore a look that seemed both grim and pleased, his jaw pulsing, his eyes alight with an excited glint.

"We journey to Maricopa with haste, Bayloo. You know the way, I trust?"

It was the first time he'd asked me a question, even a condescending one. I answered through our link, wary. "I know Maricopa."

"We had a message arrive by white pigeon last night. It was from one of our ships, reporting an attack near there. Raiders, it seems."

I almost asked why anyone would bother with Maricopa, but, of course, I couldn't do that. I wasn't supposed to be curious. Still, something about the information bothered me. Maricopa was a puny island. Indeed, it was little more than a broken mountain shell, its only settlement a tiny fishing village that existed in the peak's shadow. I knew the place only because it had once been part of Ulibon, and I'd helped to conquer it. None of the island's few inhabitants had fought; they seemed to barely even know they were part of

Ulibon, so joining Rolm didn't matter. Before the Highstar had claimed their land, the island had been too remote, inaccessible, and poor to bother with. Its inhabitants were fishermen, and not very prosperous ones. They might have a bit of food tucked away, but not enough to even fill the hold of a ship. It wasn't worth any raider's effort. I didn't share any of this information. I just played my part as a dutiful slave, speaking the kinds of words my ryder wished to hear. "The wind favors speed. We can be there before the sun reaches the lowest cloud on the horizon."

Brindisi also doubted that raiders were responsible. "Oster must be desperate after their recent losses to choose such a remote island. But all of Rolm is ours to protect. If it was them, we shall make them pay for their mistake." Brindisi said it aloud, with relish, as if I'd be impressed. He sounded idiotic, even for a human. Humans really should learn how to muster a decent roar.

Together we flew off toward Maricopa. The island lay to the southeast, an outlying hunk of rock well off any major sea lane. My route took me south, across Harcourt, over its rich pastures of cows and sheep, then to the coast. Below, fishermen climbed into their boats to risk their lives trying to harvest the bounty of the Saltstorm Channel between Ulibon and Harcourt. I flew west over the sea, passing close enough that my eyes could peer south and see the Twisted Keep of Ulibon, once the seat of the Highstar. Karthus and I had survived that battle, but many had not. Once I left Ulibon in my wake, there was only sea to the horizon. I glided with the wind for a time, soaring and drifting downward again according to whim. Brindisi paid my flight path no mind. His eyes were fixed on the water below, ever vigilant for signs of his prey.

Even with the gusts at my back, the afternoon had passed by the time the island of Maricopa finally came into view. I dropped closer to the water to ensure I would spot any fleeing ship, but I saw nothing on the sea that had been created by the hands of men. Instead, my eyes fixed upon the familiar shape of an armored dorsal fin breaking the surface.

I dutifully reported the sighting like a good dragon. "Leviathan below. Headed toward the Saltstorm Channel."

"Not our concern. Find the Osterans." Brindisi's tone told me that he cared even less about humans than I did. The leviathan would destroy any fishing boat it came across and kill its crew. The creatures surfaced only when they attacked or for air. By letting this opportunity pass, we were essentially condemning some hapless fisherman to death. Such was the way of the world. I beat my wings, leaving the giant beast to its hunt while I focused on my own.

Maricopa came upon us soon afterward. It was just as I remembered it: rock with some more rock piled on top. A cluster of three peaks congregated on the north side of the island, as if one had sprouted from the other, but only one was worth mentioning: the Kraken. The great mountain soared so high it almost reached the clouds, its far slope covered with koa trees while the opposite side, and most of the rest of the island, was scrub and bare rock. But what made the Kraken truly unlike any other peak I'd known was its inside: the mountain had partially collapsed onto itself far in the distant past, allowing a lake of clear, fresh water to form inside. I'd drank from the lake when last I'd visited, as it was the only source of freshwater on the island except for the erratic rains. I had heard it said by some of the ryders that the mountain had once been an inferno peak, much like those that made up the Wall of Fire, but its heat had fled, and the rains that had once fallen with regularity around Rolm had filled its belly with water instead.

I made a slow circuit of the island, flying at height almost equal to the summit of the Kraken. The shores of Maricopa were a treacherous maze of jagged rocks and deadly shoals waiting just beneath the shallow waters, which was another reason no humans bothered with this place. The island had no resources, no arable land, and was near nothing; there was only a single navigable harbor on the eastern side. The island's primary settlement was clustered there, clinging to a narrow patch of land large enough for a few simple dwellings made of hacked koa wood mixed with mud. As I flew toward the village, even Brindisi's inadequate eyes could spot the smoke rising from the ground.

He wasn't sentimental. "The raiders have already done their work—the village burns. Yet I see no ships in the harbor. Let us search the seas before they escape."

I brought us lower, searching the waves for signs of the Osteran raiders. It didn't take long before I was confident that no ship sailed on the waters nearby. I made several slow circles, moving a bit closer to the water each time for Brindisi's benefit. It was on the last of these circuits that I spotted the debris. I tilted my wings to change course so that we could investigate further. I had destroyed enough ships to know pretty well what the remains of a decimated vessel looked like upon the water—this flotsam had once been a ship. Scattered scraps of wood bobbed with the waves. I spotted a broken mast and the scraps of a sail. And, of course, bodies.

"Bring us as close as you can, Bayloo."

I obliged, angling myself into position opposite the westerly wind, which allowed me to almost hover, seemingly frozen above the most concentrated collection of wreckage.

"This looks more like the work of a dragon than an engagement between ships," Brindisi muttered.

He was right, except there was no sign of fire. But a clash of human warships wouldn't have resulted in this type of destruction. The hull was a splintered mess. There was another explanation, though. "A leviathan could have done this."

"A leviathan wouldn't have left bodies."

Indeed, it wouldn't have. Leviathans didn't waste food. I didn't have an answer for that.

"Pluck a body out of the water and take it with us to Maricopa."

I grabbed a human from the sea with my foreclaws, carrying the bloated mess with me back to the smoking village on Maricopa's shore. I set down on a narrow slice of rock beside the sea. The fishing boats that had once moored nearby had been burned. Most of the simple structures in the village had been toppled or torn apart. Bodies were strewn across the landscape, many with arrows sticking out of their flesh. The place stank of the dead, the slaughter, and the sea in equal measure. But there was something else as well. I sniffed at the air, trying to glean the scent.

Brindisi interrupted me. He slid from my back toward the corpse I'd dropped on the shore. "Let us attend to this man first."

He bent over the decaying man. Seawater did nothing to make humans more appealing. This one was an ugly mess. Brindisi searched the dead man's clothing and pulled out some metal coins from the corpse's pocket. He stared at them only briefly before tossing them back onto the ground.

"Coins of Rolm. He was a man of the kingdom. That was the king's ship they sank." He ground his jaw. Brindisi might not care about the men themselves, but he was angered by the loss of Mendakas' ship. One less boat to sail to Oster.

Brindisi conducted a hasty reconnoiter of the rest of the paltry village, moving from hovel to hovel with a scowl on his face. He glanced at the bodies and wrecked structures and little else. "Why would anyone want to live in this place?" he wondered.

I watched from just beside the water, trying to decide if I should care about any of this. I didn't know any of these humans and they didn't know me. If the raiders escaped, perhaps it made war with Oster less likely.

Brindisi moved from corpse to corpse. "There are only a dozen bodies, but dwellings enough for three times that number to live here. Something is missing."

He kept searching, examining the soil, looking at prints in the dirt, his scowl deepening as he moved. Brindisi's demeanor changed when he reached the settlement's largest structure. Unlike the other buildings, its walls were dark, basalt rock pulled from the great mountain, while its scorched roof was supported by the bones of a long dead leviathan. He stopped, staring at what he found inside: food. There were other supplies as well. Brindisi hacked open three storage barrels with his long sword, revealing stores of smoked fish, salted goat meat, and even a bit of grain. Two barrels were filled with stinky pommice fruit—some of it dried. Naturally, there was no ale. This island was desperately uncivilized.

"They didn't take the food," Brindisi said unnecessarily, because I also had eyes. "Nor did they bother to burn it."

Just because I didn't care that much about any of this didn't mean I failed to understand what Brindisi was talking about. Oster was starving—leaving behind this much food just wasn't something that King Galt's raiders would've done. There was no way this tiny village had such a bounty of treasure that their ship didn't have enough space in its hold to carry it all. Nor did it make sense that Osteran raiders could blast a Rolman warship to pieces.

Brindisi turned away from the storehouse, hurrying back to the nearest body. It was a woman. I knew because the hair on her head grew past her shoulders, but she didn't have any fur on her face or ears. She'd been shot between her shoulders with an arrow as she tried to run away. Brindisi placed his heel on her back, put a hand on the shaft of the arrow sticking out of her, then yanked. Congealed blood splattered onto his mailed chest. He wiped a bit of the dark crimson off the tip of the arrow, his eyes squinting. I was further away, but I saw the same thing he did. I made the same conclusion he did—that the arrow that killed the woman hadn't been made in any forge of Oster. Brindisi flicked the arrowhead with a finger to be sure. Snarling, he snapped the shaft into two pieces.

"Not metal. It's just as hard, just as sharp, but it's something else. Treated wood or whatever in the Abyss they do to make their weapons."

He said "they," but I knew he meant the Mizu.

"Mizu ships move swiftly." Brindisi knew that as well as I did, but I wanted him to know I was paying attention. "They could've come and gone."

"A waveship." Brindisi grunted at his own conclusion. "That is why we saw no sign. That is why our warship wasn't just sunk, it was annihilated. They must've had a wizard aboard."

This didn't please me. The mysterious wizards of the Mizu supposedly had powers none in Rolm or Oster understood or could match. It was said they could command the wind and sea. I had never faced one, for Mizu ships were rare, but I had heard plenty of stories from ryders who had.

Brindisi searched the horizon, as if his eyes could somehow spot a ship that I couldn't see from the air. Of course, he saw nothing. "There hasn't been a Mizu attack on Rolm in two years. Now, they return ... here. What would the Mizu want in a miserable little place like this?" He looked around again, straining to find something new in the ruins of the village. "They are metal hunters, but there are no mines here. These people had few, if any, steel weapons. There is nothing on this island that the Mizu value."

It was arrogant for Brindisi to assume that he understood the Mizu, but he was an arrogant man, even for a human. The Mizu were mysterious, appearing from their lands beyond the Wall of Fire, a barrier of smoke and fire beyond which even dragons could not fly. Their waveships moved almost as fast through the water as a dragon flew through the air, but the sleek vessels had no sails or oars. When the Mizu came, they usually came in search of metal—any metal. Weapons to be sure, but they weren't picky. They'd take coins or door hinges or jewelry or farm hoes. Once they had their booty, they sped away, back beyond the barrier of fire that hid their kingdom. No Mizu had ever been captured alive. Even my kind were wary of the Mizu. I wasn't sorry we'd missed them.

I expected Brindisi to be angry, both because the Mizu were gone and because he hadn't gotten his chance to start a war with Oster. Definitely a rough morning for an aggressive, conniving human like him. But he didn't seem angry. Instead, he kept doing a very un-human thing—he kept thinking.

"This place had a more than ample store of food in a time of famine." Brindisi returned to the warehouse. I reluctantly got to my feet as well so I might see what he saw. This mystery of the Mizu made me curious. More importantly, my current spot near the shore had a lot of sharp rocks that were itching my hindquarters.

Brindisi hacked into more storage barrels, this time making his way to a cluster in the rear of the storehouse. There was no food inside. Instead, when the wood shattered, out came gold ingots, quantities of fine, white sand, bits of flint, mortar and pestle sets, and other assorted instruments made for small, five-fingered hands that I didn't recognize.

"Not the tools of fishermen," Brindisi whispered. He kneeled down, letting the fine grains of white sand stream through his fingers. Then he picked up a small instrument that resembled two tiny blades fused together at one end. "I've seen devices like this. In the Twisted Keep on Ulibon after the Highstar died." He snarled. "It seems that the enchanters of Ulibon still live. Or at least they did until recently." Brindisi stood, his expression unusually thoughtful. "We thought we slew the last of them when their leader, Anatar, lost his head, but it seems not. Perhaps the legend of the lost heir is not all legend. Perhaps some enchanters are even now with the Mizu as prisoners."

I added my useless, obvious observation. "None of these things came from this island."

"They could've been brought here before the Twisted Keep of Ulibon fell. Or perhaps these enchanters traded with other kingdoms, or even the pirate king."

I disliked the enchanters I'd met. Their servants shot magical arrows with golden tips that could pierce dragon armor, and their magic had made the Twisted Keep impervious to the breath of the fire-breathers. Taking Ulibon had been an ugly battle.

Brindisi kept talking, although I didn't think any of his words were meant for me. "Yet, still, the Mizu didn't bother with any of these things. Not even the gold." My ryder's teeth flashed like those of a hungry predator. "They didn't even search for these materials—they left them in the building. The Mizu brought a wizard, perhaps because they knew that enchanters inhabited this place, yet they ignored the spoils of conquest. They killed, then they moved. They were in a hurry, looking for something more even precious to them than gold or other metals."

Uh-oh.

"You believe the Mizu are still here?" I asked.

"I'm certain of it."

EIGHT

I hunted the Mizu.

There were wild goats on this island begging (bleating actually) to be eaten, but rather than indulging their pleas, I flew the length of Maricopa searching for some of the most dangerous humans on this world. I had two explanations: the first was that I was genuinely curious about what the Mizu wanted on this desolate island. The second was that I wasn't sure if I could disobey Brindisi. His will spread into my mind like a pestilence. The tendrils of his desires mingled with mine such that I couldn't be entirely certain of my own decisions. Even my interest in the Mizu might've been influenced by him. The longer I stayed linked to him, the worse the situation would become. I needed this mission to end, and I needed to get away from Brindisi.

Despite its small size, Maricopa had plenty of places to hide. The most obvious spot was the eastern side of the Kraken, where the koa trees were so thick they concealed the ground beneath their lush canopy of leaves. Twisting pommice trees dominated the lower elevations of the mountain. A group of humans on foot could hack their way through the forest, but it would take time. If the Mizu were on

Maricopa, they could still be ascending the mountain. They might also be hiding in the caves of the mountainside, both on the Kraken and the smaller peaks that hugged it, but I couldn't think of a reason for them to do that.

I began my search by ruling out the rest of the island. I swept the ground so low I sent dust into the air before soaring to glimpse at the glittering lake within the Kraken's summit. I spotted goats and the tracks of some four-legged predator—perhaps wolves. But no humans. The stink of ripening pommice fruit overpowered most other scents, making the search more difficult.

Brindisi became impatient with my methodical approach. "They must be traveling beneath the cover of the trees. Traxis could hear a mouse scurrying around the castle while circling above its highest tower. Even if you can't see them, you should be able to hear them. Prove yourself worthy, Bayloo."

I don't know if other dragons grind their teeth when they're angry, but I apparently do. My ryder's words tasted like the potatoes served with a side of rancid seaweed. I was fortunate Brindisi couldn't see the crimson flashing in my eyes. To calm myself, I pretended that I had Brindisi in my jaw as I bit my teeth together. I needed to keep my anger in check. Even if he couldn't see my eyes, my emotions might leak through the rune-link. I sucked in a gust of air, then I did as I had been told.

I flew almost as slow as a man could walk over the tops of the koa trees that grew on the mountain slope. Beneath the canopy of tall branches, the spidery limbs of the smaller trees intermingled with the older, larger growths. Many of the sickle-shaped koa leaves had browned, but I still saw plenty of green as well. I listened and watched as I flew. I didn't believe that Traxis had sharper hearing than me.

I heard the calls of birds, the buzzing of insects. I detected a few larger creatures lurking about—the kind that crushed leaves underfoot—but not many. These weren't humans. I detected no sound of marching feet; I smelled none of the ugly sweat stink that I often associated with men. Still, the mountain was vast, and I continued my search, moving gradually from the hinterlands closest to the village and further up the gently sloping side. I began to hope that Brindisi was mistaken about the Mizu still being on this island.

He had no doubts. "They are here. I can feel it. They came for something, and they don't have it yet. Which means we have a chance to stop them, to kill them. Maybe even question one."

Even I cannot stay aloft indefinitely. My wings ached, my neck throbbed, and my belly rumbled (it often did that). I didn't want to tell Brindisi that I needed a break, but I doubted he was giving any thought to my fatigue. He could just eat and even piss in the saddle if he wanted. I needed meat and didn't want to scare the fauna below with a steaming yellow rain when I unlocked my bowls.

Finally, I could wait no more. "I must soon rest. To fly in this manner is tiresome."

"Not as tiresome as a whining dragon. Traxis never complained about being tired."

Traxis never hovered over a forest for most of a day after flying from Eladrell. After a bit more gnawing of my teeth, I replied aloud, "Traxis is mighty."

You should go back to being his ryder.

"Mighty old, perhaps. He sees worse than me and can barely outfly a swift pigeon." Brindisi made a sound like a dog's bark. "How much longer can you stay aloft?"

I wanted to tell him I needed to land soon—as in now—but I had nagging doubts about being able to lie directly to him without him sensing my deception. I answered honestly.

"Perhaps until the sky begins to darken, but it will take longer to recover if I push myself so far."

Brindisi snorted with disdain, as if he could flap his arms for an entire afternoon. "Go eat your dried goat meat and rest your wings."

Snide remarks aside, I was about to do that when I smelled something that definitely wasn't a goat. I was far enough up the mountain slope that the pommice stink had faded. I inhaled another deep gust of the wind to be sure. It had distinct notes of sour, sweat, and a hint of stupid. The stink of large animals, most likely men.

"Why do you wait, dragon?"

I answered through the rune-link. "Two-legged creatures are nearby."

Brindisi shifted on my back, likely notching an arrow into his bow.

I reached out with all of my senses. The footfalls drew close. I glided toward the sound of the motion, making tight circles as I floated above the canopy. I still couldn't see anything through the trees. The movement stopped. They knew I was above them. Even when I try to fly quietly, I still make a fair bit of noise, and my wing-span tends to block the sun.

I spoke through the link again. "They are beneath us, hiding under the trees. They know I am here."

"Flush them out. My bow is ready."

I flexed the claws on my forelegs. My wings burned with fatigue, but I had enough strength for this. I dropped without warning, my legs outstretched. I locked onto two of the largest koa trees in the vicinity, one with each of my hind legs. I gave a mighty beat of my wings, ripping both trees up from the ground, roots as well. It reminded me of the way human farmers harvested potatoes, only way more impressive because I was doing it. The trauma to the dirt from the roots being torn up also felled several of the smaller trees nearby, leaving an ugly, open scar in the canopy that revealed the dark soil of the mountain's slope.

Two forms dashed for fresh cover beneath the trees that still stood, like rabbits fleeing their collapsing burrow. The animals ran swift as wolves, but with only two legs, their bodies clad in suits of armor painted in the colors of fall leaves: Mizu. Brindisi loosed his arrow. It caught the slower of the pair in the back just as he reached the tree line. He didn't fall, nor did he cry out. Mizu armor was almost as tough as anything the forges of Rolm produced, even if it was made from resin-treated wood rather than metal.

I dropped the two boles I held, preparing to repeat my prior gardening exercise with two more unlucky koa trees. Bad decision.

My tail started to tickle, a bizarre sensation that felt as if a dozen rats had decided there was something delicious under my armored scales. I twitched in discomfort, which changed my flight path ever so slightly—maybe the length of two human arms—but that probably saved my life. A single dark cloud had silently appeared above me, a foreigner in the otherwise clear day. I hadn't noticed its appearance, and even if I had, I wouldn't have given it a second thought. A bolt of lightning came from the errant cloud of darkness, streaking through the sky with such ferocity that it felt as if the air itself had been torn by its passage. The blast blinded me; the thunderous echo that followed its passage shook my bones. It missed my neck, but not by much. That strange itch had saved me, but only temporarily. The lightning wasn't natural. A wizard lurked nearby.

Even before my sight returned, I swept higher into the sky, zigging and zagging as I executed a wide turn that put plenty of distance between me and the Mizu wizard's summoning. My sight gradually returned. Wary, I searched the sky for more unnatural storm clouds.

Brindisi was delighted by my near roasting. "I knew they were here." The satisfaction in his voice tempted me to flip over and see how sturdy those saddle straps really were. "We shall deal with that wizard first."

I heard Brindisi, but I kept flying on my previous course anyway, putting more and more distance between us and the Mizu. I didn't know how far the wizard could send forth his lightning blasts or what else the Mizu had in their arsenal, but being far away seemed like a good idea. I also knew I would have to go back. Brindisi wanted to fight. That was as much a part of him as eating was a part of me. He hungered for a kill so badly, I didn't need for him to say it to me.

"Grab some more trees. Drop them from above—way above, then dive hard behind them. If that wizard shows his face, I'll put an arrow through his skull." Brindisi made it sound like something appealing.

Fine. I'd risk my life again. But he'd better not make another fire-breather comment after this.

I circled again, diving to rip up two more koa trees from the furthest edge of the slope, then I climbed back into the sky, wary for lightning clouds. Brindisi probably thought dropping twenty-foot-long trunks was easy. It wasn't. Even while circling over an area, I had to keep myself steady while the wind was gusting. Furthermore, trees, with all their twisty branches and leaves, aren't made for flight. They don't go where they are supposed to go. Explaining that to Brindisi would've been a waste. I just dove. When I became confident that I had a decent feel for the wind, I dropped my wooden projectiles. I spread my wings to slow my own descent, letting the trees lead the way, hopefully providing a distraction.

The giant boles smashed into the ground with as much force as I could've hoped, their branches shattering on impact, sending debris flying all about. I came in hard behind the shield of mayhem while Brindisi shot arrows from my back. I was impressed at how quickly he fired, particularly given the dangerous angle of my descent. Even with the saddle straps, it was no easy feat to fire a bow from his position, much less with accuracy. Unfortunately, I couldn't see any of the Mizu as I flew, so I doubted that Brindisi could either. He was firing blind, hoping to hit something. I pulled out of my dive as I came upon the tree canopy, whipping my tail into the treetops and creating a rain of leaves and koa pods.

A man cried out in pain from below as one of Brindisi's arrows found a soft target. I doubted it was the wizard—I wasn't lucky. I flapped my wings for more speed and began to pull up, intending to create more distance between myself and the Mizu. I felt the itch again, a sensation on either side of my head rather than my tail this time. I swerved hard, diving away from the clouds. The air tingled. Lightning flashed again, originating from an unknown point high in the sky.

I changed my course again, spinning like a dancer in the air while tucking my wings as close to my body as I could to make myself a smaller target. For a brief moment I even thought I'd escaped. Then the world exploded and a searing pain unlike any I'd ever experienced enveloped me.

I tumbled toward the trees.

I crashed with all the elegance of one of the trees I'd dropped on the Mizu.

I smashed into the forested slope, falling through the canopy, snapping branches as I fell. My wings made the descent only slightly less painful than a complete free fall. I landed on a cluster of saplings, crushing their trunks, before rolling indignantly onto the dirt. A steady rain of sickle-shaped pods dropped onto my head, echoing through the woods like clattering drums. The smell of seared flesh was in the air. Unfortunately, I was the source. The wizard's lightning had hit my right wing, tearing the membrane just above the first joint. It felt like I was being roasted in a fire. Wings were comparatively soft. My armor had protected the rest of me from the fall. Of course, I'd landed on my feet. Cats had learned how to fall from dragons (probably).

I lifted my wing. That made it hurt even more. I'd had worse injuries, but wing damage was always serious. Dragons were excellent healers, but the precious flesh of our wingspan was prone to permanent damage. A severe enough injury might never properly regenerate. Luckily, it wasn't that bad. I expected that I would fly again, if I lived through this.

Brindisi interrupted my self-indulgent meditation of sorrow. He'd survived the fall too and was still strapped to my back. I really had no luck at all. A slave dragon's first instinct would've been the fate of his ryder. Brindisi was an afterthought to me, which I took as a reassuring sign of my independence.

Brindisi unlatched himself, slipping to the ground with a thud. He tumbled onto his knees, barely avoiding planting his face into the dirt. I had come down rather fast, and the tree branches had probably hurt as well. Brindisi puked the contents of his stomach out. It stank, but I hoped his forthcoming hunger would make him a little less condescending about my own stomach's legitimate needs.

Brindisi struggled back upright, then promptly shut his eyes and teetered backward like a poorly built castle tower. He would've fallen over. Maybe he would've hit his head. Maybe one of the sharp edges of a shattered tree trunk would've impaled him. I would never know because I panicked when I saw him fall, my blood racing with distress as if this human were my hatchling. I whipped my tail around and caught him before he struck the ground. I laid him flat on the ground. His breathing was steady, his heart strong. He seemed shaken from the crash, but I didn't see any reason he wouldn't recover. *Why had I done that?*

It had to be the link. What in the Abyss had those Sculptors done to me?

As I stared at Brindisi's inert form, I considered my unpalatable situation. I'd crashed further down the mountain from the location where the brief battle with the Mizu had taken place. They'd have to retrace their previous progress if they wanted to finish us off. I didn't think they'd bother to do that. Whatever the Mizu had come here for, they seemed to be in a rush. Also, the longer they lingered on this island, the greater the chance another dragon would arrive to investigate why Brindisi and I hadn't returned. All of which meant that we were probably safe where we were.

With my ryder unconscious, the poisonous force of his will that flowed through our link weakened but didn't disappear. I'd acted to help him, perhaps save him. It seemed I couldn't trust myself.

My injured wing made leaving this place nearly impossible. Even if I could get off the ground, trying to fly any distance risked creating an injury that would render me flightless forever. A free dragon that couldn't fly would be a dead dragon soon enough. I stretched my wings again. It hurt like bathing inside an inferno mountain. I growled in frustration. But I did nothing. I just stayed where I was. I'm rather good at that—maybe as adept as a human. There were supplies in the dragon saddle, but I needed Brindisi to get at those.

I tried to sleep, even as my wing throbbed. I managed a slight doze, but pain and anxiousness denied me any real rest. Light faded from the sky, and the stars and moon appeared. I thought I caught Rima's ill shape, but the vision disappeared so quickly I could've been mistaken.

It turned out that not sleeping was for the best. Sometime that night, the Mizu came. The attackers crept through the forest deliberately, avoiding twigs and other debris that might make too much noise. But they couldn't help that they were human and I was a dragon. I could hear better than them and my nose was way more impressive. Size matters, despite what some humans claim.

I laid my neck on the ground, hoping that this would make it look like I was asleep. But I wasn't a fool. I turned my face away from the direction of the interlopers—I really didn't want to learn what an arrow up my nose or shot into my eye would feel like. As the humans neared, I heard every step, every breath. When they got really close, I could hear their hearts beating against their chests. There were only two.

I didn't wait to let them get all the way into the clearing where Brindisi and I lay. If they realized I was alive they might run, and I wasn't in any condition to chase them. I needed to make this quick and get it done without further damage to my wing. The interlopers made my task a bit more difficult by separating before they came as close as I would've liked. When the first one notched his bow, I struck.

I shoved myself off the ground in the direction of the first Mizu, moving like a pouncing cat. My neck sprang forward. The human had positioned himself behind two trees that were thick with branches, but the scale armor on my head was strong. I just shoved myself through the obstacle until my jaw reached the Mizu, cracking any branches in my way. The Mizu screamed in agony as my teeth shut on him, his armor making a satisfying crunch as my mouth closed. The salty taste of blood leaked into my mouth before I released the dead man. His companion would die next.

I expected the other Mizu to run. That's what any other soldier would've done. However, the Mizu stood his ground. He crouched behind an interwoven cluster of trees, his bow ready. I smashed down the obstacles with a few powerful swipes of my forelegs. He fired—at my eyes. I dodged his first arrow. The second landed beneath my snout. It didn't fully penetrate my armor, but it sank deep enough to lodge itself there. It hurt, and when I get hurt, I also get angry.

I snatched the little archer into my mouth, but I didn't crush him; I didn't want to kill him. I just wanted to scare the piss out of him— which is what happened. After that warm liquid had all dribbled out, he dropped his bow. At first, the Mizu squirmed, but once he realized that moving around made my teeth sink further into him, he stopped wriggling. I brought the Mizu back to the clearing, spit him onto the ground, then placed my right foreleg on top of him with my claws on either side of his head. His eyes opened so wide he might have been trying to shoot his eyeballs at me. The man's pupils were as black as his hair, while his skin was a shade darker than the humans of Rolm.

I put my nostrils next to his face and exhaled my hottest, moistest snarl. That got me a choking howl of terror. Now came the really hard part. Dragon jaws just weren't built to speak standard Rolmish.

"Why... here?"

If the Mizu's eyeballs had been capable of rolling out of his head, they definitely would've. They must've been securely fastened. Too bad. Blind men were less likely to try to run away.

I said it again.

This time the Mizu tried to speak, at least in the sense that he made some sounds that might've been words of a language. But I couldn't understand him.

"Let me try." It was Brindisi. In the excitement, I hadn't noticed my ryder bestir himself. He looked paler than normal, but otherwise in reasonably decent condition (apart from still having only two legs and a two-holed thumb on his face instead of a real nose that could actually smell things).

Brindisi positioned himself such that his eyes stared directly into the terrified face of the captive Mizu.

"Why are you here?" He said it in Avian. Why did he think to speak to the Mizu in the language of dragons? Brindisi doubtlessly knew more of the Mizu than I did. Did his words mean the Mizu also had dragons back in their home, beyond the Wall of Fire?

Seeing a human above him—even one as mean and ugly as Brindisi—actually seemed to reassure the Mizu. The shape of his face went from twisted terror to twisted defiance (this involved smaller eyes, tighter lips, and a wrinkled nose). It was clear he wasn't going to answer.

I pushed my head closer to my little captive once again. This time I gave him a shot of hot breath (I don't spit out fire, but it still stinks so much it can be scary). I could feel his terror. I did it again. The Mizu squirmed beneath my leg, doubtlessly believing he was about to be roasted. Brindisi caught on.

"You had best answer."

The Mizu remained defiant. "May you follow me into the Abyss."

My hearts surged in surprise. He did speak Avian. What did that mean?

Brindisi plunged the tip of his sword into the man's neck. He convulsed, then died. I lifted my leg off his chest.

"He wasn't going to talk," Brindisi said. "He is Mizu."

Brindisi spoke as if his words were reason enough to kill the captive—as if killing that man had been as logical as crushing a roach underfoot. Maybe to Brindisi, that was the case. I wondered what else my ryder knew about the Mizu. Supposedly, none had ever been taken prisoner in battle. Perhaps that wasn't true. The mystery of their presence on this island became even more intriguing to me.

I had nothing to add to Brindisi's conclusion, so I didn't speak. Dragons were different from humans in that way—we know when to keep our mouths shut.

Brindisi stared into the night. The mountain was mostly invisible in the dark, but I knew that was what he gazed at. "It seems reasonable the rest of them are climbing for the summit."

"I have been to the top. There is nothing there but a great lake. Its water is fresh and clear, but it has little else of value to the Mizu."

"We must get there," Brindisi insisted. "The saddle is damaged, but I don't need it."

I dreaded my next confession. "I am injured."

"You can't fly?" Brindisi was incredulous.

"I am uncertain if I can fly or not." I tried to sound like a slave dragon. "I must share with you that if my wing tears further, the damage may be irreversible."

Brindisi grunted with frustration. "I could climb the mountain myself, but that wizard and his soldiers... I need you to go with me. You must fly."

The brutal force of Brindisi's will seeped through our link. He intended to reach the summit. He intended to discover why the Mizu had come. If he had to have my runes scraped from his chest and replaced with others, that was a price he was more than willing to pay. Strangely, I understood. Part of my mind was his mind. Within the world of Brindisi, others were mere objects. Only the goal mattered.

"You must try to fly."

I wanted to know why the Mizu had come as well. Even more, I wanted to know if they had dragons back in their homeland. Why else speak Avian?

"As you will it, I will do." That sounded very slave dragon. "But it will be much more dangerous at night. I am still exhausted from the day. And hungry."

Brindisi rolled his eyes. "You sound like my wife." At that, a rare pang of sympathy for a human ran through me—for the poor woman who was mated to this man. He opened the dragon saddle and pulled out a bit of dried meat. "Start with this." Brindisi grabbed his bow from the ground and notched an arrow. "Stay and rest yourself, little pup. I'll find you a more substantial meal to eat."

He disappeared into the woods.

Brindisi meant to humiliate me with the gesture, I suppose. No chance of that. Fresh meat was medicinal for dragons. I hoped he would find a goat. Rabbits were too little. The only thing better would be if he encountered a mountain lion, and it ate him. Then I could eat the mountain lion. But I doubted that this island had any of those.

I gazed upward at the peak hidden behind a veil of night, its outline barely visible even to my eyes. A great gust of wind ran through the forest, rustling the leaves of the koa trees and sending more pods to the ground. When the wind subsided, a sound remained—a humming, faint and distant. It was a song. Something natural, without words; peaceful, yet powerful. I strained to listen, the tone soothing. It was unlike anything I've heard before, yet so familiar. The melody seeped into me and the exhaustion of this day fell away. My eyes slowly shut, and I drifted to sleep, only to be awakened by Brindisi's noisy return. The song had vanished.

My ryder had a small boar draped over his shoulders; three arrows still protruded from the creature's body. He threw the carcass down before me. "We can't risk a fire tonight so it's all yours. It's also the last time I hunt for you."

I ate hungrily, without a word to the human. The meat was fresh, bloody, and delicious. I spit out the bones, savoring the choice flesh usually taken by the humans. Despite the unexpected feast, my mind still lingered on the strange sounds I had heard. They hadn't been my imagination. I knew I'd actually heard something. Perhaps it was magic of some kind. I wanted to experience it again. I had heard the sounds coming from above, from high up on the mountain.

To get up there, I would need to fly.

NINE

Rays of morning light woke me.

After my feast, sleep had come easily, as if something within me knew the immediate danger had passed. The rest helped me regain some strength, although not enough.

Brindisi was already awake when I raised my neck. He rubbed his blade with a whetstone, carefully honing its edge, although it was already rather sharp. A strip of dried meat hung out of his mouth. On the ground lay a waterskin. I would've eaten as well if there had been anything fresh left to consume, but I didn't require it. Last night's meat would keep me satiated until tomorrow.

Dragons heal quickly, but not immediately. My wing ached; the torn flesh still throbbed. Even greater pain awaited if I dared fly. I glanced up at the Kraken, massive and silent. We had to reach the top. I stretched my wings. I hadn't underestimated the agony that followed, but I kept at it, pushing against the pain. Once I'd fully extended both wings, I folded them again and repeated the process. After the second stretch, I flapped them about hard enough to rustle the leaves of the remaining trees.

"Are you ready to fly, little bird?"

The things I wanted to say wouldn't have been helpful. Brindisi didn't care about me, only his mission. Only killing for his king. But I wasn't sure if I could fly with my wing in that state. Worse, if I did fly, I couldn't be sure it wouldn't be the last time—wings were temperamental. What kind of dragon would I be if I could neither fly nor breathe fire? I feared that fate.

I stared at the sky, feeling the wind. I thrashed my tail, checking my balance. It was all useless stalling. I too wanted to know what was atop that mountain. To do that, I needed to fly. The only way I'd know if I could fly would be to actually try to do it. Only afterward would I discover the price I'd pay.

For all Brindisi's harsh mocking, he understood dragons. "Try first without my weight. If you are able, return for me."

The words surprised me. First, he went hunting for me, now he showed concern about my wing. It all seemed very non-human, very unlike Brindisi. Of course, it was in his interest as well. He needed me to fight the Mizu and he probably didn't want to experience another crash if it turned out I couldn't fly.

I shifted uneasily. I would've preferred to take off from a high cliff or mountain. That was what young dragons did when they learned to fly. Launching from the ground took a lot more strength, and it placed more strain on the wing's membrane, but I didn't have a choice. I backed up to create as much open space in front of me as I could in the small clearing, then hurled myself forward, first with my legs, then with a great flap of my wings.

That first bit hurt.

If I'd lain on my back and let a human chip away at my scales with the edge of a carving knife until he managed to create a slice as long as my claw, then if he poured boiling pitch in the wound, that was close to equaling the pain of returning to the air. Belatedly, I realized that I probably had done some healing last night, with a portion of the membrane reattaching itself as I slept on a full stomach; then I'd gotten up this morning and torn all the new sinew to shreds, along with I'm not sure what else.

On the brighter side, the second flap hurt less than the first, and each successive beat caused me even less pain. That wasn't necessarily a good sign. Dragon nerves dull pain to allow us to continue in a fight. The lack of agony just made it more likely I'd injure myself. I glided in a circle, trying to find any sign of the Mizu. I saw nothing and heard nothing. I doubted they would've risked climbing in the dark, but I couldn't be sure. They had a wizard of unknown abilities with them.

I set back down on the ground beside Brindisi. He wore a hungry grin—like a wolf who knew he was going to get a chance to feast.

"Ah, so it was just a scratch after all. Have a bit more faith in yourself." Brindisi climbed onto me. "I trust there is nothing wrong with your teeth or claws. We are going to need them."

I didn't bother to try to explain about wing injuries or pain. Brindisi didn't care about any of those things. I merely showed him my teeth—long and sharp—and my claws, which were more of the same. There was nothing wrong with them.

Once Brindisi was on my back, I lifted off again. My wing hurt less this time, even with Brindisi's added weight. I flapped with caution, gaining altitude more gradually than usual.

"Beware that wizard, Bayloo."

I needed no reminder to be wary of the spellcaster. I'd chosen to ascend on the far side of the Kraken, where the terrain was barren rock. The Mizu would stay in the woods, under cover. I hoped that even their wizard couldn't see and cast spells around a mountain side.

It took me longer than it should have, but I reached the top. I landed on the western side of the ridgeline that encircled the hollow crater below. Beneath me was a magnificent sight. A massive lake spread out across the center of the hidden valley, its surface glittering like diamonds in the morning light. Only the slightest ripples of a tide rolled onto the dark rock of the Kraken's belly. Vines, moss, and other assorted greenery clung to the mountain's inner walls encasing the hidden treasure. Even a few koa trees had taken root on the eastern portion of the valley. Weeds and wildflowers had sprouted throughout the rest of the enclosure. This place was a giant bowl of hidden beauty. A solitary goat drank from the lake's waters, but the rest of the hidden sanctuary appeared empty.

The song that had enticed me yesterday was absent, but something else drifted on the air, a familiar scent almost lost in the rising pollen of the wildflowers and the stink of the unwashed human on my back. But not quite. My nose continued to search, though my eyes found nothing.

The peace of the valley held no allure for Brindisi. "What is here that the Mizu want so badly?"

His words startled the goat (or it might've caught a glimpse of me). The creature looked up, saw a big dragon looming overhead, then bolted. The startled animal dashed toward the sheer wall of the crater, but not in the direction of any of the trees or bushes that might've provided shelter had I been on the hunt. I wondered where it intended to go. My only thought was that there was a cave or crevice hidden in the mountain's wall. Or it was a dumb goat, even by goat standards. It ran along on its stick legs, then disappeared. Not disappeared into a thicket of trees or anything like that. It just vanished. A moment later it reappeared, moving in the opposite direction, its pace even more frantic.

I didn't mention anything to Brindisi. Perhaps he hadn't seen it. Keeping silent about the disappearing goat was much easier than trying to explain what I'd seen to my ryder, but unfortunately the goat's strange behavior hadn't escaped Brindisi.

"That was ... unusual." Through our link I felt a hunter's anticipation rise in him. "Take us down to the floor of the valley."

I glided down from my perch, still taking care with my injured wing. I set down beside the shore of the lake. Brindisi climbed down off my back and drew his blade. He headed toward the spot where the goat had vanished.

The familiar odor I'd detected on the ridge grew far stronger within the valley. My neck tightened; my tail was restless. I followed behind Brindisi, moving as softly as I could manage (which wasn't all that softly). I kept hoping he'd stop. He didn't, of course. Instead, he moved faster as he neared his prey. Even if he couldn't see the prize, Brindisi sensed it. I hung back. I sensed danger, but I had no regrets about not warning him.

A disembodied tail whipped out from nowhere, its scales a blend of crimson and gold. It smacked into Brindisi, the force of the blow knocking him from his feet. He lay on the ground, his eyes half open, his arms limp. He'd dropped his sword. A moment later claws appeared from nowhere, curved and sharp and deadly. They reached for my ryder. I had the sudden urge to help him, but I fought that. Something more important than Brindisi was going on here. The huge claws didn't impale him, at least not immediately. Instead, five claw-tipped digits that seemed to extend out of the air itself scooped him up and held him in a fist. Then Brindisi disappeared along with the claws that held him, just like the goat. Unlike the goat, he didn't emerge again.

The urge to protect my ryder surged through me like an unwelcome shiver. The feeling grew until all of my body shook. We were linked, whether I liked it or not. I felt his life force through the rune. The magic that bound us commanded me not to abandon him, but this time I fought back.

I owe Brindisi nothing.

Well, maybe I owed him some meat, but that was all. Definitely nothing more than that. Yet the pulling didn't stop. My head throbbed. I growled at the compulsion, not willing to give in.

I will decide my own destiny. Not the magic of the human Sculptors.

Those were fine sentiments. They didn't banish the power that had been carved into my scales and my mind shortly after my birth. But I'd sucked on the sweet taste of freedom for nearly three moons. I would not surrender myself. I would be free. I would be a true dragon.

Even if I wasn't going to rescue Brindisi, I decided I still needed to find out what happened to him. There was magic here, and I wanted to know what was beyond this wall of illusion. I had my suspicions based on what I'd seen, but that wasn't enough. I needed to see with my eyes. For something this important, I needed to be certain.

I walked to the place that appeared to be mere scrub brush but must've been something else. I passed through the unseen barrier between the life I had lived and the one I desired. The air tickled my scales as I passed through the magic curtain of concealment. Something tingled at the edge of my consciousness, a tick in my head of something familiar but forgotten. I didn't have time to dwell on that thought. I became ever more certain that on the other side of the illusion awaited the joyous and the impossible. I was right.

I stared at the magnificent form of a fellow dragon.

She looked really angry.

TEN

I stared at a near reflection of myself.

The other dragon was prettier than me, of course. Even though we were of a similar size, with matching eyes of glittering amber, magnificent wings, and beautiful, long jaws filled with rows of wicked teeth, she was far more striking. Her scales dazzled in a manner mine did not. Beneath her neck was a beautiful mélange of crimson and gold, not a single scale marred by the hideous runes of a human Sculptor. I rejoiced at the sight. One of my kind lived free. In that moment, I knew that I too could live as this dragon did. This dragon must have answers about my kind—and perhaps she had great power as well. She was surrounded by magic.

The female dragon stood outside a tunnel that had been dug into the rock of the valley floor—the entrance to a concealed cave. Animal bones lay scattered around her feet. Two pillars of gleaming gold, each as tall as my head with my neck fully extended, soared from the ground into the sky as if marking the entrance to a grand palace. Symbols were carved into their surface—not completely unlike those on my chest. I had never seen their like, but I guessed they were connected to the magic illusion that concealed the dragon from view.

Based on their shape and size, I doubted a dragon had made those artifacts.

I craned my neck about. I could still see the great lake a short distance away, as well as the sky above, although my vision was slightly distorted, as if I peered at the edge of a mirage on a sweltering day. The illusion was apparently a one-way barrier: the dragon could still see beyond the magic. It was a creation beyond anything known in Rolm or Oster. The mystery of this place deepened.

I expected the other dragon to kill Brindisi. Presumably, she'd been hiding here to avoid detection by humans like him. But she hadn't done the deed yet. Instead, she'd pinned him under the claws of her digits just as I'd done when I'd tried to question the Mizu. Brindisi lay on the ground, helpless, blood dripping from the corner of his mouth. My ryder's eyes fluttered open, his previous stupor suddenly banished. Shock surged through the link between us, followed by something that might have been fear. The female dragon's eyes shifted color as she gazed upon Brindisi, the amber turning to crimson. Brindisi broke her stare, turning his attention toward me. He knew he needed me. The surge of his will struck me. I flinched at the power, at the stabbing pain of compulsion in my head. My eyes closed as my head dipped. I fought against Brindisi as well as the magic of the runes that held me.

Brindisi spoke to me through the link. *"Aid me, Bayloo!"*

A choice confronted me. I could no longer hide from what I'd become. I took a single step toward him, but not a big one. Finally, I had found another of my kind—a free dragon. Finally, I saw an opportunity to truly shake my bonds. Here I could find answers and maybe assistance. It was time to stop hiding what I was. That choice should've been easy. But the rune-link made it a struggle. Still, I did it. *"I will not be a slave. I am not a slave."*

Brindisi gasped aloud at my resistance, but I felt as if I were flying. There was no going back to hiding. I sensed the shock fade within Brindisi, to be replaced with fury; a raw anger powerful enough to make me shudder through the link. *"You obey!"*

My mind was a mountain, but Brindisi was steel, and he had the advantage of the control- runes. The magic carvings concentrated the force of his will. Brindisi's mind hacked at me; his orders felt like daggers in my head. The pain came hard, but I did not yield. My days of slavery were over.

Brindisi twisted his head to regard me with a look of utter hate. He felt betrayed. I could've told him that he and his kind never should've enslaved us, but I didn't have time to bother with Brindisi. It was the other dragon who mattered to me.

The female dragon examined me, her eyes turning a faint shade of emerald, the color of regret. I didn't understand at first, not until she shifted her gaze to the runes carved into my scales. Her eyes became a darker shade of green, as if it was she who had lost something precious.

"Not. A. Slave." I spat out each word. Yet the language of my declaration belied my defiant words: I spoke in Avian, the language devised for us by the human masters.

At my declaration, the gloom in the dragon's eyes exploded into a blaze as fierce as the afternoon sun. The power of it made my chest feel even bigger than it already was. *She understood!*

A thousand questions raced through my mind. Before me—finally—stood the opportunity of answers: an adult dragon, free and surrounded by magic. She must have an amazing story to share. I had the chance to learn about my kind, my history, maybe even more of who I was ... The heat of my need for knowledge surged through my body. My eyes glowed as brightly as hers. But I was being a selfish idiot. I'd spent too much time around humans. I needed to think of bigger things: we were in danger—this dragon was in danger. The Mizu were here with their wizard.

"Humans—dangerous ones—they have come to this island," I told her. "They must be searching for you."

The dragon sniffed at the air. There was a hint of alarm at first, but then she seemed to calm herself. I, too, sampled the wind. No scent of human fouled the air. But the Mizu's stink had been how I'd found them yesterday. They might have figured that out. If the Mizu had come to this place to hunt dragons, they'd have come prepared.

I shared my suspicions. "They hide their scent. A wizard comes with them."

The female dragon showed her teeth. We both craned our necks toward the lush portion of the valley. I saw nothing. All was still and quiet. The only noise was that of a steady wind gusting and the soft lapping of the lake water on the shore. Even the trees were still.

Too still.

Like all dragons, I knew winds. The shifting gusts had been part of us since we were babes. I fixed on each nuance of the breeze like humans obsessed with the hair on their heads. The trees shouldn't have been so motionless. A dozen different scents should've carried to my nostrils, yet these gusts smelled dull, lifeless. Like something made by humans.

Magic.

The other dragon realized it as well. She reared upwards; her wings spread as if in preparation for flight. I expected her to lift off the ground at any moment, swooping in to roast the interlopers who'd dared venture into her domain, but she hesitated for some reason. Instead of taking to the safety of the air, the dragon stayed close to her cave. Her eyes flicked back toward the tunnel that led to her home. Her hesitation was costly.

A furious attack erupted from the deceptive sky; a bolt of lightning came at the dragon, somehow coaxed by an unseen power from weather that should never have spouted such a force. Apparently, the barrier of illusion that had shielded the dragon's lair from view was no match for the Mizu wizard. The sizzling light struck her in the belly. The golden pillars toppled. We were exposed to the enemy.

The dragon roared, an awesome cry of defiance that echoed through the valley. My own hearts jumped in alarm. The dragon's scales had been broken and seared by the attack. She lifted her leg and tossed Brindisi's tiny form away from us, throwing him into the lake with as much concern as a human might show a chewed bone. I wasn't sure the depth of the lake. The dragon launched herself skyward, her wings trembling as she rose. She was hurt. I worried for her as much as I had for any other being in all my life.

The Mizu appeared like a pack of predators conjured from the air. Whatever magic their wizard had used to allow them to approach us undetected was gone. I counted ten smelly humans formed into a well-spaced line, bows at the ready, their bodies encased in resin armor from head to foot. It wouldn't protect them from me. From us. I had no doubt these Mizu had come to harm my fellow dragon, but now they had two to contend with. My anger flared. Battle called me. *Finally, a battle for me, for dragons.*

I came at the Mizu head-on, charging forward with a dog's gait, using my wings only to catch a bit of wind and make each leap quicker. I sought the wizard. He was the real danger. I could kill the rest of the humans later. Slowly, if I wished.

I found him behind the line of archers. Among these Mizu, the most powerful stood in the back—so very human. The wizard wore no armor, just a shimmering robe of silver so shiny it reflected the terrain around him. Inked images and arcane symbols covered his deeply tanned skin; his eyes, black as a moonless night, stared out at me without emotion. The wizard clasped his hands together, his fingers interlocked. The dark void of his eyes flashed like sparked flint. His palms turned outward toward me.

Chicken piss incoming.

I didn't stop. I'd committed myself to this attack; there was no place else I could go. I could survive one of those lightning strikes ... maybe. Either I'd kill that wizard, or he'd kill me. As I closed, an arrow struck me—not bounced off me, but struck me. It hurt, but those pricks were nothing compared to what I knew the wizard could unleash. I roared, the anger of a lifetime of human-induced slavery reverberating in my cry.

The wizard flinched. Indeed, he went to a knee, pointing his hands and head at the sky as he did so. For a moment I thought my terrible roar had caused that, but then the shadow of my fellow dragon passed overhead. She descended upon him, her claws outstretched, her jaws open. She intended to end this human, but wizards do not die easily.

The air around the Mizu wizard crackled and the chill of a winter storm shot through me. Tiny flames, no bigger than the light of a firefly, flashed around the dark-robbed Mizu. In the next instant, a wall appeared between the attacking dragon's claws and the wizard's soft body. The barrier was one of ice and flame, its structure pulsing as the confluence of forces clashed within. The dragon smashed into the magically summoned barrier with a terrific force that would've shattered a ship's hull, but the wizard didn't flinch. His black gaze flashed with a shiny gloss, and his hands glowed as he summoned more energy for the shield. The dragon scraped and bit before retreating into the air. Dark clouds rolled across the sky, moving with the swiftness of a hawk. A streak of lightning flashed, and for a terrifying moment I thought all was lost, but the latest bolt did not strike the dragon nor me. It plunged into the shield protecting the wizard.

A wizard-dragon!

The barrier didn't buckle. The mage stood his ground, his face set with determination.

I lunged to attack. Another arrow found its way into my scales as I moved, but my fury whipped my pain. This wizard had to die. I just had to get to him, and he would—assuming that his protective barrier only worked in one direction at a time. When I was close enough, I leapt, coming down with both my forelegs targeting the Mizu's face.

The wizard was faster. He hadn't turned his head as I came at him, but he somehow knew my intent. I collided with another of his conjured shields. I hit and chomped and scratched at the barrier. Its surface burned with the intensity of freezing ice, biting through even my scales, yet it was as slick as wet glass. I smashed my tail into the wall, but the magic shield defied my strength. I paused, staring through the translucent barrier at the wizard, my blazing eyes letting him know that I intended to transform his bones into powder via a slow grind of my teeth. The mage took note of me. The shield grew hot. So hot, my claws heated and smoked as I attacked, but I didn't stop pushing. A bead of sweat dripped down the wizard's face; this wasn't easy for him either. His lips moved, his eyes glowed, and a new force awakened. I felt the wind surge around me. Tendrils of an intense whirlwind wrapped around me. Like an invisible hand, the summoned torrent hurled me into the air, flinging me toward the opposite side of the valley. I spun out of control, unprepared for the ferocity of the force marshalled against me. No human deserved such power as this.

I unfurled my injured wings, but even that wasn't enough to right myself; I spun, plunging into the lake tail first, my hind legs following. I barely escaped falling backward onto my wings. I twisted at the last second, keeping the essential parts of me dry. I beat my wings hard in an effort to keep myself out of the lake. I felt my injured wing tear again. Dread bubbled inside me, but I didn't have time to dwell on the severity of my latest damage. I had to keep flapping—I could neither swim nor breathe water. Pain ripped through me, but I managed to steady myself. With my jaw clenched, I beat my wings, lifting myself into the air. I struggled to balance myself, but I did it. I flew to the battle, toward the wizard. If I had to die, this would be the right day for it.

The female dragon had been thrown off the shield as well, although not as far as I. She righted herself and was closing again at high speed, her eyes fixed on that deadly Mizu wizard. I thought she would unleash her fire. That is what I would've done, if I could've. I wondered how the magic shield would fare against the power of dragon breath. But she let loose no flames. Instead, when the dragon opened her mouth, something far more magnificent came forth: a song.

It wasn't the soothing tone I'd heard on the mountain. To a human, it probably would've sounded something like a soft roar, but human hearing is limited. To me, to a dragon, it was like the call of the wind mingled with the answer of the rustling trees and the soft echo of thunder in the distance. I sensed the power in that song. The dragon's eyes flashed with determination. The air buzzed as if a thousand invisible bees swarmed around us. The female dragon's eye flashed a brilliant indigo in triumph. The wizard's shield trembled for an instant before it disappeared. He froze, not realizing—not believing—what had happened. The time of his death approached.

The dragon bore down on him. She roared a single word. "Drasu!"

The Mizu wizard moved his hands, trying desperately to muster another spell. The dragon had too much momentum, though. It looked as though she would land on top of him, squashing the wizard into the rock, but at the last moment her head jerked upwards, as if something impossibly urgent in the distance demanded her attention. The triumph in my fellow dragon's eyes became panic. She veered right, changing her course. She managed to swipe the wizard with a single claw as she passed overhead, slashing his side up to his face and sending him to the ground, but it was far less than she intended. I looked to see what had panicked her. In that moment, I finally understood why the Mizu had come here and risked so much. It was the cave.

The Mizu archers we'd mostly ignored in our desperate fight against the wizard had reached the tunnel where I'd first encountered the female dragon. All but a pair had slung their bows. Six of the Mizu held a net—a huge one, with golden laces.

Trapped inside was a baby dragon.

ELEVEN

I released an echoing roar like none I have ever uttered.

From the depths of my being poured my despair at this unjust world, my fury as it became worse before my eyes; raw emotion passed into the world from my cry. The other dragon's roar intermingled with my own. I trembled at the misery in the companion cry—a mother's desperation for her hatchling.

Our combined roars became more than mere noise. Ten soldiers surrounded the newborn dragon. All ten fell, knocked from their feet by a gust of raw fury unleashed by air itself. The mother dragon came at the Mizu warriors faster than any other creature of the sky. I continued toward the fallen wizard (I've noticed bad humans have a tendency to cling tenaciously to life), but with an eye on the hatchling as well. My fellow dragon was swifter to her target than me. She rammed a claw through the heart of the first Mizu soldier just as he struggled to his feet, slamming him into a second soldier, skewering both. She grabbed another Mizu by the head with her hind leg, separating his body into a small and large section as she passed, picking up just a bit of altitude as she made a tight circle back toward her hatchling, intending to land amidst the recovering soldiers. Three

Mizu had managed to scramble back to their feet with bows ready, but there was no way that arrows were going to stop an angry mother dragon.

As I'd guessed, the wizard lived. Lines of bloody crimson intermingled with the ink symbols on his face, but his eyes were focused as he struggled to a knee. The mage saw me bearing down on him, his gaze a sea of black calm despite my threat. I showed him my teeth and that my unspoken promise about grinding his bones into small particles remained valid. The mage spoke some hasty words, once again summoning the unseen hand of wind that had recently hurled me into the lake. Except it wasn't as powerful this time, or perhaps I was more prepared. The wizard's power slammed into me, but I slammed back. The gusts slowed me, grabbing at me. I wanted to keep going, but my mangled wings failed me. The wind drove me to the ground, with my legs being forced to battle for each step on the rocky ground. I wouldn't stop. Step by step I moved closer, or, more accurately, my jaws moved closer. *Crunch your bones, bones, bones, little human.*

An arrow pierced my hind quarter, right into the gap around my left leg. Blood leaked from the wound, dripping onto my limb and the ground. My hind leg weakened. From the corner of my eye I caught sight of the marksman—a Mizu who had fled from the mother dragon and taken cover behind a koa tree.

The wizard exploited my added distress. The whirlwind of magic wind surged. The unseen hand of air grasped me, tossing me backward. I fell about halfway between the tunnel and the wizard. A second spell followed—a net of some kind, its coils formed of the same translucent ice and fire as the shield, fell on top of me. The trap pinned me to the ground, my legs facing upward. I wiggled and twisted to turn myself, to have leverage against the spell's weight. The magic net tightened in response, its tendrils burning on my scales. My injured right wing exploded with pain. The intensity of my utter failure was the worst of this. Darkness mingled with the anger in my heart.

The wizard flexed his fingers as his eyes gleamed black. My bones shook. My throat tightened; my chest felt as if I was falling from the sky once again. My final fate came for me.

No. No. No.

It happened anyway. Power doesn't care about justice. Or contrary opinions.

The wizard unleashed his lightning. The deadly bolt wasn't directed at me, but I wished that it had been, so I wouldn't have had to witness its aftermath. The mother dragon had devastated the Mizu soldiers while I'd been locked in combat with the wizard; only two still stood, spread apart and desperate, their net abandoned, although the baby dragon remained entangled within it. The wizard's new blaze of magic energy struck the mother dragon in the flank. She roared in pain as her legs failed her and she sank to the ground. I shared her agony. I too roared. Oh, how I roared. For all the good it did.

But the dragon wasn't beaten. She raised her neck even as her body failed. No fear showed in her crimson-tinged eyes. From her came another song, this one formed of the sound of anger. It started as a rumble but rose to a scream. The surviving Mizu dropped their bows so they might cover their ears. All except the wizard, who stood defiant. At least until the ground beneath him shook; his eyes grew wide, and I dared to hope. A crack opened beneath the wizard's feet —small at first, but rapidly spreading in both directions. The wizard darted to his left, fleeing the spreading hole that threatened to swallow him. He stumbled, falling to the ground. He rolled, frantically fleeing the abyss chasing him. I thought he would attempt some spell to seal the chasm, but instead he focused again on the mother dragon. With some poisonous words and a flick of his hand, he summoned his lightning once again. He could muster only a small bolt from the charred sky, but it was enough for his purpose. The bolt struck the mother dragon's neck. Her song stopped and so did the spread of the cracking ground. My fellow dragon lay still in the dirt. I was empty.

The wizard stumbled on his feet, bloodied and battered, but still far too alive. He barked at the surviving Mizu soldiers, who scrambled back toward the net and the trapped baby dragon. Once that happened, the wizard turned his attention back to me. His dark eyes were faded, circles of exhaustion beneath them.

While the wizard had dueled with the mother dragon, I'd managed to flip myself over onto my legs. The net that held me seemed to weigh as much as a small castle, but I still moved, bearing its weight on my back. Only three of my legs worked properly, but I dragged the fourth along. I moved at a snail's pace, but still I moved. I didn't know what I could do even if I managed to reach this wizard, but I came at him.

My adversary shook his head, weariness in his motion. He spoke some words in a language I didn't understand; they weren't words of anger. They sounded more like regret. He bowed his head toward me, deeply. I kept marching toward him. When the wizard's head rose, he slowly raised a palm toward me.

The wizard spoke in Avian. His words surprised me. "I am sorry."

His hand trembled, but I knew he still intended to kill me. So be it. The Abyss was better than watching that helpless hatchling get dragged off to become a Mizu slave. Death was mercy.

The wizard's invisible hand came for me, its grasp feeble. The spell betrayed his fatigue; he had barely triumphed against us, but he had won. The Mizu mage still had enough magic to command his wind-hand to lift me from the ground and toss me into the lake, the magic net still entangling me. I crashed into the cold darkness.

I'd sometimes heard humans speak of the afterlife, of journeying to live forever amongst their Sisters in Haven—some kind of promised land of delights, where the desires of heart, stomach, and mind were forever satiated. I'd wondered if dragons had anything similar.

I would know soon enough.

TWELVE

I tumbled through the watery depths.

I didn't know how to swim. Dragons didn't voluntarily get into the water, and no one was stupid enough to try to force us. I'd seen humans swim, though. I had also watched ducks traverse the ponds in the gardens of Eladrell, and I'd eaten plenty of fish. Swimming didn't look hard. I probably could've done it if I hadn't been stuck in the magic net. The wizard's cage had stopped glowing as I sank further into the water, loosening slightly, but not enough for me to free myself. I twisted, and kicked, and bit, and thrashed. It all just made me sink faster. We dragons were made to fly in the clouds, so we can hold our breath and don't need as much air as humans, but we weren't fish. I expected to drown, alone and in the dark.

Brindisi saved me.

The mother dragon had hurled him far into the great lake when the Mizu arrived. He'd apparently survived, shed his armor, and begun the swim back toward the shore. Either it'd been a long distance, or he'd bided his time until his adversaries killed each other. Brindisi had only his dagger with him. It wasn't much use against dragons or the Mizu, but it was enough to cut the ropes of the no-longer-unbreakable net. Indeed, the net disappeared—vanishing completely—shortly after Brindisi sliced the first coil, perhaps because the mage that had conjured it was no longer present.

Brindisi helped free me, but he couldn't teach me how to swim. I thrashed about, I swished my tail, I moved my three non-crippled legs. None of it did much except tire me. Swimming wasn't as easy as I'd thought. I kept sinking. Somewhere, a duck was gloating.

The solution came when I hit the bottom. My feet dug into the rocky floor. The water made me light. I still had plenty of air inside me. I simply started walking toward the shore. Let a duck try that. But I made it only a few steps before I realized this wasn't going to be so easy.

I kept losing my tenuous grip on the lake bed and floating upward. Each time my claws left the bottom, I would kick my legs frantically and get nowhere; Brindisi tried to keep me moving in the correct direction, swimming to the surface for air and then returning to try to guide me. It was more than annoying how easily he navigated in the water, while I could barely make any progress at all.

I would've drowned before I reached the surface trying to walk the whole way, but I soon figured out I could use my folded wings to propel myself forward. Somehow, it hurt less than trying to fly. With an awkward dance of pushing with my wings and crawling with my legs, I managed to reach water shallow enough that I could extend my neck above the surface. I got there just before I ran out of air. I gasped into the sweet daylight, filling my lungs, before resuming my journey. Even with the certainty that I wasn't going to drown, it took me a frustratingly long time to get to shore. I eventually dragged myself out of the lake, my wings dragging on the ground, soaked and damaged beyond any hope of healing. I doubted I'd ever fly again. What was a dragon who could neither fly nor breathe fire?

The desolate shore shattered my hearts. The Mizu were gone, as was the hatchling. The sun had passed the apex of the sky and was sinking toward the horizon. The mother dragon still lay on the ground, her eyes shut, ugly black holes in her scales. Brindisi followed me, silent for now, but I was still all too aware of his presence.

I dragged myself to sit beside my fellow dragon. She didn't stir, yet there was warmth inside her still. The Abyss had not yet claimed her.

I could've tried words of Avian, but that seemed so inadequate. She'd shown me another way. I opened my mouth, pushing out sounds that none of my kind on DragonPeak ever uttered. The noises I made were awkward and clumsy, neither roar, nor growl, nor speech, but the emotion was there. Quickly, I adjusted my tone. I sang my sadness to her as well as my longing to speak with one of my own kind. If she could hear me, I'm sure she would have understood. My hearts hit against the inside of my chest hard enough to make it ache. One of her eyes opened followed by the other, although both were a sickly shade of yellow, the color laced with veins of blood.

The mother dragon cooed with relief.

"The Abyss calls to me ... but I held on ... kept hoping for you ..." She spoke in a language close to Avian, except that the sounds were more elegant, as they were meant to be. I had no trouble understanding.

My eyes flashed a smile of joy that she still lived, but it was a tainted gladness. I didn't understand why this noble creature would've placed hope in me. There was nothing I could do except watch her die. My flash of happiness quickly faded to despair. She saw it.

"You must believe." She made a difficult swallow. "You must believe, my child."

My chest nearly exploded upon hearing those words. I couldn't breathe; I forgot my pain. I must've not understood her. *My child. My child.* But there was no mistake, no delirium. With a single sniff, my nose confirmed that I sat beside my own blood. The world spun as my mind raced. *I had found my mother!*

My eyes spoke because no other part of me was able to move. "How?" asked the confused light there.

My mother answered me in a manner that was unknown to me until that instant, sending to me raw emotion of the most wondrous and powerful character. Her eyes pushed away the ugly yellow that marred them, shifting to a soft violet, tinged by an amber that gleamed so bright that it resembled gold. Only the veins of blood spoiled her gaze. A scent surrounded me, sweeter than any other I had experienced, something beyond the ripest fruit or the choicest honey. It made my hearts ache, but in a good way. For the first time in my life, I knew the kinship of another being. This was my mother.

I struggled with my mouth. The words came drenched in conflicting emotion. I found my mother. "But ... you're still here. After all this time."

"You mean to ask how I am here. I carry a great burden, and I hold true to the Way. But I am a mother as well. I never gave up on you after you were taken—you and all the other dragons who are our brethren. We are all kin, we dragons. We are all beings of destiny."

At the precipice of the most profound loss, I now experienced an unrestrained joy without equal. *I had a mother, and she hadn't forsaken me. She had never forgotten me.* A hole in my being, of which I'd been only vaguely aware, was suddenly filled. There was nothing a child lost in the dark desired more than this, and here it was, laid before me. Perhaps today was a good day to die after all, but for a different reason—today I could die happy. Of the infinite questions that flooded my mind, I asked the most mundane, indulging the unanswered mystery that had lingered since I'd become aware of my true self: "What is my name?"

"Only humans would think it the place of the parents to give a name that carries through a lifetime. Dragons—free dragons—earn their names. Our name changes over our lives, as we change. A true dragon's name will grow over time, a failure will be called less. The greatest of us have many names. Earn yours."

"What are you called, Mother?"

Her eyes flashed and a trilled song escaped her mouth—or part of one. It was a melody of sounds, conjured from deep in her throat. I shivered at its power, its reassurance, but most of all its determination. Just hearing the sound made me want to roar with hope. This was her true name. It was a song of light against the void.

"In Avian, it would be perhaps, 'Bring Forth the Dawn,' or something like it. Even Avian cannot capture the true meaning of a dragon name."

"Where is your mate—my father?"

My mother allowed her eyelids to close. I thought she might not answer me, but finally her eyes opened again, and she spoke. "He was on Veralon, if he still lives, but do not bother to seek him. What is left of our kind there is just a wild, lost colony, driven to madness. He is one of those now, a wild creature without thought. His spirit has left him, as it has left the others. Their minds did not survive the shattering that changed magic. I thought I could help them, but they are beyond my power. Perhaps there will be a way to restore them one day, but I will not live to see that dawn." Her eyes, which had glowed so brightly, faded. My throat clenched at the unspeakable pain she felt, which I could do nothing to salve.

"But if my father is this way, then why would you... you know... mate with him?" I wasn't sure if this was a polite question among free dragons.

I think she would've laughed if she had the strength. "We females are the more generous gender, but there is no time to teach you that lesson. Let me say simply, there were none other suitable. No other dragon would understand my path on the Way other than those lost ones clinging to life on Veralon." An ugly cough came from her throat as she spoke the last. After sucking in a long, pained breath, my mother spoke again. "We are the last of our kind, my son. The last of the ember dragons. The remaining light of this world is slowly dying. Everything depends on us, as it always did."

"I don't understand."

My mother's eyes fluttered shut, even as she struggled to keep them open. Both my hearts stopped until her eyelids rose again. "Save them—your sister, the other dragons, the other life of this world, even the humans ... they are all in peril."

"Humans?" I said the word with contempt. They were the cause of all of this.

Despite what had just happened, my mother had more kindness in her than I did. Even though her hatchling daughter had just been stolen—*her daughter, my sister*—she drew on some deep reserve of will. Her voice strengthened, her eyes glowed a bit brighter. "They are not all evil. Some helped me. Some helped you. The humans here tried their best ... risked much to try to free you. Without humans, you would still be enslaved."

I couldn't believe that. Humans cared only for themselves. Certainly, none ever risked their lives for a dragon. "A human helped me?"

"More than helped—sacrificed," my mother told me. "Those runes on your chest ... they were a secret of dragons, stolen by humans."

"Stolen?"

"The magic was stolen from our kind; now it is used to enslave and destroy. It is part of something vast, something for us. But the rune magic, such a powerful magic, even I didn't suspect ... It took so long to find a way to undo it. Even then, I could only give you a chance at freedom with the thorns. I didn't understand their power either ... but that is not important now. You had to claim your chance, and you did. But the humans made it possible. One most of all."

"Who?" I dreaded her reply. Already I suspected.

My mother hesitated, as if she suspected she was about to cause me pain. "Jona."

The air in my nostrils became sour and poisonous. I'd killed the man who had tried to save me. A human who had known my mother, and I'd killed him. It couldn't be true. I didn't want it to be true. "He was like the others. A bit kinder, but still a ryder," I insisted. Even as I spoke, I knew I was wrong, but still I kept speaking like the idiot I'd shown myself to be. "His kindness was only to bring me food and drink. To even be a ryder, he would've had to have passed the Tell. He could not have been there to help me."

"I sense such powerful emotion in you—grief, fear, and much else besides." I couldn't tell if she approved or not. A twinkle seeped into my mother's stricken gaze. "The humans of Rolm may think themselves masters of the rune magic, but they would be wrong in that vanity. These Sculptors are mere imitators—we are the masters. When Jona submitted to the Tell of the human Sculptors, he carried an item of magic made by the enchanters of this island that shielded his thoughts. He is bound by nothing. With this and the aid of my magic, Jona easily ascended the Arrow Peak to win the Rite to replace your dead ryder. Only once he had won the right to be bound to you could we risk him trying to free you. Any other ryder would've sensed your mind awakening and told the Sculptors."

"Jona never spoke of any of this." I said it desperately.

"Of course not. You were a slave. If it didn't work, you would've exposed him, and he'd have been killed. The sacrifices we made would've been for nothing."

"Even if the Tell could be beaten, the runes are carved into us ... these chains of magic that control us. How is such power defeated?"

"Not defeated, but ... reduced for a time. To give you a chance." My mother paused. This time, not from pain. I think she was reluctant to continue, but she did. "A very special material—it resembles a plant—was brought here ... at great cost." Her voice failed her. Only after a painful breath did my mother speak again. "The humans call it aurathorn. The archive speaks of it by a different name ... it is said to be ancient as this world, infused with the power of the last one ... a relic that can dampen the power of magic. I hoped it might work on the control-runes where no other magic could. The people of this island have some knowledge, some lore of our kind. They knew where to obtain aurathorn, when even I thought it lost forever, when even the great archive offered no clues." My mother sucked in a breath that must've been painful. "They agreed to help."

"This aurathorn can break the control-runes?"

"Maybe in its true, original form it could do this." I didn't understand what she meant, but I didn't dare interrupt. "The aurathorn vine I obtained for you only gave you an opportunity—a chance for your will to assert itself. The rest was up to you. For years, we failed. Some thought we had been tricked, that aurathorn wouldn't work after the initial light of its thorns faded in those first days. But I believed there was enough power left for you to break free."

I thought of Jona's late night visits, of fish he had brought me. How he'd tried to engage me in conversation, in stories and history. It hadn't worked. My mind had been stuck. Had he slipped the aurathorn into my food even before that? It seemed likely. But nothing had made a difference to my trapped mind, until the ale.

It was too much. "Why would humans help free dragons?"

My mother stared at me, a look that carried a lifetime of regret. "What is important is that they did. It was a great risk for both those who volunteered and our kind. The decision I made ... know that I had to follow the Way. Such a price ..." The breath left her, and a dribble of blood leaked from her mouth. Both her eyes fixed upon me. "But here you are. Free."

A hole had opened in my stomach so large that every scrap of food I'd eaten for the past two days should've been pouring out of it. "At what price?"

My mother's eyes faded. I was losing her. "The Way dragons follow demands that we do what we must for something greater than ourselves."

"The Way?"

Her eyes shut again. "It is not for you. Your mind is different. You must find your own path. It is destiny that you return to me now, just as your sister has been stolen."

I had almost forgotten the hatchling. *My sister!*

My mother sucked in a noisy, difficult breath. "Save her. In the clutches of the worst among us ..." Her voice trailed off and again her eyes shut. I knew she was not gone, though. Her chest heaved with effort, but she still had strength. "Only you can save her now."

I still didn't understand that part. And I was no use to anyone. "I'm nothing, Mother. I can't fly, I can't—"

"You have power, my child. You are an ember dragon."

I knew my mother drew upon an incredible will just to keep herself alive, to give me this time with her. There was so much I wanted to ask, and even some things I wanted to tell. I cursed time, as it escaped. I raged that I'd been denied the opportunity to know the remarkable being beside me. She knew so much; she had such power. "That song—you have magic, but I know nothing of it."

My mother's eyes became dark as the night, with only a faint light shining near the center. "You can be—"

She never finished. She never spoke again.

An arrow plunged through my mother's eye, an arrow that stole the last of her life and robbed me of whatever knowledge she would've had time to pass onto me. The arrow of a human. Fired by Brindisi.

I spun in a mad spasm of fury, an anger without equal. The human was crouched a hundred human paces away, a Mizu bow in his hand. I leapt across the distance, roaring with hatred so intense that my limbs trembled. My eyes burned with the light of the flaming sun. From my tail to my nose, I was rage given form. I was death.

"Bayloo, stop!"

A force as strong as the Mizu wizard's lightning struck me; carved into my body was my vulnerability, a chink in my armor that I could not mend. Brindisi had poured every bit of his will into the command, the power surging across the inseverable link between our minds. He held the chain of my collar. His mind choked my will, struggling for a master's dominance over his wayward slave. But I fought. I was a dragon. I faced his onslaught of will. I'd beaten back his commands earlier. I could do so again.

I think Brindisi knew I wouldn't break from force alone, so he spoke to me, his words echoing inside of me. "The twisted lies of that other dragon have confused you. Remember your mission. Remember your duty. *You exist to serve.*"

To serve. Always, I had served. I remembered my service, my training, and the humiliation that came with it: the heeling, the saddle, the locked cave-prison, the scraps they fed us. I remembered the battles and the deaths of my brethren as they fell in service to their masters.

I had no duty to humans.

Slaves knew only the brute force of a master's command. I managed to slip from the fog of slavery that held so many of us. Others had died so that I might be reborn. Jona had died. If I bowed, all they had given would be for nothing. I pushed myself; Brindisi's will was like an avalanche, a constant pounding on my exhausted mind. Still, I struggled toward him. I moved a mountain with each step. Closer and closer.

"Bayloo, stop." I didn't obey.

He yelled it again, with just a hint of fear. "Stop."

Pain coursed through me, my blood was fire, my eyes bled. But still I came at him—this human who had killed my mother, this human who may have also killed Jona rather than allowed him to heal.

My shadow fell over Brindisi. He didn't stop trying to bring me to heel, but he was also no fool. Through the bridge that joined us, I sensed his desperation. He raised the Mizu bow, taking aim at my face.

I stopped. Not because I had to, or because he commanded me, but because at that moment, I wished to stop.

"Why do you enslave us?"

I watched Brindisi's eyes, his hand, the tension of his pulsing jaw. His mouth stayed clamped shut; his chest heaved. I thought he might just fire his arrow, but something stayed his attack. I forced myself to be patient. Eventually, this servant of the human king answered me. "Your kind are destroyers. You would set the world ablaze, as you did before."

It wasn't the answer I expected.

"How would you know this?"

"It is written in the Book of Ages. We humans can write, we can record our knowledge. We know history, which gives us wisdom. The Sisters of Haven saw the evil of your kind and so granted us the power to control you. And controlled you must be, all of you. But you can still be useful. In service you can find honor. It is not too late, even for you." He lowered his bow. He tried to tempt me with an offer. "I know you want to get that hatchling. So do I. We must pursue the Mizu. They may be at sea already, but we must stop them. They must not escape beyond the Wall of Fire. Together we can do it."

That was as close as Brindisi could come to decency: a mission to kill. He pushed at me once again, a last, desperate surge of will commanding me to drop to the ground, to kneel to him. To be ridden once again.

That wasn't going to happen.

"Did you kill Jona?" I came closer. "Did you kill him so you could claim me as your slave?"

Brindisi's eyes narrowed. His lips said no, but the link between us allowed me to sense that he hid something from me. I pushed for the truth he wanted to conceal, but he laughed at me. His thoughts remained clouded.

Brindisi gritted his teeth. "I hadn't thought it possible. You attempt to read my mind ... clever beast."

I came at him again with my own will, seeking his protected memories, but he was on his guard. Whatever secret he held about Jona, he wished to deny it to me. But I knew Brindisi well enough to know that he would kill to get what he wanted—even a fellow ryder. In a flash I saw it, and I knew what Brindisi had done. It had been so easy to snuff out the ember of Jona's life, helpless as he was on the sickbed where my own selfishness had put him. A hate hotter than any inferno mountain ignited inside me. Brindisi sensed my blood lust, my desire to kill the slayer of those I cared for, and he realized he would never again command me. In that moment, he attacked.

I moved faster than he did, coming down on him with my open

jaw. He tried to raise his bow, but I had my teeth around him before he could pull back the arrow. I bit down, crushing his ribs between my teeth. I did it again and again. Thankfully, he had lost his armor in the lake. Brindisi's blood gushed into my mouth. I ground his bones and his flesh until there was nothing recognizable about my former ryder. Then I swallowed him.

After all my waiting, it turned out that humans tasted like chicken.

What a disappointment.

THIRTEEN

I returned to my mother's side.

It hurt even to look at her, but I did. Dried blood stained her face; the warmth of life had fled her body. The enormity of my loss paralyzed me. How quickly I'd gone from a place of sublime hope to bottomless despair. I nudged my mother gently, not quite believing that she was truly gone forever. She stayed dead.

I released a deafening roar, a sound of mourning and loss, of longing for what might have been. I hollered until my lungs were empty. At the very end, my rage turned to something like a song, my tone turning from grief to anger about what had been taken from me —stolen by the humans. When I finally stopped, and the valley became quiet again, I realized I was not alone. Other creatures had gathered. A dozen wolf-eagles, their heads a beautiful shade of silver, perched above on the rim of the mountain, staring down at the scene. Those birds were dangerous, even to a dragon if they attacked as a pack, but these seemed to have no interest in fighting. From the trees came boars and goats, and even a mountain lion, which should've sent the other less fearsome animals to flight but had not. I didn't understand quite what had drawn them here—lesser creatures, all of them—but I was nevertheless grateful for the respect on my mother's behalf. I bowed my head in acknowledgement.

I stared once at the body of my mother. She had given me so much during the scant time we'd had together. I was grateful for the knowledge and the lore, and to finally have heard her name spoken. To have her ripped from me was a pain unrivaled in the world. I lay flat on the ground next to her, wishing I could be even closer. I was a child in need of warmth, but there was none to be had here. Instead, I sang a farewell, a melody deep and sad. At the end, I learned something else: dragons' eyes do sometimes leak water.

I rose to take a last look at my mother. She had freed me, but my kin were not so fortunate. They would live out their lives as slaves, unless I changed that.

If I'd been a fire-breather I would've set my mother alight. That seemed the right thing to do, the proper thing for a dragon. But I lacked the ability, as did she. We were something else. In our brief time together she'd given me that precious knowledge. I wasn't a freak or a misfit. I wasn't an ash dragon at all. I was an ember dragon (or at least half of one, since I didn't know my father). I had never heard of such a thing before this day, and apparently neither had the human Keepers. We were something different, something special.

Using the last of my strength, I dragged my mother's body to the lake, bringing her as deep as my claws allowed. The gentle water covered her. She deserved better, but at least it was something better than being left in the open for the bird scavengers.

What now?

I possessed free will. I'd proven it against everything Brindisi had thrown against me. No human, nor any other creature, would ever command my mind again. I could choose my course, but I lacked a guide.

What would my mother have wanted me to do?

She would not have wanted me to waste time mourning her. She had spoken of the Way of dragons. I didn't understand precisely what she meant, but I sensed it was some kind of code of conduct for my kind. Leaking water was unlikely to be part of its teaching. I would spend no more time this day dwelling on my loss.

I would honor the dead with my actions. I would give meaning to my mother's last words, and what I knew to be her first wish of me: I would save my sister. I would not allow another dragon to fall into slavery. The sweet vengeance of killing the wizard and all the other humans who had been a part of murdering my mother was just a convenient benefit.

There was the matter of my battered body to contend with. Reluctantly, I forced my wing to move as I stretched my neck to examine the tear. What had begun as a tiny injury, no bigger than a human pinky finger, had grown to a length of twice that of one of my claws. I could do nothing about that. I tended to the other wounds I could reach.

I plucked as many of the arrows from my scales as I could manage, yanking them out with my digits or my teeth. I accidentally broke one shaft but got the others, except for two implanted on my backside. There was nothing to be done about my injured hind leg. Either I would survive and it would heal, or I wouldn't.

I took a bit of water from the lake to wet my throat, then dragged myself with my three good legs to the end of the valley. With my jaw clenched, I started to climb the rock face using my working legs. The mountain's surface was more brittle than that of the cliffs above Eladrell, and it didn't offer the benefit of carved staircases. I had to sink my claws deep into the stone crevices to pull myself upward. The pain inside somehow gave me strength. Each moment I delayed made the chances of finding my sister more remote. A trail of blood leaked behind me, but I would not fail to reach the top. Claw after claw I climbed until I was there.

Once atop the Kraken, I had a vantage point to search the seas in every direction. My eyes remained intact. I hunted my quarry.

I hoped the Mizu would be delayed leaving the island. There had been no ship within sight when I'd arrived, which meant there must have been a prearranged retrieval time. Or the wizard was able to signal the ship. With any normal vessel that would've given me plenty of time. They'd be below at the sole harbor giving me time to destroy themor die trying. But Mizu ships were different from all others—they moved with uncanny swiftness. No one knew how they did it, but having experienced the strength of their wizard's power, I guessed it had to do with magic. But as fast as the Mizu waveships could travel, they couldn't match the speed of a dragon in flight. Unfortunately, I wasn't able to fly at the moment.

I reached my desired vantage point and realized that my speed (or lack of it) didn't matter. I saw no ship, Mizu or otherwise, only the monotonous churn of the sea's waves. I kept searching, scrutinizing every current, every shadow, every ripple of water in each direction. There was nothing. I unleashed an ugly roar of frustration. Even the Mizu could not have moved so quickly. They were still men, wingless, and therefore shackled to the ground or the ocean.

The wolf-eagles who had come to my mother's vigil flew out from behind me. They squawked as they plied the sky. I could only guess if they spoke to me or each other. The pack moved with an easy grace, their feathered wings barely moving as they rode the wind to whatever place they called home. The darkness of my mood lessened slightly at their passage. To my surprise, they chose a flight path closer to sea, rather than toward the clouds as I would've expected, breaking their tight formation as they flew. The birds moved in a southern direction, each keeping in a tight pack formation worthy of their land-bound wolf cousins. I had thought of these birds as lesser creatures, because they did not think as I could, but they knew their task better than I in this instance. Of the dozen wolf-eagles, eleven continued on their path without interruption. One disappeared into nothingness. No predator had claimed her—one moment she flew, the next she had vanished into the horizon. Then she appeared again, untouched and seemingly unaware of what had just transpired. But I knew: *another of the wizard's illusions.*

One of the birds circled back toward me. I thought it bowed its head, or maybe I imagined it. But I preferred to believe the bird had acted intentionally. Even a feathered flier understood the need for vengeance.

I fixed on the point where the lone wolf-eagle had disappeared, imagining the distance from that point to where she had reappeared. Within that area I knew I'd find a ship and a wizard. The vessel would be moving swiftly, so I didn't give it more thought than that. I intended to destroy that ship and every human aboard. Some portion of my mind struggled to remind me I could barely move my wings; and even if I could glide to the vessel, there would still be the matter of getting back to shore again. Those pesky details arose from the cowardly part of me. I had no time for such thoughts. Needles of fiery pain erupted as I attempted to unfurl my wings. The agony swept through me. I fought it off with an image of my mother's corpse. That pain was nothing compared to what I planned to inflict on the Mizu wizard. I spread my wings as far as I could, then I leapt from the mountain toward the sea.

I made full use of the altitude of the Kraken's peak to angle myself toward the unseen target. I pulled my wings back and straight-ened my neck, becoming an arrow in the sky. The pain intensified, then numbed—an advantage of being a dragon. It also meant the injury worsened further still. I didn't care. I would be fury.

The emerald water drew closer quickly. No ship had yet been revealed. Anyone watching would've thought me mad as I fell toward the depths. I didn't consider changing my course. I couldn't have slowed myself without further damaging my wing anyway.

About three heartbeats before I hit the water, the elusive Mizu ship appeared, as if someone had ripped a veil from my eyes. I gave silent thanks to the wolf-eagle who'd assisted me with my prey. I intended to make this opportunity count. Unfortunately, speed had a cost that sheer willpower could not overcome. My trajectory was going to send me into the sea rather than give me an opportunity to crash into the ship, as I'd intended. I shifted and twisted and did all the things that I'd been born to do. If my wings had both been whole, if one of my hind legs hadn't been shambles, I might've been able to make the necessary adjustment. My injured body couldn't do it. I had enough time to glance at the grim faces of the Mizu archers on deck as I smashed into the cold waves.

Unlike my previous unintentional swim in the lake, I was prepared this time. Rather than flail about as I had in the water of Maricopa, I took full advantage of my speed and momentum. I had missed destroying the Mizu, but their ship's hull was directly in front of me in the water—its unprotected hull. Even better, beneath the surface, there was no ballista, no archers, no mage. I was like a leviathan hunting in the depths (except leviathans were decent swimmers). With my wings tucked to my back, I pointed my head toward the Mizu ship.

Even with the tremendous force accumulated from my dive off the mountain, I was barely faster than the ship, and my speed was fading. Fortunately, my entry angle had sent me at the Mizu's starboard side, otherwise they would've outrun me. Even leviathans couldn't match the speed of a Mizu waveship. I was certain that I was the first human or dragon to ever confront a Mizu vessel from beneath the surface. I was also the first to discover the secret of their waveship's speed: slaves.

From the bow of the craft extended two chains of enchanted gold, each a twin of the other in thickness and length. Secured to the far end of each of the tethers were ghastrays. The creatures were almost invisible, their skin and most of their internal organs translucent in the murky water. Only the glow of their eyes and edge of their fins revealed their eerie presence. And the noise.

Before this moment, I'd only seen pieces of the ghastrays I'd killed in battle. None of those had involved me diving in the sea because I hadn't really been interested in swimming, particularly with things that wanted to kill me. Seeing the creatures alive and moving did nothing to improve their appearance. I figured the powers of Haven probably made them nearly invisible for a reason. Except for their stealthy coloring, ghastrays bore some resemblance to giant mundane stingrays with the notable exception of their heads, which were like nothing else to be found on sea, land, or air. They had the mouths of gigantic worms (round and large), the eyes of spiders (six altogether), and the esthetic beauty of sea squids (none). Each of the slave-ghastrays had a tail longer than mine, but as thin and fearsome as a whip. From prior encounters, I knew those things shot poison, in the sea and into the air. These creatures were more dangerous than leviathans because they came in packs, and they were far more cunning. I'd not imagined that they could ever be made into slaves, much less the equivalent of underwater oxen to pull a ship. Perhaps someone had once thought the same of dragons. Humans excelled at stealing the power of others.

The sea vibrated with the ghastrays' calls or cries or whatever it was that the creatures did with those hideous mouths. The noise made my throat clench—it was worse than a drunken human singing about the wondrous taste of potatoes. One of the ghastrays moved its head in my direction as I neared and at least three of its bulging eyes fixed upon me. My own gaze was on those deadly tails. Those were formidable weapons against even an airborne adversary. In the water, I wouldn't have any chance. But they didn't attack. Slaves did as they were told, nothing more.

I closed on the ship, maneuvering myself toward the surface just as I reached it. I jumped out of the water with a kick of my legs, getting enough lift to sink my claws onto the vessel's low-lying deck. It wasn't an elegant pose; I probably resembled a dog trying to climb onto a table to grab dinner scraps, except my jaws weren't cute. The first thing I grabbed was a Mizu sailor between my teeth. I bit him in half and flung the carcass into the sea. Other Mizu scrambled to either side of the deck. I kicked the hull with my functional hind leg, expecting to punch a hole, but the planks held—that damn Mizu resin. I tried again before giving up. There were plenty of other ways to take this ship down.

A ballista on the foredeck swung around in my direction. I was ready for that. My tail came up from the depths, curling behind the men trying to put an arc-bolt into my head, knocking their feet out from under them with a single swipe. On the way back, I swept them off the deck into the sea. Archers fired as I pulled the rest of my bulk onto the deck. It was a testament to the fine construction of the vessel that my weight neither sunk nor capsized the ship, but the arrows kept coming and I wasn't enjoying it. Three sharp tips stuck into my scales. A few intrepid fighters had even drawn swords, but there was still no sign of the wizard. Or my sister.

I went after the Mizu crew before they organized themselves. My tail swept to the rear as I bit and clawed at a concentration of seamen and archers massed on the foredeck. That was too easy. I crushed two more Mizu in my jaws, perforated three with my claws, and knocked most of the rest into the sea. My tail bashed at the deck and anyone foolish enough to approach me from behind. I roared as I fought. There was anger in that cry, but I also hoped my sister was near, and she would hear me and answer. The only reply I got was the noise of panicked humans as I devastated their ship.

I spun on the deck to face a final group of archers. I blocked an arrow headed for my eye with a foreleg, but another struck me just above the jawline before I bit the archer's head off. I was going to look like a porcupine at the end of this—if there was an end to this. I kept inflicting carnage.

The waveship wasn't large. Soon the deck was empty except for bodies, abandoned weapons, and some debris that had once been the railing and wheelhouse of the vessel. I smashed my tail into the deck. It held for three strikes, but even the Mizu's resin-treated wood wasn't indestructible; it gave way to my furious strength. My claws finished the work, peeling back the planks the way the humans ate oranges (I liked them too, except I hated the outer skin, and nobody would peel them for me).

I was thorough—I didn't just rip up the center deck. I ravaged the bow and stern as well. As I methodically searched the Mizu ship, I came across its unusual steering mechanism (I'd destroyed enough ships to have an understanding of the general construction of human vessels). Apart from being located at the bow of the ship, the wheel of the Mizu ship wasn't a wheel at all. Instead, the ship's controls appeared to be a pair of rods that intersected to form a single handle near the top. The instrumentation glittered with what I presumed to be some kind of enchantment—this was how the humans commanded the captive ghastray-slaves chained below. I gazed back toward Maricopa, barely visible even to me in the distance. My digits were agile enough that I could've used the controls to turn the vessel. But I didn't. Touching those mechanisms meant controlling creatures that didn't want to be controlled, the same way I'd been controlled. Ghastrays might be a bunch of vicious killers, but I liked slavers even less. I stared at the helm and vowed never to become what I hated most in this world, whatever the cost. If I died, I would do so free, with... well, if not honor, then a clear conscience. Instead, I ripped off more of the deck around the control mechanism, exposing the golden chains that led from the ship's bow down to the ghastrays. These were the Mizu version of control-runes. With an angry snort, I shoved a claw from each leg into two of the interlocking rings and ripped it apart. The chain broke easily. I enjoyed the taste of bestowing liberation, even if the first creatures I'd set free were ghastrays who would kill me if I gave them the chance. This noble task completed, I resumed ripping the Mizu ship apart.

There were living quarters below the main deck, but no humans and no sign of my sister. I kept destroying, smashing the vessel piece by piece even as my hearts wobbled with fear about what I wasn't finding. After disassembling the crew quarters, I ripped still more deck away, accessing the ship's main hold. It was filled with weapons, nets, chains, and human foodstuffs. Finally, in a dark corner of the hull, hid the wizard. His mirror-like robe shone even in the faint light, not that he could've hidden from me anyway. Live humans smell differently than dead ones.

He was bent over a chest made of a black wood that I'd never previously encountered, a black orb of glass in one hand. For a moment, I thought it was some kind of weapon, but he dropped it as soon as he realized he'd been discovered. He couldn't hide. It was time to fight.

The wizard's hand twirled and his eyes glowed. I had no intention of enduring another lightning strike. I struck with force, intended to smash the wizard before he could end me. The little man was quicker. He dove out of the way just as my claw collided with the spot he had stood in a moment earlier. I hit the outer hull instead. The wood cracked and I lurched downward, off balance. My attack had been quick, but sloppy. Now, I was vulnerable.

The wizard waved his hands and the air heated. A tendril of wind came at me—a small one. Nothing like what I'd experienced on Maricopa. Indeed, I can fart a bigger gust. The spell washed over me without noticeable effect. I snarled in contempt, realizing the only thing this cowardly Mizu mage had in common with the more powerful wizard I'd faced on Maricopa was a similar robe. His eyes were the wrong color, and they were filled with fear. I knocked him from his feet with my tail, then pinned him to the ground with a claw. Sea water was coming through the hole I'd made in the bottom of the ship. It surrounded him up to his ears.

I lowered my head close to my prisoner.

"Where is the hatchling?"

I let my saliva drip all over him.

The minor wizard closed his eyes, mumbling some sounds I couldn't decipher. The words sounded memorized. He wasn't trying to speak to me. I asked my question once again. When he failed to answer, I stuck a claw through his belly. He quivered violently as he died, a fate he deserved. This one had barely been worth my time to kill.

Where is the real wizard?

There wasn't much left of the ship but debris. I had no place left to look. I'd failed. Again.

I roared my grief. This one was probably loud enough to be heard in Eladrell. It might have been my final farewell. My wings were broken. I was stuck on this sinking ship.

FOURTEEN

My sister was gone.

Or she'd never been on the ship at all. That Mizu wizard had beaten me again, and probably for the last time. I would soon be testing my swimming prowess again, and this time I didn't like my chances.

My experience in the lake had taught me a few things, mostly that I wasn't as adept a swimmer as I'd fancied myself when my only experience had been watching ducks. I'd survived the lake, but the sea was considerably deeper, and it had big waves along with strong currents. Running and gliding along the bottom wasn't going to work this far from shore. I probably shouldn't have set those ghastrays free. They could've pulled the ship back to Maricopa.

Isn't it perfect that my one selfless act is going to end up getting me killed?

The only choice was to try to fly. I wasn't optimistic about how that would work out, but it was fly or die. For my sister, I would endure the pain of trying.

I climbed out of the ship's hold, back onto the remnants of the deck. The highest, driest part was the foredeck, where the ballista had once been situated. I stood upon the rotating mount of the giant weapon and judged the distance back to Maricopa. I could've flown there easily if I'd been my usual self, but I wasn't.

I tried spreading my wings. The pain had been mostly turned off, but even without the constant agony to remind me, I knew that my right wing was a disaster. The jagged tear stretched almost a third of its entire length. I closed my eyes, feeling the wind. The gusts were at my back at least, but I doubted I could even lift myself. If I'd been on this ship a day ago, I'm not sure I would've cared if I died. Meeting my mother and my sister had changed that. I had an inkling of who I was. I had blood kin that needed me. I had a purpose. I didn't want to die, which was just so human.

I clenched my jaw and thrust my wings. Or at least I tried. I got airborne—a little. I flapped as best I could, struggling to lift myself. I pushed desperately, but with all my efforts I only managed to lift myself a tail length above the waves. I wasn't going to make it, but I tried anyway. I pushed until my chest burned and my head spun. I thought of my mother and sister, and all my brethren back in Eladrell who would be condemned if I failed. I fed on the anger; I didn't quit, but my body had its limits. I tired, slowing until there was nothing left to give. Then, I fell into the water, too exhausted to repeat my futile attempts at swimming. I sank, falling through the depths, the water growing colder and darker as I went down. The chill seeped to my body, banishing the burning fire in my wings.

It was a relief to not have to fight anymore.

At the very end, my mind failed me. I saw visions of the unreal, of frightening creatures coming up beneath me, of moving through the water into the light, of land, of rock and solid ground. Finally, I succumbed to darkness.

I awoke to someone tickling my nose.

Who in the Abyss does that?

I opened my eyes to find a tail in my face, and not a pretty dragon tail. It was a ghastray's tail, stinger and all. I brought up my own tail, ready to fight, but I faced no adversary. I lay on a rocky beach, the massive form of the Kraken looming nearby. Stars lit the sky. A ghastray floated in the shallows of the beach, its strange body seeming to hover within the glittering waves, somehow unaffected by the tides. All six of its eyes stared at me, unblinking. I stared back. It no longer was shackled with the golden Mizu slave chain, but I had no doubt this was one of the ghastrays I had freed from the waveship. Otherwise, it would have been feasting on my carcass.

The ghastray's frightening head rose above the water. "A life for a life, dragon." It spoke Avian, although its voice sounded like a very old human talking with a mouth full of stones. I wondered how the creature came to understand the language. It seemed the ghastrays were far more formidable than anyone—including me—had thought.

I tried to be polite. "My thanks for saving me."

Ghastrays weren't into polite. "When next we meet, I will consume your hearts."

It seemed that this would not be a lasting friendship. I didn't care. This creature had knowledge I desperately needed.

"Where is the other dragon—the hatchling?" I had trouble speaking, but the ghastray understood well enough.

The nearly invisible creature before me sounded like it was choking on fishbones for a moment. Perhaps I'd insulted it by asking it a question. Its mouth twitched, and each eye opened and shut in succession. "Two man-boats, dragon."

It was my turn to choke. I had attacked the wrong vessel. "That wizard has many tricks."

"Drasu." Even by the standard of a talking ghastray, the word came out with chilling hatred. "I shall eat his heart and that of his children. He and all the slavers will die."

Drasu.

My mother had said the same word. It was a name—the name of her killer. She had known the wizard. That was important. It told me my mother had once dwelled across the Wall of Fire.

There could be no mistaking the creature's malevolence toward the mage. I was okay with that. "I will help you find him, and you may have him to feast upon. Humans taste like old chicken."

More choking noises followed from the six-eyed creature. "We are done, dragon."

He sank beneath the water. I hurried toward him even though it hurt to move, splashing into the shallow water. "Wait."

The ghastray raised its tail out of the water, warning me to keep my distance. The poison tip twitched. I was in no condition to fight, but my need was great. "The ship heads west, back to the home of the Mizu. How do you intend to cross the Wall of Fire?"

The ghastray's tail twirled in a circle, reminding me of an angry hornet. It took all of my self-restraint to remain still. After the third circuit of its poisonous stinger, the ghastray's head came back to the surface, its beady eyes opening and shutting one after the other. "For this answer, a debt is owed to us. You agree, dragon?"

It was just my luck that I had freed a ghastray who could not only speak but was a mercenary trader of its knowledge. I couldn't imagine what this sea creature might ask of me, but I needed its information. If I couldn't cross the Wall of Fire, my sister was lost forever. "Agreed."

"Seek out the crescent island changed by the lost humans. To find it, fly from here directly toward the tip of the setting sun. That place... is different than the others. There, the billowing smoke of the fire peaks is false. It may smell the same to your stretched dragon snout, you may feel peril, but it is only your mind tricking you. In that place only, you may pass through the so-called Wall of Fire." It dipped its head beneath the water. I thought our conversation concluded, but it rose once again. "Remember, dragon. A debt is owed." Its eyes looked at the horizon. "Your kin come for you. Through the night they fly. Our time is at an end, but first I would know your name, dragon."

I thought of my mother's words, about how we dragons earned our names. Had I earned anything? I was free, but even that might not have been something I had done on my own. I'd failed to free my sister, or even find her. My greatest accomplishment in my life was freeing two ghastrays, and I wasn't going to name myself for that. I wasn't yet worthy of a dragon name.

"The humans call me Bayloo." I dipped my head slightly (very slightly). "Have you a name?"

The noise that came from the ghastray's mouth was a horrific mix of a cock's crow and the crash of a great wave against a sheer cliff. "In human-speak, I can be called Vengeance."

I had to admit, it was an excellent name, particularly for a freed slave. One day, I would earn myself something even better (and more original).

Vengeance blinked his many eyes at me, then submerged. A moment later, the waves of the sea were my only companion on the shore. I craned my neck, searching the skies for the dragons that Vengeance had foretold. I didn't have to wait long before I heard them coming from the north—the magnificent sound of dragon wings pushing through the air. I stared anxiously at the giant form of the Kraken until they appeared above it: two giant ash dragons set against the night's low clouds, human ryders on their backs. As graceful as they looked in flight, sadness came along with them. These were my brethren, and they were slaves. They had barely known any other life.

I would change that, but only if the humans were stupid enough to rescue me.

FIFTEEN

I blacked out.

That was how my brother Lothar found me—face down on the beach. My sister Narsis accompanied him, along with their ryders. I always liked Narsis. Slave dragons weren't usually social with each other, but there was something in her manner that gave me the impression that she would've been kind, but for the runes carved into her.

The scent of dragon pulled me from my stupor. In the moment before I opened my eyes, I dared to hope that my mother's death had been a terrible dream, but the grim scene around me was all too real. A pair of humans with different colored hair but nearly identical scowls stared at me as their slave dragons looked obediently behind their masters.

The blond ryder's eye fixed on the blood dripping on my torso. "Bayloo, what happened here?"

I wasn't ready to answer that question, particularly from a ryder. I closed my eyes again, intending to feign unconsciousness. Instead, I really did slip back into a void of delirium as my body shut down, devoting all its energy to healing.

I have some recollection of my fellow dragons carrying me in their claws back to DragonPeak, which must've been a challenging display of flying. I wouldn't have thought Narsis and Lothar could've managed by themselves. Another dragon must have assisted, but I didn't remember that part.

I awoke in my cave, battered but not yet broken. Pain roused me from my slumber, the sour odor of humans clogging my nostrils. I kept my eyes shut. More sniffing and listening told me that three humans scurried about nearby.

While all humans stink, they do it differently. I recognized Lisaam Payne's distinctive rotting onion scent, but the other humans weren't familiar to my nose. One reeked of the sour-sweet fragrance of alaga flowers, which grow in higher altitudes and are prized by female humans. The other person smelled of blood—my blood. A few sharp stabs of pain on my wing later, I realized that someone was sewing my wing with a needle and sutures made of sheep guts. Apparently, I'd bled all over the place. The work being performed hurt, but compared to what I'd been through, that pain was a mere nuisance. The fact my body was again letting me feel pain meant I'd been healing.

Sweet-Flower stood near the sewing person. Based on the various sensations, I deduced that Sweet-Flower's role in all this was rubbing an ointment on the newly mended wing sections. This substance was the source of the alaga flower odor I detected. Since it had been generously lathered onto my wing, I would be smelling a lot of it for the foreseeable future. Excellent.

The humans toiled without speaking, sewing and rubbing, their lone heartbeats steady until finally they finished their task. My wing had been stitched back into a single, whole piece. Even without moving, I knew there was no way that those sutures would hold if I stretched or tried to fly.

"Will this truly work on a dragon's wing, Elkra?" I recognized Payne's rasp of a voice, but it sounded unusually concerned—almost as if he cared about what happened to me. Considering he'd tried to sell me to Prince Dayne, I didn't want his concern.

"I've never seen damage this severe." A human sighed so hard the dragon in the next cave could've heard it; no good news would follow. "The rip is through the muscle and almost across all of the wing's surface. Even if it mends, it is uncertain if the dragon will be able to use it to fly again. Their wings are complex things, frames of cartilage and hardened skin, propelled by breast muscle, but also the strength of—"

"I understand dragon flight, healer. That wasn't my question. I need to know if your mending will be successful. A dragon that cannot fly or breathe fire is just a very inconvenient way to waste meat."

Hesitation followed. "I cannot guarantee—"

Payne cut him off. "Your excuses bore me, Elkra. You claim to be a master of your art. The test of a true master is results."

The other human spoke. The voice of a female, softer and calmer than the others. "Elkra's stitches are close and tight. The essence of the alaga flower will ward off infection and speed the healing. If we were to compare this damage to an injury to a human arm, there would be scarring and likely some permanent impairment of mobility due to muscle damage." A low growl emerged deep in Payne's throat, but the woman kept speaking. "However, dragons' ability to regenerate themselves vastly exceeds ours. I have hope that the dragon will heal completely, Master Payne."

"Hope." He said it with distaste. "The tides of war are coming to Rolm's shores. Hope is useless, whoever you are."

"I am Valis, Master Payne. And while I am still a senior apprentice, I take my master examination on the next moon."

Payne's displeasure gurgled in his throat. Elkra heard it as well. "Master Payne, leave it to us."

The Keeper only grunted. "What about the rest of the dragon's injuries?"

A human hand ran over several scales on my neck. I didn't like it, but I managed not to shiver in distaste. "A few arrows made their way into the gaps between his scales—I've never seen so many fired with such accuracy. They have unusual tips. We cleaned the wounds, removing any debris. Those pricks are nothing for a dragon of this size. Apart from the wing, we expect he will regain his strength quickly, so long as he is properly fed."

Properly fed. Finally, some real healing talk.

"His life would not be endangered by... further stress?"

I didn't like the sound of that at all.

Elkra answered with caution. "I'm not sure I understand."

"You don't need to understand. You only need to answer."

"Except for the damage to his wing, he'll be as strong as ever within three days or so."

Valis interrupted. "Unless the wing injury is so severe it slows his other healing. Dragons aren't immune to infection either. These injuries must be kept clean."

"I think you must do a better job training your assistants, Elkra." Payne sounded dangerous. I was familiar with that tone. "You said three days, healer. You had best be correct."

"It will be as I said," Elkra replied.

"Excellent." When Lisaam Payne sounded pleased, it worried me. "Send word to me when he awakens. We still need answers about what happened on Maricopa. And what happened to Brindisi too, I suppose." There was no mistaking Payne's lack of distress about my late ryder's demise, although he might have felt differently if he knew that at this moment the man's remains were moving from my stomach to my ass, and not very smoothly.

I relaxed slightly at the sound of the cave's gate opening and the foul smell of Payne disappearing. My gate locked behind him. Even with Payne gone, the scent in my cave still bothered me. Humans were bad enough, but my head began to ache from inhaling the powerful odor of those fragrant flowers. I had expected the other humans to follow Payne outside. I wanted my solitude.

"Valis, there is nothing more for us to do here. I'll ask one of the

Keepers to check in on the dragon. We just need to ensure he doesn't tear the stitches when he wakes."

The female healer replied immediately. "I will stay. The Keepers are lax."

It's hard to hear a shrug, but I was almost sure that I did. "As you wish. I must return to the guild house. Have the Keeper send for me if I'm needed. I don't fancy another climb up those stairs soon, but the hoist has broken its ropes again."

Elkra called for a Keeper to let him out of my cave. Soon afterward, I was alone with the female human. One human is better than three, but it turned out that this Valis was a talker. Worse, she was also a toucher.

Valis laid a hand on my side, then actually pressed her ear against my scales. She might've heard some gurgling. Fortunately, Brindisi wouldn't be spilling any secrets from in there.

"Your heartbeats are amazing ... they work in such harmony that I barely hear that there are two." Two soft fingers glided down my body to my tail. "Such a remarkable creature, like none other in this world."

An excellent observation. I'd prefer she leave, but at least this Valis was perceptive.

"The perfect fighting machine, but intelligent as well."

Yeah, I liked her more than most humans.

Valis went to my damaged wing next, careful not to touch anywhere near the stitches. "Elkra did an excellent job with the needle." I was glad to hear that. However, she released a heavy sigh afterward. "But dragon wings are so unique. It is impossible to know the outcome of our work."

This time I wished she'd keep talking about my wing, but she didn't. After completing her examination, Valis backed up to the edge of the cave, from where she seemed to just watch me, humming an annoying melody that reminded me of frogs trying to whistle. Eventually, she allowed herself to sink to the floor. I pretended to be asleep through all of this, but keeping my eyes shut became tedious. I tried to focus on my own plan, specifically, how I was going to get out of here before the Sculptors returned to give me yet another ryder. I found the human's presence distracting. Or maybe it was the flower smell. My head spun every time I tried to focus. I didn't like people in my cave. I realized the only way to get rid of her was to give her what she wanted. I opened one eye slowly, as if my eyelid were heavy.

Valis bolted to her feet. Tiny even by human standards, her skin lacked almost all color, which matched the stringy snow-color strands that hung down from her head to her shoulders. I knew white was popular with humans in the summer. Valis was probably well liked by other humans during that season. Only her eyes had color—a smoky blue tint. For a moment, I thought she had dyed the left side of her face to add a bit more color as some humans inexplicably do with the hair atop their heads (but not the ear or nose hair for some reason, which might indeed make them more attractive), but I quickly realized I was mistaken. Her skin was simply a different shade—a not unpleasant crimson that ran from beneath her eye down to her neck. The contrast made her face more interesting than other humans, much as my magnificent mane further enhances my own irresistible attractiveness.

Her Avian was excellent. "I am Valis."

I glowed a smile at her with my open eye. I couldn't help it—she was only the second human who had introduced themselves when they first met me. Jona had been the other, but I didn't want to think of him now. I needed information from Valis.

"That was a smile!" Valis' voice squeaked with excitement.

I held back a compliment about her fine Avian. A slave dragon would never presume to evaluate a human. Instead, I craned my head to make it obvious I was studying the stitches on my wing, even as I took great care not to move any part of my body except my neck.

Valis jumped like a startled squirrel. "Please do not extend your wing. Do not move it at all." She placed both her tiny hands on me, as if she had the ability to stop me from moving it if I chose.

I kept it simple. "Is it healed?"

"We have rejoined the tear—mended it like sewing a tunic, but with special thread. That should allow the cartilage and skin to fuse back together without too much scarring. That is all we healers can do. It is up to you to do the real healing."

She spoke in a warm tone without condescension. I risked another question. "How long until I can fly?"

She pursed her lips. "I don't know."

Ah, honesty. So useless.

But Valis wasn't done. "On a human, it might take up to a week for the skin to mend, and even longer if there was muscle damage. But dragons heal quickly, overcoming injuries that would be fatal to any other... well, to any other living creature."

She had no idea if I'd fly again, and neither did I. But I did know that Lisaam Payne had plans for me that involved pain. He also had a debt to pay to a furious prince and his dangerous mother, the queen. It wasn't hard to put those pieces together: Payne intended for me to be joined with Prince Dayne. That didn't appeal to me, but I would be far more prepared than I had been before Brindisi. I knew my strength. No mind would ever dominate my will again. I was free, now and forever.

I also had far more knowledge of my kind than I'd ever had before. I was an ember dragon—a unique breed of our species. My mother had commanded magic like a human wizard, which meant I too might have such power. I was ready to take on Prince Dayne or any other human. The problem was my mangled wing. I needed humans to help fix that.

I focused all of my senses on Valis. She looked different than most other humans due to her coloring, but that was only superficial. Her heart beat faster than normal. By her own admission, she didn't have much experience with dragons. I think she was excited to be speaking to me. I took a risk. "I have no ryder."

Valis tilted her head as she considered my words. I held my breath, fearing I had alarmed her, but instead her voice changed to something even softer, its tone dripping with human sympathy. "I am sorry about that. I know it must be terribly difficult to lose Brindisi. Master Payne wanted me to send word as soon as you were awake to learn more about how that happened."

This woman actually believed I cared about losing Brindisi. Clearly, she hadn't known the man.

"Our ryders are joined to us," I told her. Then I steeled myself for the huge lie. "I have a great void within me."

Valis' eyes actually shook. For a moment, I feared water might leak from them. "Is there any way I can help you?"

I began to understand why humans lied so much. It helped them get what they wanted far more easily than the truth. "Crema's ryder has always been very kind." Actually, she'd never been anything like that, but I still needed to speak with Bethy Rann. My hearts thundered as I spoke the last. No slave dragon would've spoken as I did, nor made this request. Any Keeper would have known something was amiss, as would most healers, but only this one particular healer mattered. I studied Valis' eyes, her breath, even the beating of her heart, for signs of distress, but there were none. She acted almost as if she was speaking to another human. I dared to hope.

Valis smiled using her mouth in the human fashion. "I shall go to her myself if that would give you comfort. With my kind, comfort and the proper company often make a difference in their healing. Let us hope the same is true of dragons."

This woman had to be the kindest (and most naive) human in all the world. I considered asking for a bit of ale as well, but it seemed too great a risk. Instead, I flashed Valis another dragon smile before I laid my head back down on the floor. She left my cage to attend to the errand I'd given her. I took some satisfaction in that as well. It seemed like the more natural way for the dragon-human relationship to flow.

My wing hurt, my neck ached, and I was running out of time to escape before the Keepers discovered that I had disposed of Brindisi via my stomach. My tail ticked with impatience as I stared at the entrance to my cave, waiting and listening. The sun had set so I hoped Valis would take her time before sending word to Lisaam Payne that I was awake.

To my relief, Bethy Rann arrived before anyone else. Ryders often spent their nights on the huts built on top of the peak, while a man like Lisaam Payne would be more likely to be sleeping in his warm bed in Eladrell.

Rann came to the gate of my cave, a torch in one hand, her curved blade at her side, and suspicion in her eyes. It was safe to assume Rann had never been summoned by a dragon before. I moved closer, but not too close.

I let her speak first. I didn't want to show too much initiative. She was already spooked.

"The healer, Valis, came to speak to me. Apparently, you would heal better with my company?" Her voice dripped with suspicion. Perhaps she thought I wanted to cuddle, which I didn't—she didn't even have a tail.

I sniffed the air to confirm there was no Keeper nearby to over-hear us. Satisfied we were alone, I told myself to be patient, to act more like what she expected as I tried to determine if I'd concocted a plan of genius or madness. "The honorable healer asked if there was any other master that might be with me while I am without a linked ryder. She thought it might aid the healing process. It seemed impor-tant to her that I answer."

I had learned some valuable lessons from listening to humans lie to each other. Blaming the person that wasn't present was among them. My words seemed to have the desired effect. Some of the tension in Rann's shoulders eased—but only some—and in her eyes I saw something else: disappointment. It flashed in the form of a flicker of her eyes toward the floor, but I was sure of what I'd seen.

"Healers can be as strange as any creature bred in the depths of the Pits of Gargen," Rann said, placing her hands on the bars of my prison door. "Is my being here helping you feel better?"

She mocked me. I stared at her and she at me. Rann's eyes were tinged red, the edges swollen. I didn't know how long we had before

Lisaam Payne arrived. My behavior was odd for a dragon, but she wasn't acting like a typical ryder, either. I'd made some guesses about her, and I was almost certain now, but there's a chasm of consequences between almost and correct. At least she'd come alone. I'd have to try to kill her through the bars if I'd misjudged her. After my last meal of Chicken-ala-Brindisi, that was hardly an incentive to mess this up. The silence between us stretched. I decided to break it by gambling my life.

"You miss Jona."

SIXTEEN

Bethy Rann's eyes grew wide with shock.

Her hand moved to her blade. As if that piece of metal would save her. I gritted my teeth, forcing myself to hold still. She pursed her lips, calming herself. Finally, she nodded. "Yes. I miss him. He and others who have died."

The thunder of my beating hearts was so loud Rann should've been able to hear it in the cave. I understood her meaning. "You and Jona are both from Maricopa."

Rann tilted her head, her gaze narrowing. "Why do you believe that?"

My eyes pulsed with satisfaction. "That terrible pommice fruit—only you and Jona could stand it, but it's all over Maricopa." Rann's lips formed a tight smile, an expression I'd not seen on her before. "And it made sense there would be more than one of you."

She pressed her head against the gate, her eyes still locked with mine. Her voice cracked when she spoke next. "At least my brother did not die in vain."

I sniffed her scent, paying closer attention than I ever had in the

past. I had previously ignored those humans who rode horned dragons. That had been a mistake. "You are his blood sister."

As soon as I said it, I knew it made sense—it explained her
emotion out on the Shelf. Bethy Rann had been mourning her
brother, who I'd gotten killed.

"Yes." Rann sounded relieved to admit it. "My dead brother.
Already word of what happened on Maricopa has spread through
DragonPeak."

My inside wobbled with guilt. First her brother, now this. Still,
Rann was strong. I did not try to hide the truth. She deserved that.
"Your people on Maricopa are dead. They tried to help my mother.
Now they are dead." I could've apologized, and that might have been
the human thing to do—but what purpose did it serve? Those people
would still be dead. Instead, I spoke as a dragon. "My mother is dead
as well."

"Oh, Great Dawn ..." Rann whispered it. It took me a moment to
realize she spoke of my mother, using something like her Avian name.

I made a vow as a dragon should. "I shall hunt the killers of your
people and my mother to the ends of this world."

"They were not my people," Rann said. This surprised me. "Jona
and I came to Maricopa as refugees. Those people took us in. They
gave us sanctuary."

"You were not born there?"

Rann spoke in a distant voice. "No, but our people were related
to those of the island, so they accepted us. The people of Maricopa,
like my own people on Ulibon, originally fled the Empire of Ni-Yota.
We fled the tyranny of the Mizu during a great purge—or so I was
told."

My understanding of Avian must have failed me. "You are from
beyond the Wall of Fire?"

"Not me, but my grandfather came from there. Our ancestors
were known as the Illugar in our homeland. But those are only stories
to me—my brother and I were born on Ulibon."

This surprised me. "Ulibon?" I had many memories of Ulibon,

none of them fond. "The humans there were fierce. The magic of their enchanted weapons killed many of my brethren in the battle for the Twisted Keep. You and Jona are from that land of enchanters?"

"Only the Highstar and few others know the craft of enchantment. Jona and I fled the aftermath of Mendakas' war there. After the last Highstar of Ulibon was killed, there was chaos across the land as Mendakas burned the countryside along with the keep of any lord who dared to remain loyal to the Highstar. Like many others, I fled as far away as possible. We went to Maricopa."

"That is an odd choice."

Rann shrugged. "It was a forgotten island no one cared about. The people there were my distant kin. They once even dwelled on Ulibon. They were more likely to accept us than Oster or the pirate king."

I thought of Brindisi's discovery in the devastated village. "There were enchanters on Maricopa. The same magic that allowed the Highstars of Ulibon to conquer that island."

Rann wore a hard glare and deep frown as I mused at these revelations. "Let us not waste time with histories. You fought at the battle of the Twisted Keep. You know our magic—my people know the art of enchantment. But even that was not enough to save the Highstar and Ulibon. Nor was it enough to save your mother or the people who lived on Maricopa. It wasn't enough to preserve my brother's life either." The end of Rann's mouth curled even further downward. "Tragedy stalks you, Bayloo. I hope their sacrifices were worth it."

She had the truth of it. But I had no assurances to offer. Instead, I told her my name.

"I am the First of the Free, also known to humans as Bayloo. Jona gave me a chance at real life. I mourn his death, and my role in it, but his bravery and sacrifice shall be sung loud through the skies when dragons are again free."

Rann opened her mouth to reply, then closed it without uttering a sound. Her lips were tight. She nodded curtly. "Welcome to the world, Bayloo, First of the Free. I think you have a story to tell me, of a battle and more."

I did. I had a story, and I had a plan, but there was no time to share any of that. I had only time to give a warning: Lisaam Payne had returned.

SEVENTEEN

Rann fled.

She ran up the peak as Payne and his companions made their way down the winding mountain path that led to my prison. There were many humans—more than on Payne's previous visit. Indeed, enough heavy footfalls scraped along the path that descended from the Shelf that I feared a parade would soon arrive at my cave. To come from above in such numbers meant that a horned dragon had flown the humans to DragonPeak (the highest point accessible by winch lift was below the location of my cave). I backed myself against the rear of my cave as I waited in the gloom for these humans who deemed themselves too august to climb with their own feet.

Lisaam Payne stepped inside first. His face told me trouble followed in his wake. And so it did.

A soldier clad in heavy mail came next, followed by two fighters in matching armor, the image of a rearing fire-breather beneath a pair of crossed dragon claws emblazoned upon the metal that covered their chests. I recognized the crest of the human who called himself the King of Dragons. These men-at-arms fixed their gaze upon me as they took up position against the wall, their faces chiseled with wariness. The king himself followed.

Lian Aradrel Mendakas moved with presence. He stood a head beneath the tallest of his soldiers and wore no armor, only a doublet of lush purple. Yet there was no doubt he was the more formidable man. His frame looked to have been carved from the stone of a mountain, with wide shoulders and thick, powerful arms. He wore a beard of sheer black that matched the hair of his head, but I smelled the tell-tale odor of the dye that humans used to stain away their graying wisps.

Mendakas' eyes were unique among his kind—hard orbs of silver that pierced like the tip of a sword. Only at the corners did the spidery wrinkles of his skin give evidence that men did not live forever. The king wore a single circle of gold atop his head, but he didn't need it to proclaim himself ruler. In Mendakas, the humans had found a true specimen.

But even the greatest of men were not without rivals. King Mendakas' equal in presence entered my cave just in his wake. Queen Florin had a swan's grace, moving beside the lion that was her husband, although her eyes told of the deadly cunning that lurked behind a beautiful facade. Her skin was almost as pale as Valis' and her head was covered by flowing waves of golden hair that glittered beside the king's silvery eyes.

The rest of the royal party numbered six, but Lisaam Payne directed them to remain outside, allowing only the healer, Elkra, within the cave, while the others lined the narrow ledge beyond my prison. I was pleased that the Prince of Sapphires hadn't been included in the party, but slightly disappointed that Valis wasn't here. That left me surrounded by humans I didn't like—pretty much as always.

Mendakas stared at me as if he expected me to bow to him as other human suppliants might. The intensity of his gaze pushed at me in the way that a ryder might command me through our link—except Mendakas needed no runes to do it. His will was tangible even without evident magic, although not nearly as strong as the bond of a control-rune. Still, I sensed his demand for respect and supplication. I held myself still, waiting. That was the advantage of being a slave. I merely needed to react.

"Bayloo, to heel," Payne commanded.

I did it even though I hated it. The top of my head was level with the king's when I pressed my neck to the ground.

"Bayloo." Every eye focused on the king when he spoke, including mine. His voice echoed in the cave, deep and powerful even the second time I heard it. "You flew with Triton and I at Ulibon at the Battle of the Twisted Keep."

"I have that honor, Master."

"Triton praised your speed. You moved with such swiftness, even their enchanted arrows could not catch you in the sky. And last year in the Thunder Straits you tore the back fin off a leviathan and then lifted the rest of the beast halfway out of the sea to save one of my warships that had foolishly ventured too close."

I remembered that great beast. It ate a fisherman's boat whole. I didn't understand leviathan appetites; wood was just a bunch of splinters bunched together—it was like eating trouble.

I puffed up at the king's praise, and it wasn't an act. "You and Triton are both too kind, the honor is too much. The power of my brother's breath has no equal."

The king's eyes darkened. "Perhaps that was once true. But all creatures under Haven fade." I got the impression he wasn't just speaking about Triton. "You know this well, as you've now seen the death of five ryders. Some of whom were more precious to me than others." His eyes flickered to the queen, whose face grew colder. The king fought a battle of his own on that front.

"Tell me of the death of my great general and friend, Brindisi."

I hadn't spent any time concocting my story, which meant I'd have to adhere as close to the truth as possible—without actually telling it.

"He died in battle, Master, as he would've wanted. A great warrior. His foe was the Mizu."

The assembled gasped in near unison, except for Mendakas whose face might as well have been a painting for all the reaction he showed. "That is a result, but not an explanation. I wish to know how he died."

Lisaam Payne edged his skinny body forward a step. "Your Majesty, if I may, their minds are limited. It is best to ask one question about a single matter to them, one that requires only a simple response."

Mendakas didn't acknowledge the words of his Chief Keeper, but the queen had a reply. "Do not think to instruct the king, Payne. My husband knows the nature of each of his dragons. He was riding when you were still wetting your bed sheets." Her voice was a dagger of jagged ice. "He needs no further guidance from you on how to ask questions."

If I were a human, I would've rather eaten chicken feathers than shared a meal with the royal mated couple. No wonder the little prince wanted to lose himself in the sky.

Mendakas' face told me he didn't intend to repeat himself, but he still expected an answer to his question. I strained my mind to produce a worthy lie. "With the Mizu traveled a wizard of tremendous power. The wizard was able to call lightning from the sky. Brindisi and I did battle with them and their wizard, but the Mizu were too many. The arrows of the Mizu archers ended the life of my ryder, Master."

The king's jaw rolled slowly, chewing on my words. "Yet you survived. How is that?"

If I told him the truth, he wouldn't have believed me. "I tried to attack their ship as they fled. The wizard's magic struck me. They thought me dead in the sea. I thought I was as well."

Mendakas' stony gaze lessened as his face assumed a more thoughtful pose. "The lightning wizard." He spoke mostly to himself.

The queen seemed far less interested in my words. Her eyes remained upon me, but they were there to evaluate a piece of chattel.

Another man entered the cave at the king's summons. He was an old human, his skin worn, his ear hair at full bloom—as good a measure of human wisdom as any that I've found. The ugly yellow color of his teeth further portended the august knowledge that his shriveled head likely held.

The old man spoke with a graveled, well-worn voice. "A spellcaster who could summon the power of Haven you say, dragon?"

"It is so, Master."

"Tell me of his eyes."

Those I would never forget. "They were as black as a raven's wing, Master."

The old man turned to his liege. "The eyes of night. It must be Drasu. There cannot be two with such power. Only the greatest of prizes would tempt one such as he to leave Ni-Yota to come to our shores."

The king regarded me again. "What did the Mizu want?"

It's often painful to be thought a fool by those who are themselves fools, but there were times I was grateful for the human ego—such as now. The existence of my mother and sister would remain locked in my hearts, a secret forever unknown to these creatures if I could help it. "I do not understand, Master."

"Simple minds, Your Majesty," Lisaam Payne said, before he could help himself. The queen frowned but didn't rebuke him. "Bayloo, what did the Mizu take with them?"

I tried to think of something plausible, something unrelated to dragons or the lake within the Kraken. "Barrels from the village storehouse, although they left many behind as well. Brindisi thought the items inside unusual, Masters. There was gold, flint, a strange white sand, and other creations that I did not understand. Brindisi called them items of enchantment, though he did not speak to me of what they were."

Ugly-Yellow-Teeth tugged on a dropping lobe that hung low from his right ear. This gesture may have stimulated the old human's mind, for a somewhat-correct notion actually spewed out of his mouth afterward. "That desolate rock was once part of Ulibon... before that, it had been recorded as uninhabited. Sometime in the not-so-distant past, people came there and settled that place. We do not know their origins. It seems they chose that desolate place for a reason. They were not just simple fish-folk as they appeared."

These words caused the king to furrow his thick brow. "Anatar of Ulibon was a formidable man. His enchanters were worthy adversaries. And there is the matter of his heir."

The queen's eyes lifted off me and flicked upward to inspect the inside of her skull at her husband's pronouncement. "The dead heir."

I knew the story to which King Mendakas referred because I had been there. After the great battle for control of the Twisted Keep of Ulibon had been won and its Highstar sent to the Abyss, the soldiers of Rolm had searched for the dead leader of Ulibon's wife and young son, his sole heir. Hundreds of humans had died fighting their way up the spiraling walls of the Twisted Keep, until they'd reached the residence of the ruling family. The Highstar's wife and son had supposedly leapt from a tower window rather than be captured. Two days later, a pair of bloated, mutilated bodies had washed onto the rocky beach beneath the tower. The face of Egriss Mare, wife of Anatar, had still been distinguishable, but the boy who came ashore nearby had been mauled by some beast of the sea. His clothes had been right, but some said that was merely a clever deception, that loyalists of the late ruler had spirited away the true heir, and his mother had taken the child of a servant to ensure her own son would live to seek revenge upon his father's killers. I had no opinion on the matter. Before this moment, I hadn't cared about the fate of some human boy without whiskers. I still didn't, except to the extent this tale kept the humans from searching for my mother.

When the queen next spoke, the sound that flowed out reeked of contempt. "Always wary of the imagined danger of the dark while ignoring the actual threat in front of you." She directed her withering gaze to the old man beside the king. "Gedrick, do you believe that the son of Anatar has been on Maricopa all these years, and has become a man grown?"

The king's counselor shuffled his weight between his feet. "I believe the king suggests one possibility for what might bring the greatest of Mizu wizards beyond the Wall of Fire to the shores of one of the most isolated and desolate islands in the domain of Rolm."

The queen greeted Gedrick's evasion with a contemptuous smile. "Perhaps if the dragon had a ryder linked to it again, we could glean more useful information from it. What say you to that, Keeper Payne?"

My sensitive ears allowed me to hear the actual blood draining from Lisaam Payne's face. His eyes flicked between the king and queen. Here was a man who wanted to please all masters. "A ryder's link is indeed far superior to anything we can glean from their limited speech in Avian. A ryder could tell us more."

Florin beamed with triumph. "By the fortune of Haven we have an impeccable man who has already undergone the Rite and shown his worth, a young man of pure blood. Surely this is the time to fulfill the will of Haven, my king?"

Mendakas appeared as pleased by this prospect as I do when presented with a meal of asparagus and chicken feathers. Queen Florin was a dagger poised to strike and her mate understood danger.

Gedrick spoke into the silence. "We might send another ryder to Maricopa to search the village again. And the rest of the island as well."

Mendakas didn't hesitate. "Do this. Send Del Quickblade."

That wasn't what I wanted to hear. Humans never seemed to do what they were supposed to do.

Even after the king issued his command, the queen did not relent in her expectant gaze. She moved closer to Mendakas. "What of our son?"

Mendakas looked at me rather than his mate. His voice took on a determined edge. "I know what you seek for my younger son." The unspoken accusation was there.

Florin didn't back down. "It is the right thing."

The king's face remained frozen. "To mount a dragon is a sacred thing. The power—"

The queen's scoff cut him off. "Do not talk to me like some drug-addled Seer. It is a beast. It is to be ridden. Left alone, these dragons would devour all the food and starve every person in Rolm and beyond. They would slaughter each other like those mad beasts on Veralon. It is not anyone's fault but your own that your son Horace fell off one of them. My boy will not fall. Dayne can handle this creature."

This human had been hatched in a cold nest.

The other occupants of the cave shuffled about uneasily. All except the king. "This dragon has buried five ryders, Florin."

"All the more reason for one with the right blood to hold his reins."

Gedrick moved closer to his liege. "The beast's wing is injured. It may not fly again. It would be a tragic thing to mar Prince Dayne for the sake of a flightless beast."

Mendakas offered a regal (but relieved) nod at this. "Gedrick speaks wise counsel to us."

The queen was unimpressed. "Then this too shall be another indication of your son's dedication and bravery."

Mendakas turned to face his wife. The paramount couple of Rolm locked gazes in a contest of wills, their stares like unseen horns attempting to drive the other to submission. Mendakas looked away first. "If Dayne is bonded to Bayloo, there will be no other dragon for him. The dragons fade from this world. No other can be spared. The Pale Wrights of Oster breed ever stronger beasts for their ruler while our strength fades. We must defeat Oster soon."

Queen Florin's eyes hardened so much I thought they might crack, but instead she dipped her chin in acknowledgement of the king's bargain. Just like that, I'd been given away.

"Chief Payne, Bayloo shall be bonded to my son, Dayne. Send word to the Sculptors to prepare the ceremony for whenever the dragon is deemed ready."

EIGHTEEN

I waited like a captive bride.

I didn't have a choice but to wait, because I didn't have a way out of my cave-prison. Also, my wing was damaged. I needed Bethy Rann to return soon. Prince Dayne would be coming. Once he knew he could be my ryder, he would use every means at his disposal to make that happen as soon as possible.

Rann had fled in haste when I told her that Lisaam Payne and the others approached. She'd vowed to return, but there hadn't been time to discuss when. I hoped it meant tonight, but Rann didn't know about Prince Dayne. She didn't know how badly my wing was injured or what I had done to Brindisi on Maricopa. She didn't know that my time was leaking away.

My next visitor wasn't Rann. It was Valis.

She smiled at me when she arrived at my door. A bored Keeper allowed her inside.

"I'm here to reapply the ointment," she explained.

I didn't like the smell, but I'd tolerate anything that would help my wing heal.

"Your healing is remarkable. No infection, and already the muscle seems to be rejoining."

I liked hearing this. "How long till I fly?"

Valis considered as she carefully probed the area around the tear with a gentle finger. "At this rate, the wing may be mended in two days, as far as my eyes can tell. What I see is superficial. Only you know when it is truly mended. You must move it, feel it. My advice is not to rush. There is plenty of time."

She was very mistaken. Del Quickblade had been sent to Maricopa. There was no telling what he would find.

"I'll be back in the morning to check again." She rubbed her hand against the scales on my side. I think she meant it kindly, as if she could pet me. Why do humans do that? I didn't do petting. "Goodnight, Bayloo. Get some rest, it should help you heal."

I considered asking her to fetch Bethy Rann again, but I didn't think she'd fall for my sorrow act again. I let Valis leave. Then I could only wait.

Rann returned to my cave in the depth of the night. I hadn't slept —my wing ached—and her noisy human footsteps would've woken me in any case. I was relieved to see her. I needed her help. She placed her hands on the metal of the gate that held me. I made my way over so that we might speak quietly, without waking a Keeper.

Rann didn't bother with greetings. "You're to be joined to Prince Dayne."

"I know."

Maybe she expected me to panic, to need her help. I did, but not with escaping the little prince. The skin on her forehead crinkled as she stared at me. "You don't seem worried. Perhaps you should be." Her voice dropped to a harsh whisper. "Many have sacrificed to free you."

I snorted at the notion of Prince Dayne's mind overwhelming mine. "Brindisi was steel. The Prince of Sapphires is rabbit fur. I will not be a slave again." More gently, I added, "I do not forget those whose aid to my kind cost them their lives, Bethy Rann."

Rann's angled brow softened, but she didn't say anything.

"I made a mistake in failing to protect Jona. It is a scar that I will carry with me, Bethy Rann."

"It would've brought Jona great joy to know you are free, Bayloo. He would've given his life for that, and it seems he did. He was the better of us. He believed in what your mother was trying to do—to free you. And more, I think." She took a hard swallow.

"My mother died trying to protect my sister. She failed in that. I shall right that wrong. Her purpose is now mine."

Rann arched a brow. "Do you even know her purpose?"

It was a fair question. I blew a sigh out from my nostrils. "Not completely. My own freedom, and the recovery of her daughter, shall be the start." Reluctantly, I added, "She seemed concerned about humans as well for some reason—until the wizard killed her. Drasu is his name. He shall die."

A whisper came back at me. "I understand the need for vengeance on behalf of a lost mother."

I heard the smoldering anger in her voice, but this wasn't the time to ask about that. I needed to understand what my mother had been doing on Maricopa. "After the fall of the Twisted Keep, I flew to that village on Maricopa. Those who lived there displayed no outward sign of magic. Their village was poor, almost completely devoid of metal or wealth. How is it that they were enchanters who made an alliance with a dragon?"

"I told you of my ancestors, the Illugar. When their ships fled Ni-Yota and landed on Ulibon, there were some among the original refugees who disagreed about using enchantment to construct weapons, to use magic for conquest. They split from the rest, leaving Ulibon. In Maricopa, they found a land no one wanted, a place they could live in peace, or so they thought. My mother told me about these lost people, which is how I knew to go there. The elders of the island kept their knowledge well hidden, and those that lived there had little interest in the affairs of others. They wanted no bloodshed. They believed in the *Ka*, that all creatures are bound together by some unseen force that held together a fragile world. To kill was to disrupt that tenuous balance." Rann's bitterness was as subtle as a rooster's crow.

"You don't approve of them or this *Ka*."

"There is nothing delicate about this world. It is brutal. The strong rule the weak." Rann's face flushed and she looked as if she would say more but held her tongue at the last instant. I had no interest in her human grievances at that moment anyway. I needed to know more if I was to help my own kind.

"How is it that my mother came to your island?"

Rann emptied her tiny lungs in a deep sigh. "After Mendakas and his dragons destroyed Ulibon and claimed Maricopa, the refugees on Maricopa feared the King of Rolm would discover what they were and kill or enslave them for the knowledge of enchantment that the elders still possessed. They went to work on something—I believe it was an illusion like the one that shielded your mother's cave. The elders worked for years, journeying up the mountain to perform their works of enchantment. They exhausted their supplies many times and had to trade for more. I'm not sure with who. I was young. Perhaps the pirates. Perhaps Oster, or another distant people. In any case, strange sand, metals, petrified wood, herbs, other things I didn't recognize, would mysteriously appear in the village, then be brought up the mountain. Whether your mother's arrival was connected to what the elders tried to do, I am unsure. She didn't reveal herself to the village. Rather, she came in the depth of night, in silence, to the great lake within the crater of the Kraken. Only a few of us were permitted up there. I was not among those until I was needed."

"And the villagers did not fear having a dragon in their midst?"

Rann looked at me, her lips tight. "Among the Illugar, and in my ancestors' home of Ni-Yota, the attitude toward dragons is very different than that of the people of Rolm. They are feared, yes, but also revered. Jona was captivated by your kind. Perhaps that was why he was anxious to do what he did." She shrugged, indicating she had no more to say about this. "I only know that a bargain was struck with the Great Dawn. Your mother wanted help to free a dragon—you. To do that, she needed something that only the elders on Maricopa could provide. Some kind of strange vine. Aurathorn, they called it. In exchange, I believe she offered the elders assistance with the magic they had been toiling to create. Or perhaps it was something else—something to do with the *Ka*, the balance they so desperately believed in. Whatever the promise, they devoted themselves to the task."

Aurathorn. That was the key to unlocking our chains. That is what I must find.

"But even with the magic your mother and the elders created, they still needed help to free you—it is not easy to get close to a dragon and live. Jona volunteered." Rann rolled her eyes. "He was such a believer, my brother. Despite all he knew of the ugliness of this world, he thought that freeing you would make a difference. Just like the elders."

I was offended by Rann's skepticism. "And you?"

"I know my destiny." I wasn't sure what she meant, and she didn't give me a chance to ask before continuing. "Over two years passed after Jona became a ryder. There is no reliable means of communication between Maricopa and DragonPeak. Twice a year we sent a messenger, to meet and bring back news. And always, that message was failure. Then came yet another war with Oster, where Jona was gone from DragonPeak for months. Even after the fighting ended, we didn't hear from him. We feared he had been killed. I was *asked* by the elders to find out what had happened, and, if necessary, to take his place. I was *asked* by your mother to help free you, her child."

"You did not want to become a ryder."

"Do not take offense, for I did not know you then, but at the time I did not have Jona's strength of belief in this task. The elders considered me rebellious. An outsider. However, I was best suited to win the Rite—there were few youths on tiny Maricopa, and among those, I was the quickest, the best with a bow, and I cared the most about Jona. Even with Dawn's assistance, only I could triumph in the Rite and earn the right to ride a dragon. So, I came to be a spy. I was relieved to find my brother still alive. But he was fearful that Lisaam Payne suspected he was a spy, and so Jona had to be particularly careful in his movements and how we behaved around each other."

"What else did my mother promise you?" I asked. "Merely asking you does not seem like it would be enough."

Rann actually laughed, but it was a cold, rocky sound. "You do not think mere benevolence motivated me?" She pursed her lips. Then Rann held up the metal bracelet she wore on her arm. "She told me about this. It was a gift from my mother before she died. But Great Dawn explained to me what my own mother could not before her death."

I guessed the bracelet was magic—enchanted. "What does it do for you?"

Rann's lips hardened with annoyance. "It steadies my arm when I wield my blade." She didn't pretend to be telling me the truth. "I did what I have done for my own reasons, my own quest. That is all you need to know."

Rann's secrets did not concern me as much as the imminent return of the Sculptors and the loss of my sister. I needed her help. "You have sacrificed to be here. I know that. What is it that you do seek, now that your people are gone?"

The question seemed to surprise her. When she did answer, it was with a request for the impossible. "I want my brother back."

"If I could do such a thing, I would," I told her truthfully. "Jona was a good man. Even your Sisters of Haven cannot pierce the Void of Death, is that not so?"

Rann smiled like a jackal. "You cannot bring back a life, this I already knew. But I wish to kill someone as well."

"Who do you wish to kill?"

Rann's lips barely parted. She answered in a whisper, so low only a dragon could hear. "King Mendakas." Her eyes were cold with determination. "Now we're bound together."

"Why?" Not that I disagreed that Mendakas deserved a painful end, but her voice and expression told me that it seemed very personal to Rann.

"Does it matter to you?"

"No," I admitted. Her reasons were her own, so long as I got what I needed. "In this we have a common purpose. He who has enslaved my kind shall have no mercy from me."

Rann's eyes flashed with the hunger of a wolf. "I will help you, because that is what my brother would have wanted. And it will help me get what I want." She pushed at the bars of my cage. "To open this, I need a Keeper's key. Easily accomplished, but you must be ready to fly once I do that. When I let you out of this cave, we fly first to the Fist, to find Mendakas, to kill him."

This sounded like a stupid plan, and Bethy Rann wasn't stupid. "What then?"

"Take me to a place of my choosing, leave me there, go find your sister."

"Where shall I take you?"

Rann's eyes were cold. "I shall reveal that once Mendakas is dead."

"My wing is injured. I cannot fly."

"We can wait, but time is short," Rann said. "War with Oster comes. The ryders can speak of nothing else. Any day we will fly into battle."

I needed Rann's help, but I wasn't prepared to do as she asked. "I must do more than merely kill Mendakas and find my sister."

Rann's eyes squinted in displeasure. "What do you mean?"

"My kind will not be slaves anymore. I need the aurathorn that you spoke of. I need it to free the rest of the dragons, and I need your help to deliver it. Once that has been done, I shall kill Mendakas and I shall go to free my sister."

"That is impossible."

Heat flared from my nostrils. "Why do you say this?"

"Jona used the last of the aurathorn two months before he died. The aurathorn we had is long gone. And even if it was not, only your mother knew the alchemy that went into preparing it for consumption. Something about reactivating the essence within thorns. That's what Jona told me, but I had no idea how to do it, even if we had more thorns."

This must be what it felt like to be struck in the face with a dragon's tail. My breaths became labored, but I wasn't ready to give up. "Where did aurathorn come from? It is a small island; you must have some idea how it arrived there."

Rann pressed her lips together hard enough that they became white. "I could make a guess where it came from, but that would be all, and it would do you no good." She shook her head. "Even if you could get more, your mother did something to the thorns with the help of the elders. The people that might have known are all dead. You cannot save the rest of the dragons. You can save your sister, though. You can help others." Rann stared at me with pitiless eyes. "The aurathorn is gone."

NINETEEN

I roared from my gut.

I shouldn't have done that.

"You giant fool!" Rann hissed. "Even the laziest Keeper can be roused from his bed if the cause is important enough. You make enough noise to shake DragonPeak!"

She was correct, but my blood still boiled. I growled because I could not yet bring myself to answer with words.

"Dragons have endured for generations like this," Rann hissed at me. "Find your sister first, as your mother wanted."

I gathered my wits, battling anger in my mind for control. "Are my kind to be condemned to slavery because you can't find the thorns of some plant?"

Rann held her ground in the face of my barely controlled rage. It helped that she stood outside the bars of my cave. "Even if we had more of the aurathorn, it only worked on you. We'd tried for years with you, and even a few other dragons with no results. Jona wasn't even certain that it was the leaves that allowed your mind to escape. He said you got drunk, and only then did he notice the difference. After all those years of trying."

The spikes of my mane pricked up. "I wasn't drunk."

"He said you were rolling around in your cave, singing about sheep bones. Badly. At one point you began dodging non-existent potatoes."

I had a vague recollection of those potatoes. The memory helped cool my frustration.

"I tried the aurathorn on Crema, of course. I even got her drunk once." Rann allowed herself a smirk at the memory. "Other dragons don't share your particular appetite for brew. Crema doesn't sing, thankfully. I think it made her dizzy but had no other effect that I could see. You seem to be unique, Bayloo."

What I unlike other dragons? Did this have to do with my heritage as an ember dragon?

I didn't want to hear about my uniqueness. Freedom could not only belong to ember dragons. I needed to find another way to free my kin. Having the assistance of Crema and Bethy Rann would be important.

"Would Crema fly with you anywhere?" I asked.

Rann chewed on her lip as she considered. "I could get her to fly almost anywhere, I think. But she will not knowingly betray Rolm. That is seared into her by the runes—I can feel it anytime I've probed such things. There is a wall in her mind, a boundary that I fear to cross. If I tried to force her to act against Rolm, I'm not sure what would happen."

I did know what happened. Rann was right to be cautious about forcing a dragon to commit treason. To push a slave dragon beyond the limits permitted by the Sculptors' magical carvings brought horrific results. "The control-runes form a block in our mind," I confirmed for her. "The rune-link weakens our will, substituting the desires of our ryder. But they also impose upon us an overriding duty to Rolm." I spoke even as I explored the reaches of my own mind, struggling to remember the fog of my enslavement. "Before my mind awoke, I wasn't even aware of the barrier within me. I simply could have never contemplated betraying Rolm. If a ryder tried to force a dragon to go against the magic of the rune, it would shatter the drag-on's mind, possibly the mind of the ryder who attempted such a thing as well. I have seen it."

Rann's eyes bulged out at me. "A ryder betrayed Rolm?"

I huffed out a long snort. "Not willingly. There is the Tell that all must survive before being linked with their dragon. The ryders are pathetically loyal, except Jona and you. But, in the first Hunger War with Oster, when Karthus still rode me, one among us—my brother Jaxis—fell in battle. He was captured, as was his ryder, Dorane."

Rann's brow furrowed. "No dragon has ever been captured. According to the Keepers, Jaxis died from the poison of a fury's sting while fighting at the Shard. Is that not true?"

I closed my eyes, struggling for the distant memory that was both vivid and elusive. The images came reluctantly. "I remember that morning. We flew at the heart of Osteran power—the Shard—that shining diamond mountain, impenetrable and undefeatable. We thought ourselves so powerful, Triton at our lead. But it was a trap."

"The furies awaited," Rann said.

This part of the story every ryder knew. Before that day at the Shard, we hadn't seen the furies in battle. It was on that day we understood the awesome power of the Pale Wrights of Oster to breed ever more deadly beasts to send against us.

"Yes, but what isn't known is what followed. As I think on it now, I think King Galt wanted us to come," I told her. "The songs of the human minstrels say Galt wanted to kill his rival king—he wanted to murder Mendakas. But I think Oster's true aim was to capture a dragon for the use of its mysterious breeders—the Pale Wrights. And they succeeded. That is a secret that is not told and known by only a few."

"How does one capture a dragon?" Rann asked.

"After we fled the Shard, grateful for our escape, we realized Jaxis was not among us."

Rann peered around her on the dark ledge, looking for Keepers.

She needn't have bothered. I would've heard anyone approach. "He was captured inside the Shard?"

I grunted my confirmation. "We thought him dead. That is what the ryders believed. The introduction of the furies to the battlefield changed Mendakas' calculations for the war—he could no longer rely on surprise and dragons. The next morning, most of the dragons flew west to rendezvous with the Rolman fleet. But five of us remained."

"You went back to Oster to find Jaxis?"

"No, we all thought Jaxis and his ryder to be dead. We returned to Oster to destroy their fleet, to clear the way for the Rolman ships that would be coming to harry and burn the Osteran coast. But most of all, we came to scout the approaches to the Pits of Gargen."

Rann grimaced. "Even the most arrogant ryders don't want to go near the Pits."

"We knew the Pits were where the breeders of Oster toiled, hatching their griffins and breeding war wolves. Deep underground where no dragon can venture, none in Rolm dared attack, but with the emergence of these furies, Mendakas' thinking changed. But we never got that far. I flew with my brother Lothar in the depths of night toward the isle south of the Shard, to the near lifeless clay flats where the boreworms dwell. It was there, traveling across that desolate expanse, where it was thought no land creature could venture, that we saw Jaxis. He walked, slowly and deliberately, his head hung low. Osteran soldiers marched around him like ants escorting a queen.

"At first, we didn't understand. There was nothing in my experience that explained Jaxis meekly plodding along with Osterans. Then Karthus focused on the wagon trailing behind my poor brother —his ryder Dorane sat tied between a pair of Osteran soldiers with long knives in their hands."

"A hostage?" Rann arched a brow. She sounded more interested than horrified.

"As slaves, we would rather die than cause harm to our ryders. Meek submission was Jaxis' only choice."

"What did you do?"

"I was a slave; I did as I was ordered," I reminded Rann. "Karthus, however, did not hesitate once he understood the situation. We went to kill the Osterans. Jaxis tried to stop us."

Rann choked in surprise. "Impossible."

"No, the Osterans held his ryder hostage. An Osteran soldier kept a knife on his throat. I will spare you the details of the battle. It ended when my ryder Karthus gave me orders and I followed them. I killed Dorane."

I felt no shame at the time, but as I recounted the tale aloud, I found guilt clawing at my insides. It had been a merciless act.

"Karthus had you murder a fellow ryder." Rann said it in a whisper, as if that made it better.

"Dorane's death didn't calm Jaxis. Instead, it sent Jaxis into a frenzy of madness. My brother did not come easily or painlessly. That is among the reasons the story was kept secret."

Rann was silent, her breaths deep as she thought. "Then it is as we thought. Aurathorn seems to be the only way to free a dragon, and it only works on you."

I would not accept that. I could not. And that hadn't been my purpose in reliving those memories. I had another idea. "I believe Galt's plot went deeper."

Rann's brows lowered. "Tell me."

"Do you remember your carving, when Crema was first linked to you?"

"I remember," Rann said immediately. "They give you some potion to dull the pain, but it's nothing compared to the intensity of the experience. It is not something I could ever forget, even though I was blindfolded."

"Dragons are not permitted to watch either. As hatchlings, a hood is placed over our heads, and when a ryder is re-linked to a carved dragon, we are ordered to stare downward with our eyes shut. Besides the Sculptors, none but ryders and Keepers are ever permitted to witness a carving, and none have—until me."

"I had not given it thought before now. Crema's eyes were indeed covered. What did you see during the carving?"

"Do you remember a small pot with a dark liquid inside?"

Rann shook her head tentatively. "I heard something like a box open. There were sounds like a ceramic lid. That is all I know, until a sharp object as hot as any fire struck my flesh."

"In the box they keep a black substance that they use to carve the runes. Brindisi called it the Flux. Have you heard of it?"

"No, but that's typical for the Sculptors. The magic of the runes is the most precious secret in Rolm—the key to its very existence. No one but the Order of Sculptors, and perhaps the royal family, is privy to those secrets."

"I find it curious that the Sculptors are meticulous to not let dragons see what they are doing—even dragons that have already been enslaved by the runes."

Rann's eyes locked on me. "You believe this Flux may offer a chance to free dragons as well as enslave them?"

"A Sculptor used it to erase the rune on Brindisi's chest—the ones that linked him to Traxis. Then new runes were carved for my link."

A spark of excitement entered Rann's eyes. "The rune can be removed?"

"From human flesh at least. Dragon scale may be different." I mashed my teeth as I searched my memories. "In the days before Mendakas attacked Oster, there was a great fire in Eladrell. Houses near the Grandquell were set alight, along either part of the Guildquarter and the area near the Sculptors' temple."

"The king accused an agent of Oster of trying to burn the city," Rann confirmed. "Some said they saw a griffin rise from the smoke, flying into the night. King Mendakas himself rode Triton out to look for the supposed intruder, but no sign was ever found. But the Sculptors' temple was damaged in that fire, part of its golden roof destroyed, and the ArchSculptor Dananak was killed."

My eyes glowed as hope rose within me. "What if men from Oster started those fires as a diversion? What if their true objective was the Sculptors' temple and this Flux? Then they lured us to the Shard, where the furies awaited, where they hoped to trap a group of dragons. Why use such a weapon and why else take such risk to capture Jaxis if not to change his control-runes? To have a dragon of their own."

"A risky ploy."

"Perhaps Oster found a way to wipe out the control-runes. Perhaps the Flux is the key to it all."

Rann rubbed the bottom of her chin. "If that is so, it seems even your mother did not suspect it."

"She had never been a slave. No dragon knew of the Flux. The Sculptors are meticulous about their secrets. As a dragon, how would she have known?"

"Even if the Flux can somehow remove what it has created, it is in possession of the Sculptors, kept within their temple, except for a small amount they bring out to do a carving. How would you get it in sufficient quantities to free all of the other dragons?"

I released a reluctant growl. I didn't like the path before me, but it was the only one that offered hope to my kind. "There is a way."

TWENTY

The prince came for me the next morning.

Dayne stepped into my cave, his greedy eyes alight like a child expecting presents. His mommy wasn't with him, but that brought me little solace. In her place walked a crimson-cloaked Sculptor, his acolyte trailing like a ghostly shadow. Lisaam Payne entered last, completing the quartet of crappy humans. I guessed Prince Dayne (or perhaps his mother) had deliberately kept his entourage small. When the carving began, I was pretty sure he would be a screamer.

Had the rune-link already been established, I might not have been able to fully conceal my contempt for Prince Dayne, although I was partly to blame for the prince's idiotic behavior—I had encouraged him in his misguided belief that it was our destiny to be joined. Now, I would have to deal with the results.

The other humans were almost as unwelcome as Dayne. The mask of the ArchSculptor was identical to that of the one worn by the man who'd done the carving for Brindisi, but I was fairly sure this was a different person. The face covering sloped on this human's forehead and his eyes were smaller and meaner. The acolyte was relatively young, with drooping eyes and uneven shoulders. He bore the locked box with the Flux inside with a puffed chest and skinny arms.

I had experience with carvings. As soon as the Sculptor ordered Lisaam Payne out of the cave, I decided to play good dragon, rolling myself into position even without being told. That surprised the Sculptor and put a sloppy grin on Prince Dayne's face. The smile lasted until the carving started.

I surreptitiously kept one eye open again. I wanted to search for additional details I might have missed the first time I'd watched a carving, but also, I wanted to witness Dayne's agony.

The Sculptor opened the iron box with his key from around his neck and withdrew the implements of his trade. He wielded a similar stylus to the one I'd seen earlier, but this time I studied it even closer. My mother had told me of the duplicitous origins of the Sculptors' rune-magic. With that knowledge, I recognized the stylus anew: it was a dragon claw, honed and worked and maybe with some enchantment cast upon it, but I had no doubt that it had come from one of the corpses of my kind.

The acolyte withdrew the small pot that contained the Flux from the metal box. Once that had been done, the Sculptor dipped the bone instrument's tip into the mysterious magical liquid and began to carve on the prince's bare chest (he resembled a plucked chicken). I took the terrible risk of raising my neck to get a better look at the Flux while the Sculptors were focused on mutilating Dayne's flesh. I sniffed at the air. My suspicions of the origins of the Flux grew, but I still could not be sure.

The carving was a noisy affair. Prince Dayne had lived a life of privilege and pleasure, protected by his heredity and his mother, so screaming and crying were natural to him. I would've thought that the son of a man like Mendakas would've at least tried to control himself, but if Dayne made any attempt to hold onto his dignity, there was no sign of that in his childish wailing. He commanded the Sculptor to stop.

"To leave a half-complete rune upon you would mean your death, my prince."

The Sculptor resumed his work. I expected to enjoy Dayne's agony, but by the end, I wanted the carving to end as much as Dayne did. My ears were rather sensitive, and his cries pathetic. At least Dayne hadn't called for his mother. Unfortunately, his damp pants and the small pool of stinking yellow liquid at Dayne's feet by the time the Sculptor had finished his work lessened the meaningfulness of even that small accomplishment. The Prince of Sapphires, better known as the Prince of Pee-Pee. How could I not be proud to carry such a man upon my back?

If Dayne's performance embarrassed him, he gave no sign of it. He didn't even order anyone to clean up my cave. When the Sculptor pronounced the carving complete and the pain stopped, Dayne rose to his feet with a triumphant glow in his eyes, as if his extensive wailing had been a fever dream, and just as easily forgotten. He stared alternately at me and his chest with a look of wonderment—as if he'd been bestowed with another appendage of supreme maleness.

"Bayloo, we are joined!"

I didn't like his terminology or his excitement, but I gave him a fake smile with teeth that humans expected and dipped my head. But Dayne also spoke the truth. The rune had indeed linked us. I sensed Dayne's presence through the magic corridor between our minds. His emotions leaked into me: satisfaction, pride, but most of all, ambition. It was a part of him as much as my tail was a part of me. This boy wanted to rule, and not just that. He desired respect, and revenge upon those who had defied him and ridiculed him through his life. Most of all, Dayne nursed a bitter resentment of his elder brother that was never far from being foremost in his twisted mind. The hate was potent.

I'd expected the prince to be weak-willed. His actions had always seemed clumsy, his mother's shadow lingering over him. I didn't expect that his desires would be a challenge to me the way Brindisi's had been—and I was still fairly certain in that judgment. But there was more to Dayne than a spoiled prince. There was a darkness in him that took me by surprise. And surprises from humans were almost always bad.

Lisaam Payne rejoined us, sliding into the cave. Dayne indicated he should leave the gate open. My new ryder motioned me toward him. "We must take to the sky."

I would've liked that as well, albeit on a solo flight. Instead of answering, I lifted my healing wing as much as I could within the confines of the cave. An ugly crease still ran along its surface, but at least the flesh had been rejoined. My wing's muscle felt strong but stiff. I might have been able to glide, but to truly fly was another matter.

Lisaam Payne intervened. "As we spoke about earlier, my prince, we must ensure the wing is fully healed, lest the dragon be permanently damaged."

Dayne scowled with petulance. "I bet that Bayloo could fly, if I willed it."

His desire surged through our link. Dayne was smitten. That was to my advantage. "I'm yours to command, Master." I made myself want to puke, but the words pleased the prince.

The Chief Keeper's eyes grew panicked. "I must send for the healer, Prince Dayne. Your father's enemies are upon us. We dare not lose this dragon from our forces for a meaningless flight of fancy."

Dayne laughed, as if his fervent desire had been a mere jest. "Relax, Payne. We shall just get a bit of air. My dragon has been in this cave for too many days. I feel his longing to return to the sky."

Payne scowled with annoyance, but he stood aside as the prince and I made our way through the gate to the ledge outside my prison. The Keeper's hateful eyes bored into me, as if I cared.

I rejoiced at being under the open skies. The sun shone and clouds sailed across an azure background. A thousand scents flowed through the late morning air. I heard the sound of one of my brethren in flight before I saw her—Saba soaring overhead, riding the wind with her magnificent silvery wings pulled back for extra speed.

Dayne noticed her as well. "The dragon flies east, in the direction of Oster. Toward the warships that raid the outer islands, killing our farmers, stealing our livestock."

Lisaam Payne and the Sculptors had left us, so I risked a snort, letting my new ryder know I shared his disdain for the island kingdom that raided Rolm's shores, although, in fact, I had far more respect for King Galt of Oster than for Dayne or even his own father. Rolm's power was derived from the stolen magic used to enslave my kind.

"War is coming, Bayloo. Our war. This will be my opportunity to show my father he needs a true dragon ryder for an heir. Horace was thrown from his dragon, an unworthy pretender. Just as he is unworthy to take my father's place. But I shall be the new king of dragons. I alone of the royal line have the strength to rule."

To rule. The words echoed from Dayne's mind to my own. This boy wanted the throne as much as I wanted to find my sister. Maybe even more. My quest was newly born. For Dayne, the fire had been building inside him his entire life; every slight had fed the flames, every honor that went to his brother was kindling. His mother had stoked the inferno. I'd underestimated Dayne. He was formidable in his own way. His desires tugged at me, amplified by the magic of the runes.

I reared up and unfurled my wings as if anxious to take to the skies and do Dayne's bidding. In truth, I wanted to fly. I beat my wings, cautiously. The area around the tear was taut, and uncomfortable. There was pain when I stretched. As badly as I wanted to be in the air, away from this place, now was not the time. Another few days would see me healed. But that was only part of it.

We shall rule the skies, Master, I told him through our link.

His human teeth shone white at my words. "Bayloo, destiny has brought us together: the greatest of men and the greatest of dragons. The fools say you are somehow less because you do not spit flame. But I sense the power in you."

Could that be true, that he senses my power? I hoped he was just deluding himself. But delusions could be useful to me.

"Let the healers come, Master. I ache to fly."

"As do I, Bayloo." Dayne gazed outward, drawing a great breath into his lungs. I presumed human smell was so limited that he could ignore the urine that stained his breeches. I couldn't. Dayne's hands formed themselves into fists.

"I shall return. We need be only a bit more patient." He walked off, leaving me outside my cave. For a moment, I thought I'd actually be left outside to my own ends, but Lisaam Payne was more diligent than Prince Dayne. The Keeper appeared soon after the prince stalked off, ensuring I made it back into my homey prison. Before I returned to my cave, I caught sight of another dragon in the sky. I recognized the pale, sun-colored scales of Organa. On her back was her surly ryder, Del Quickblade. They headed toward the Dragon-Peak, flying home from the direction of Maricopa.

I was out of time.

TWENTY-ONE

What did the humans know?

In the devastated village on Maricopa, they would find implements of magic and plenty of bodies. A lazy human might stop upon discovering those items of enchantment, but ryders weren't typical humans. A more diligent person would take the time to explore the island, including the Kraken. There, they would find the bodies of the Mizu warriors (or at least the bones if the scavengers had been there first). They might even find my mother's cave, although what would be left there?

I considered the ryder who had been sent to Maricopa. Del Quickblade had earned his name from his sword arm, but his skill didn't end there. Quickblade was precise. He made no mistakes. I didn't think he would be lax in his search.

I really needed to learn to lie better. Or heal faster.

I wondered how long it would take the ryder to make his report and who would show up at my cave after that happened. Indeed, I wondered on that question deep into the night. To my surprise, no humans came. I saw dragons flying around the peak even after dark and heard noises from below, but that was all. I finally slept, only to be awakened by Valis at my cave entrance at first light, a Keeper at her side.

She entered, her eyebrows scrunched together in a look of concern.

"Prince Dayne is your new ryder?"

"I have that honor." I twisted my tongue as I said the last.

"I do hope you'll be more cautious with him than your other ryders, Bayloo. He is loved by the people."

I hadn't known that. Well, there is no accounting for taste, is there? "Nothing is more important than the safety of my ryder."

Valis forced a smile. "He does so much for those of us who live in the city. He sponsors a kitchen for the needy in the Beggar's Quarter, and at Deliverance Day, he supplies free wine for the city watch."

That didn't sound like my Prince Dayne. I suspected his mother's hand in such supposed largess. Still, I saw no harm in allowing Valis to keep her illusions. "Generous and brave. I have felt those things in him."

The lies were coming easier. Excellent. I would need that skill.

Satisfied, Valis walked over to inspect my wing. "This is remarkable. There's a bit of scarring, but it's largely mended from what I can see. How does the wing feel when fully extended?"

"It is not normal. Too rigid. It does not feel fully a part of me."

"I will remove the sutures." Several edged metal instruments appeared from a satchel Valis had slung over hershoulder. "Please hold still." She cut and plucked the sewing from my wing. It hurt more than I thought it would. "Keep still." I did—mostly.

"Is movement easier now?"

Alas, it wasn't, and I told her so.

Valis tapped her teeth together. The sound irritated me. "There may be damage inside I cannot see. Scarring. We don't know as much about dragons as we should." After a pause she added, "You may just need to give it a bit more time."

"Time is precious."

"Prince Dayne sent a royal messenger to Master Elkra and I." She seemed impressed, even though a royal messenger just meant that the human parchment carrier wore an itchy tunic. "Prince Dayne was most insistent that you fly as well." Valis took another long look at my wing, running her hand along its length, tracing a line parallel to the healing wound. "There is a poultice I've seen Elkra use—a cloth soaked in the essence of Mitar root, which grows only in Oster. He tried to use it on Fortax, during the war with Oster. It may be of some help, although Elkra will be hesitant to part with any of his remaining root."

I'd never heard of Mitar root—which wasn't surprising, since I wasn't a healer—but I knew that my brother Fortax had died from the arc-bolt that had pierced his belly scales, despite the efforts of the human healers. I wasn't fond of strange, human concoctions, but I also wasn't fond of getting called out for my lies about what happened on Maricopa. I'd take any help I could get.

"The honorable prince will help you convince Elkra, if you let him know the situation."

"You wish me to speak to Prince Dayne?" She seemed both terrified and enthralled by the prospect.

"Get a message to him that you have an idea to help me fly. On this matter, I am certain he will do all he can."

Valis nodded as if she understood, leaving me soon after. As I waited in my cave, dragons came and went from the peak. I heard Lothar's growl and Albion's hiss, and there were sounds of other dragons I couldn't identify as well. So many of my brethren in flight could only mean an engagement with Oster. *It is beginning.*

The afternoon came and went. I had an inkling of hope that more urgent matters of impending war might distract from Organa and Quickblade's discoveries on Maricopa. Valis returned with the Mitar root after midday. It smelled like a mix between Prince Dayne's piss and rotten leviathan flesh. Valis applied it to my wing as if it were treasure. She probably enjoyed eating vegetables, too.

"Prince Dayne truly cares for you," Valis practically gushed.

I didn't reply, saving my stomach for more important lies.

The Mitar root warmed my wing, but beyond that I didn't know if it had any other effect besides stinking up my cave. Valis seemed to enjoy applying it anyway. "Elkra is furious and is taking it out on me. He's given me a list of chores that'll take me days to finish. I need to get back to the city, but I'll return tomorrow to check on you. Try not to move the wing when the medicine dries."

As she left, I caught sight of a horned dragon—Presta, I think was her human name—flying upward, likely headed to land at the Shelf. On her back were humans I didn't recognize. I had a bad feeling in my belly.

I made one more request as a Keeper opened the gate to allow Valis to depart. "Will you please ask Prince Dayne if he would come lay his hands upon my wing?"

Valis' eyes grew wide. "Why?"

"I beg you to tell him that the bond between ryder and dragon may help heal me."

Valis scrunched her nose with skepticism. "It grows late, and he has already done so much for you. I don't think we could ever dare ask more."

I couldn't let her go. "Tell him I ache to fly this very night. I hear my brethren in flight, and I wish to join them in the battle. Prince Dayne will understand, I promise. He will be *grateful* to get this message."

I was really reaching on this one but Dayne's gratitude seemed to impress her. Her eyes glazed over for a brief moment.

"I will try. I'll send—"

I was too impatient to even let her speak. Other humans were coming. "Seek out Crema and Bethy Rann. Crema will fly to the Fist and carry you and Prince Dayne back here with haste."

"I don't understand." Valis squinted at me. "Why such a rush?"

"Please, Valis. I need to fly. The need for my ryder is even stronger. I know you will have Prince Dayne's gratitude for this. You are the only person who understands."

Valis' face flushed. "Very well, but don't move that wing till I get back."

I didn't move it. I tried to imagine myself healing. I even tried to sing to it a bit, trying to mimic the sounds my mother had made. My voice echoed back to me in the cave, mundane and rough. I didn't have my mother's talent for it, and time had run out on me. Heavy footsteps made their way down the peak. The humans who arrived at my cave came laden with grim purpose.

Payne and the royal counselor who I'd met before—Gredrick-Of-Many-Ear-Hairs—shuffled into my cave. A masked Sculptor accompanied them, albeit without an acolyte. He moved with a slight limp, dragging a foot that didn't seem to quite cooperate with the rest of his body. The last man to enter was Del Quickblade, his long gray hair pulled back into a flowing mane, his skin so weathered it resembled the dark scale armor he wore on his chest. He alone wore a blade, the hilt so worn that I could see the imprint of Del's hand.

Lisaam Payne was the first to speak. "Bayloo, to heel. Allow Aylin of the Order to inspect you."

That couldn't be good. They must have suspected a problem with the link. Payne expected instant obedience. If I was going to kill these humans, I had best do it before I laid myself out before them. But there was still the problem of getting out of my cave, and escaping now would mean the failure of the rest of my plan.

I let the moment pass. I obeyed Payne's order.

The Sculptor—Aylin—approached, his steps awkward. He bent over before me, staring hard at the runes that had been carved into me. He squinted so hard I thought he might be simultaneously pushing a particularly troublesome stool from his bowels. The Sculptor withdrew a stylus from inside his robe—definitely a dragon bone—and poked me several times with its end. I wondered which of my kin it had been taken from. Was it the bone of an ember dragon like me? Was this how the humans had stolen our magic?

"There is no flaw in the carvings," Aylin declared. "As I said, it is quite impossible for anything to be amiss with the control-runes."

Lisaam Payne made a rumbling sound in his throat. "What about the other side of the link. What about the runes inscribed into Brindisi?"

"We do not have a body to examine," the Sculptor pointed out. "But even in the case of a flawed carving on a ryder—another impossibility—it would not change the power of the original control-rune placed upon Bayloo when he was a hatchling." He pointed to my chest. "The five sections of the holy circle, symbolic of the human hand, bind him to our race; the crossed claws at its center ensure loyalty to the Kingdom of Rolm; the ancient symbol of our order at the center of it all. The circle itself is the conduit by which the dragon is linked to its ryder. The greater size of the human circle on the ryder's chest ensures that the will of the ryder is concentrated as it flows into the dragon's mind, like a mountain stream narrowing as it flows downward. The system is intricate, perfect, and unbreakable."

"Nearly unbreakable." It was Quickblade who spoke, his voice sharp like his blade. "I've seen dragons go mad, lose control. I know of Jaxis."

Aylin tensed at the reply. "The occasional errant behavior of a controlled dragon is not because the rune's power has been broken. Once carved, a dragon is changed forever." The Sculptor spoke with such arrogant certainty that I laughed inside. "The sculpting cannot be undone any more than you could re-form the bark of a tree after it has been felled and crafted into a longbow. But just as even the best trained, most loyal hound can succumb to the madness of the frothing mouth disease, so can dragons. In very rare cases, they can have their minds damaged by the same powerful magic that binds them. But that leads to madness, not betrayal. All dragons serve Rolm as their foremost duty."

Quickblade stroked a finger beneath his chin. "Borolon burned half of Eladrell. He circled the city, killing, until Traxis tore open his neck. That dragon wasn't mad. He knew exactly what he was doing."

"Borolon had been carved in his fourth month of life. The control was never firm. We know better now." The Sculptor turned away from him toward the humans. "Look elsewhere for your explanations. There is nothing wrong with this dragon. Doubt whatever discoveries you made that prompted you and Gedrick to summon me. But do not doubt the craft of my order, ryder."

The Sculptor's conviction made me worry about my own hope to free my people. I needed the Sculptor to be wrong about more than just me. But first, I needed to lie my way out of the mess my earlier lies had landed me in.

The ugly purple vein in Lisaam Payne's thin neck stopped throbbing at the Sculptor's reassurance. He focused on me. "Bayloo, you may rise."

I did so with relief. It would be a lot easier to kill these humans now, if I must.

Lisaam Payne glanced at Quickblade before his eyes found my own. "On Maricopa, did you encounter another dragon?"

My mind raced as I debated how to answer. I felt the Sculptor's eyes on me. Despite his tone and his arrogant manner, the masked human's heart beat quicker than the others. I suspected he was far less confident than he let on. Lisaam Payne's question told me that Quickblade had likely found my mother's cave and the evidence of the battle with the Mizu. I decided there was no way to reconcile my earlier story with that omission. I needed to survive this interrogation.

"I was the only dragon on Maricopa, honored ryder."

Something within me ached as I boldly lied to my former masters. However, one of the many great things about dragons is that we don't sweat.

Quickblade stepped closer. "I found the cave. The corpse. The bodies of the Mizu soldiers." He took another step, his eyes as hard as dragon scales. "The cracked egg."

I've never been so grateful for the inadequacies of human hearing as at that moment. My hearts wanted to escape my chest. "I do not understand, Master. The Mizu we fought were in the village and at sea."

"Yet there were no Mizu bodies near the water. Only in the great crater."

Oh. That. "I do not understand, Master. I am sorry."

Quickblade dared to come even closer. He could probably feel my breath from my nostrils from where he stood. You'd think he'd be backing away. Didn't he realize I was dangerous? He might be fast to draw his blade, but I could chomp metal if it came to it. Crapping that metal out was a whole other matter, however. "You never flew with Brindisi up to the crater within the Kraken?"

I smelled trouble coming—I just wasn't sure what I could do about it. If I didn't answer, they would know. Behind his mask, the Sculptor's eyes danced nervously.

"We flew over the crater," I offered carefully.

"Ah, but you never landed there, never landed beside the great lake at the mountain's heart?"

"No, Master."

The ryder's sword was in his hand an instant later. Fast indeed. My instinct was to defend myself, of course. I could crush him, bite his head off. That was what he wanted, though. A slave dragon would never do that. I flinched but kept myself in place.

"This dragon lies," Quickblade declared, his sword poised to strike.

Lisaam Payne's mouth had dropped open, Aylin's eyes were wide with fear, and the king's counselor had edged himself toward the exit of the cave (the wisdom of the old hairy-eared).

"Explain yourself, ryder," the Sculptor demanded.

Still holding his sword with one hand, and without taking his eyes from me, Del Quickblade pulled three objects from his pouch. I recognized them immediately. I cursed my own stupidity. Lies were only useful when there was at least some possibility the listener thought they were true. The contents of Quickblade's hand made my false tales useless.

In his open palm, he held three arrowheads, taken from the quiver of my late ryder, Brindisi. His bow had been lost in the lake, but the quiver easily could've washed ashore. When I'd concocted my lies, I'd thought of the fight of my mother and I versus the Mizu, but I hadn't considered Brindisi or his weapons.

"I found these among the dead, washed up on the edge of the lake within the heart of the Kraken. I found the remains of a longbow as well. They belong to Brindisi."

The other humans stared at me, still not quite believing. Even Lisaam Payne's hands trembled. He'd been deceived by a dragon. I think they all wanted me to have an explanation for it. But I had no more words to offer. I was done lying.

I'd fallen into the ryder's trap.

TWENTY-TWO

The first to die had to be Del Quickblade.

He was the only warrior. But there was also the Sculptor to contend with. I didn't know the scope of their magic. I would have to be quick. Four humans were no match for a dragon. Still, I hesitated. My wing was improved with the application of the Mitar root, but I wasn't sure if I could outfly my pursuit. Also, killing them meant I had failed my fellow dragons and my sister.

I was trapped in a nest infested with humans while my brethren were still enslaved. Once I'd slain the occupants of this cave, I'd have to flee—destroying any hope for the others. Unfortunately, I didn't see any other way out of this prison except by tearing every one of these humans to shreds. The cave door was closed, and none would be able to run out in time.

Quickblade and I stared at each other. I dropped the veil of ignorance from my eyes. The standoff lasted for mere heartbeats but felt much longer. My claws should've already been covered in human blood, but I hadn't moved. Neither had Quickblade, though his hand remained on the hilt of his sword.

The clattering of feet approaching saved these hapless humans. I counted at least ten humans and no sounds of dragons. A familiar tickle in my mind confirmed my suspicions. These new arrivals meant me no harm. Quite the opposite. When an indignant voice commanded some lounging Keeper nearby to stand aside, Lisaam Payne's expression turned from confusion to distress. I savored that change nearly as much as a sip of ale.

Into my cave came my unlikely savior: Prince Dayne. Resplendent in his gem-studded black scale armor, sapphires flashing on his hand, my ryder arrived with heat in his eyes and royal guardsmen in his wake. The newly arrived soldiers had smooth skin on their faces and eyes that brimmed with the impatience of youth. They moved with arrogance that mirrored the prince they served. Valis slid inside as well, although she hung at the back of the group. The cave was crowded with the human stink, but they all made room for Prince Dayne as he approached me and Del Quickblade. Dayne's confident gait made it obvious that he'd never seen Quickblade in a fight.

The prince spoke to Del as if he addressed a wayward servant. "What are you doing with my dragon?"

Quickblade could've carved Dayne into pieces before the prince could've managed to get his bejeweled blade from its scabbard, yet I sensed not a trace of fear in the young prince. How could it be that stupidity so easily substituted for courage? Had I been going about life the wrong way?

Quickblade's chin twitched as he returned his blade to its scabbard. His voice was as tight as a bowstring. "My prince, I fear this dragon belongs to nobody."

Dayne uttered a haughty scoff. "My father calls his dragon ryders to battle and here you are, wasting time telling me about my dragon."

Lisaam Payne found his voice. "My prince, I fear there is indeed something amiss here."

"Amiss you say, old man?" Dayne turned upon the Keeper like he'd bitten the prince's tail. "I smell jealousy in this cave."

Lisaam's dead eyes darted to the Sculptor. I think it was a plea to intervene, but the masked purveyor of the stolen magic said nothing.

Humans always think of themselves and their own desires first and foremost.

Into the breach stepped Gedrick, his voice graveled but firm. "Prince Dayne, what I have heard this day troubles me as well. All is not as it should be here. It must be reported to the king, for your own safety and that of the kingdom."

Dayne flushed at the unexpected rebuke from his father's advisor. A rush of uncertainty surged through him, and into me through our link. Three humans had spoken against me, with only the Sculptor remaining silent. I worried Dayne's arrogance might have a limit.

I can't lose him.

I had hoped to wait before attempting what I had to do. I had hoped to be certain that I could fly before I endangered myself, so at least I could still escape if I was wrong about my own strength, but I had no other choice.

Since that fateful day when my mind had awoken, I'd been scrupulously careful about revealing my own true thoughts to my ryder. I had kept the secret of the power of my own will buried deep inside me. I could sense my ryders' emotions, but I had guarded against their sensing mine, forcing the bridge created by the control-runes to be a one-way channel. Indeed, that was the way the link was supposed to work. The magic of the runes fed me the concentrated will of my ryder, allowing him to control me, but it didn't work the opposite way. However, even in the current of the strongest river, a determined fish can travel upstream. That's what I needed to do.

If I tried such a thing with an experienced ryder—a man like Quickblade—he'd have tried to slice off my head. It was one thing to defy a human's command, it was quite another to attempt to reverse the roles, to attempt to invade the mind on the other end of the link. But Dayne wasn't any ryder. He hadn't really won the Rite. He had no experience in using his mind to control a dragon. I doubted he had truly transmuted the bone of a dragon. He'd cheated to become a ryder. His will wasn't the same as the others. That's why I'd encouraged his attention to me, letting him believe our link was his destiny. Humans were more receptive to being told what they wanted to hear, and Dayne was particularly receptive.

I began cautiously, playing on Dayne's own dark suspicions.

Beware your brother's schemes, I told him through our link. *He covets that which belongs to you.*

Only it wasn't just words I sent across the magical bridge that joined us. I also fed my ryder my best imitation of the suspicion I'd already felt emanate from Dayne himself. I gave back to him his own fears, and his own hate of his brother.

Dayne's eyes widened. He sucked in a sharp breath. He went completely still.

Had I gone too far?

A moment later, Dayne's eyes filled with a new wariness—not at me, thankfully. His suspicion focused on the men who tried to reason with him, who tried to make him see the truth. The poison seed I'd planted in his mind grew quickly. The prince's gaze hardened.

"More lies." His venomous voice was my sweet music. "I see through your plots."

Gedrick tried again. "I assure you, my prince—"

"A new era will dawn!" Dayne shoved a bejeweled finger toward me. "Dragons are our power, and I shall have it. No one will keep me from my destiny." Dayne's face shone red as he stepped even closer to Lisaam Payne. "Not even my dear brother. He couldn't handle a dragon. I shall show my father and the kingdom that I am worthy!"

Quickblade's hand flexed on the hilt of his sword, but he didn't draw it from its scabbard. This was his prince, and he was a sworn ryder of Rolm. Also, if Quickblade had started to yank out his steel, I would've bitten his head off. That's what any good slave dragon would've done.

"Oster has invaded!" Dayne declared. That caused several audible gasps. "My father calls his dragon ryders for the great battle to come. Bayloo and I shall be among their number. What of you, Quickblade?"

"Invaded?" the ryder repeated. He glanced at each of the other men who had accompanied him to the cave but found none willing to fight by his side with either words or deeds. Gedrick might still bring the matter to the king, but for now, he held his tongue, which was likely how he had remained alive and in service to a man like Mendakas for so long. The news of Oster's actions had shifted priorities.

"I fly where my king commands," Quickblade offered through a clenched jaw. He snapped his head back toward me and added, "Battle may bring finality to this matter."

Perhaps he referred to my slew of dead ryders. He probably meant it as an insult. I took no offense.

Prince Dayne basked in his triumph, his giddy relief spilling into my mind. I was surprised how easily the stupidest human in the room dominated the others. "Bayloo, come to me. Let us fly."

Oh. Flying.

I'd been hoping for more time. It would be cruelly painful to escape this cave only to plunge to my death. Or suffer irreparable damage to my wing. Still, this was the gamble I'd made. I wanted Dayne to get me out of there, and here was the opportunity.

I moved toward the exit. Quickblade hesitated before standing aside. Lisaam Payne, Gedrick, and Dayne's soldiers quickly followed. Valis, too, gaped as she stood against the wall. I winked at her as I passed.

Just like that, I, Bayloo-the-Liar, walked out of the cave-prison and into the swirling wind above Eladrell.

Then, the real trouble began.

TWENTY-THREE

Rolm prepared for war.

Beneath me, soldiers marshalled inside and outside of the Fist. Light footmen with swords and pikes gathered along with a large contingent of archers. Separately, the king's elite harriers—human scouts who could run at near preternatural distances at speed—gathered nearby. Accompanying support and supply wagons were being hooked to oxen in long rows in staging areas beyond the keep's walls. Great banners had been unfurled. I had no idea what purpose those served, but humans really liked them.

Whatever King Mendakas had planned, it would be big. There were too many troops mustering to be carried by all the horned dragons in Rolm. Some must be planning to travel by ship or by foot. The day was quickly slipping away as the army prepared. Even if the soldiers marched immediately, it would take several days for the foot soldiers to travel to the far coast. But soldiers carried on the back of my horned cousins could be there before daylight left the sky. The ash dragons could be there even quicker, flying faster and higher than their smaller kin.

Dayne strode up beside me as I stood on the ledge outside my cave, as if we were friends sharing the view. His pet soldiers crowded behind us. I think he sensed my curiosity, or at least guessed it.

"The Osterans tire of the cat-and-mouse game of raid and chase. Particularly since our dragons have roasted four of their ships. Yesterday, we received word that they arrived in force—at least a dozen ships laden with soldiers and war wolves along with griffins have landed on the far coast. Lord Azdraw's keep at Hartspass is under siege. Maatrex with his ryder Nitan Giles was sent to scout and report but hasn't returned."

At a primal level, the news angered me—the Osterans had no right to this land. They deserved their fate. Nor could they stand against dragons. I ached to fly, but not for the correct reasons. I had to remind myself that the legacy of the runes made me think this way. My true loyalty had to be to my own kind. "The Osterans are formidable. They will have furies with them as well."

"They are not as powerful as we are," Dayne said with his ignorant confidence. "My father will lead the main wave, but an advance force leaves now to relieve the sorely pressed defenders at Hartspass. Are you ready to retake your place in the sky, Bayloo?"

Valis came up behind us at that moment. "My lord prince, the dragon ... We still don't know if his wing can withstand the rigors of flight."

Dayne scoffed. "I know my dragon, girl. If he didn't think he could fly, I'd sense it. Be off with you. There is a war to fight."

Knowing how Valis felt about the prince, his dismissal must have stung. Still, the healer didn't shy away. "Bayloo has no idea if he can fly or not. It's our responsibility to take care of these creatures."

Dayne's anger flashed. "As I said, I know my dragon. I lose my patience quickly, little one."

I didn't like Dayne's tone. Valis meant well. She had the good sense to care about me. What more could I ask of a human? Still, I knew there was no choice. If I didn't fly now, I might never get the chance again. Dayne had surprised Lisaam Payne and the rest, but Gedrick would speak to the king. Mendakas would soon hear of all that had transpired in the cave. Unlike his youngest son, Rolm's ruler was no fool. I needed to act for the sake of my kind and my own freedom.

I spread my wings, but not easily. "As you say, my prince, we must return to the sky."

Dayne spun toward me, his teeth gleaming with delight. He wasn't the only one. Pleasure surged through that part of me that was compelled to please my human. I hated that part of me. Even with my mind freed, I loathed having these runes on my body. I wanted them gone.

At Lisaam Payne's signal, several Keepers hurried to place a saddle on my back. Dayne slipped off the first time he tried to climb onto me, landing on his rump on the rocky ground. Payne barked for a Keeper to attend to him, but Dayne was having none of it. The prince got himself onto the saddle on the second attempt. I felt him fumble around with the saddle straps that would keep him from falling off my back should I have to perform tricky maneuvers. It wasn't long before he was ready to take to the sky. Given the lack of assistance by the Keepers, I suspected that Dayne had secured himself incorrectly. Lisaam Payne did as well.

"Shall I have a Keeper come up to confirm that everything is in order, my prince?"

"I need no help. I was born for this."

Sure, and I was born to raise potatoes. Dayne had likely trained on the back of other dragons, but he'd never been in the sky alone. That experience couldn't be replicated, and nothing was quite like flying with me.

I couldn't decide if Lisaam Payne cared if Prince Dayne died on his first dragon flight or not, but I had no intention of letting anything happen to this ryder. I would protect him. For now, I needed him.

I tested my wings as best I could on the ground, extending, retracting, and flapping. There was no pain. The root-based medicine Valis procured for me seemed to have made a difference. However, there was still stiffness. My maneuvering would suffer. I thought I could deal with that. The bigger question was if the mended tear would hold or if I would fall out of the sky, permanently damaged.

Dayne had his eyes on the horizon. "The others move at speed, Bayloo. Now is our time. We fly with the vanguard, but we must fly!"

One way or the other, Dayne had the right of it. There was nothing further to be gained by waiting. His desire tugged at me. I launched myself skyward, but not for long. My injured wing dropped. I lost control of my flight, careening into an uncontrolled turn as my wings balked. It wasn't just the stiffness—I wasn't able to move them the way I should have. I panicked, beating my wings and twisting my body, barely avoiding a collision with the sheer face of DragonPeak. Dayne's fear fed my own distress, his raw human emotion mingling with my own. I struggled to clear my head even as we fell in an uncontrolled spin.

For the first time in my life, I had to think about how to fly. It had always been something I just did, like breathing, chewing food, or emptying my bowels. I was aware of the mechanics, of course, but I'd never really needed to focus on them before. Dayne's surging fear made trying to do so now challenging. I started simple: calm down. After that, I forced my legs to stop wiggling about. They were useless except for landing and impaling enemies, but for some reason I had the urge to move them about like some silly human. Why did they keep wanting to move as though I were on the ground? I forced my wings to straighten, even though they wanted to flap. Like a hatchling, I need to learn to glide first. Having already fallen half the height of the Peak, it was frightening to hold myself still, but failure meant death. I had too much to accomplish to die right now.

I got it done. No pee-pee either. I hoped Prince Dayne paid attention to that kind of courage.

Once I steadied myself and the ground stopped racing toward me, I relaxed. The taste of the wind flowed through my nostrils, granting me a certain peace. Humans have their mother's milk to nurture them. I'd never had a mother or milk, but I'd had the wind. As a hatchling, it had sung to me, it had caressed my body, it had awakened a primal instinct within me. It did so again now. I glided, I calmed, I quieted Dayne's unpleasant echo inside my head, and eventually I truly flew. The first time I flapped my wings, I broke into an unwanted turn, but this time I didn't panic. I glided, and tried again, gently, as if I were a hatchling. I learned the contours of my new, mangled wing. I flapped again, gaining altitude. Gradually, I picked up speed and confidence. I regained the height of the peak, then went further. I found the winds of the lift-stream and soared upward on its warm air toward the clouds. Dayne became giddy on my back, his own terror turning to elation, just like a hatchling who had survived his first jump from the mountain. I beat my wings harder, keeping us away from the rigid air of the clouds lurking above the lift-stream, instead turning us in the direction of my brethren.

The sky was mine again.

One of my brothers flew toward me—it was Lothar, the giant fire breather ridden by Amos Gilder, who circled back to meet us. He had seen my distress. Lothar was a fearsomely handsome beast, his scales a dark cobalt that was nearly black, although his eyes shone a dazzling amber. His ryder couldn't have been uglier, even by human standards: Gilder's chin stuck out beyond the tip of his nose and his head, face, and ears were all devoid of hair. Usually, the ryders used hand signals to communicate with each other, or, if there was time, they could relay commands to their dragons, who could better communicate the same to their fellows. Gilder was motioning to the prince, but I had no idea if Dayne even knew the ryders' signals or not, nor could I see his response, if any. However, I understood: Gilder wanted us to follow him into the formation ahead.

I trilled my understanding back to Lothar. My fellow dragon swept under and around me in a loop before heading back toward the larger flock ahead of us. Lothar flew slower than he was able, keeping a careful watch on me, which I found annoying. He behaved as if I couldn't keep up with him. Worse, Lothar's presence made it impossible for me to break ranks and fly back to Eladrell without being noticed. I didn't want to fight Oster, but there wasn't any way to avoid flying east toward battle at the moment. I took my proper position off Lothar's wing as we flew back toward the rest of the formation.

When we joined the others, it was Joren-El, the ryder of Apex, in command. Our force was four ash dragons (including me) and three horned dragons. We tore across the sky, while Triton and the king remained behind as the larger force of ash dragons and horned dragons mustered. The foot soldiers would be last to arrive, if they were needed. I wasn't sorry for the king's absence, nor was Prince Dayne, although he grumbled even at accepting Joren's authority.

"Joren-El is close to my brother," Dayne whispered to me, although he could've used our link. "We cannot trust him."

I sent a surge of agreement to Dayne. That we were placed on the rear flank of the formation only added to the prince's paranoia.

We traveled over the great expanse of the Island of Harcourt, Dayne's unfettered exhilaration fading only slightly as the land of his father's kingdom passed beneath us. I kept pace with Lothar in my assigned position on the flank, but occasionally lagged behind to gauge how closely I was being watched. Each time I slowed, so did Lothar. There would be no easy escape from this. Battle awaited, but also the solace that I would have an opportunity to fight alongside my kin. I wanted no losses, at least among the dragons.

The sun was headed rapidly for the horizon when Hartspass came into view. Dayne and the rest of the humans could not yet see the fortress, but their dragons would already be feeding them information about the terrain ahead. What I saw made me wary.

The keep at Hartspass sat on a plateau overlooking the valley passage that led from the sandy far coast of Harcourt, through the eastern mountains, to the lush heartland of the Kingdom of Rolm in the interior of the island. There were other passes, but Hartspass was the largest and most accessible, and the other routes inland were also defended by stout keeps. Attacking this castle was a sensible decision for an army that had no horned dragons to ferry its soldiers by air and was desperate to reach the plains on the other side of the peaks, where all the terrible vegetables and other food crops lurked. The Osterans' true strength was in their war wolves, their furies, and most of all, their griffin flocks. I spotted a small pack of war wolves among the Osteran soldiers, each as big as an oxen, but there was no sign of either griffins or furies. Which meant they concealed themselves somewhere, because invading Rolm without these beasts was suicide.

The Osteran army had set up a siege line beneath the keep and had wheeled several trebuchets up the winding mountain paths that led into the plateau. It seemed a pathetic arrangement. I counted less than two hundred soldiers and perhaps a dozen great wolves. They had no hope of anything except dying if this was the entirety of the Osteran force.

Dayne finally saw the interlopers, and immediately hungered to attack. "So few! We shall send their entrails back to the Shard."

I could've told him how we were once ambushed at the Shard by King Galt, long ago. I could've told him what a war wolf's bite could do to his soft flesh. I could've told him about the sheer number of griffins that Oster could deploy, but I knew that would be a waste of my effort. Instead, I blamed everything on Joren-El, reminding Dayne of his orders. For the sake of my fellow dragons, I was relieved that Joren had more battle savvy than Dayne.

We kept in formation as we drew nearer to the Osteran force. The invaders looked terribly vulnerable down in the valley. Yet Maatrex had not returned from her reconnaissance to the east, which likely meant she was dead. Danger lurked.

Rather than indulge in the temptation to devastate the entirety of the Osteran force while it sat in the valley, Joren-El passed the command for the formation to keep its distance, circling the keep from far above, but not attacking. But we couldn't remain in the clouds indefinitely. Dragons tired, just as humans did, and there was the matter of the horned dragons. My cousins had less endurance than an ash dragon, and they carried armored soldiers on their backs.

Apex swooped downward, Renfax on his flank. I chafed at that. I had always been the fastest. I should've gone in the vanguard, although I recognized my recent injury precluded that. My inexperienced ryder probably played a part in Joran-El's decision as well.

I'd almost forgotten about Dayne until he spoke his nonsense. "The Osteran army is trapped in that valley. They cannot advance through the pass without being devastated by Hartspass' defenders. Why does the fool not attack?"

"Joren is wary of an ambush. The Osterans know about dragons. They are too savvy to leave themselves so exposed. We have far less space to maneuver if we fly into the valley. The caves and peaks offer many places for furies or griffins to hide."

Despite my words, nothing untoward occurred as Apex flew into the gap between the mountains, dipping below the peaks where I'd expect any ambush would've been set. Arrows rose from Osteran soldiers encamped below, a ballista hidden among the rocks fired, but nothing that posed a true threat to a dragon. Apex responded with a blech of fire that sent a group of Osteran soldiers scurrying. It wasn't until Apex and Renfax passed directly over the walls of the keep itself that the Osterans sprang their trap.

Furies launched skyward—originating not from the valley or even the crevices of the surrounding mountains, but rather from the keep itself. Hartspass had already fallen. The siege below was a ruse, the first trigger in some Osteran trap that had yet to fully reveal itself.

The initial wave of insect-like projectiles came at my brother and sister. Each turned in opposite directions, but the looming mountains that flanked Hartspass limited their space to maneuver anywhere but upwards—and the furies seemed to recognize that. The creatures made their trajectory more vertical than the evading dragons, seeking to trap my brethren in the valley. Amos Gilder shouted as Lothar plunged into the fray. The rest of my kin followed. That was what the Osterans wanted.

I roared a warning. A single horned dragon heeded me; the rest didn't.

A horn sounded from within the keep, a deep, ominous sound that echoed through the valley. I beat my wings, moving to join the

fray as a dozen griffins appeared from the east, soaring over the mountain. I was wary. I awaited a greater storm behind this first wave, but
no more appeared. A mere twelve griffins versus an almost equal
number of dragons was no contest. Where were the other griffins?
Oster had hundreds at its command.

This formation of giant birds carried in their talons a cage of
wood, dragging the container through the sky as if they were beasts of
burden in the field. It took four griffins to hold the contraption aloft.
Inside, furies buzzed about, straining against the coils of the net that
the griffins carried. The formation rose ever higher into the sky until
the net was above the altitude of the dragons who had plunged into
the emerging fray near Hartspass.

I roared again, a warning and plea, even as I knew it would be too
late.

As I beat my wings, pushing through a stab of pain in my wing,
another horn blast sounded in the valley. At the command, the
griffins obediently released their cage. I shot toward the still-trapped
furies as the contraption fell, coming apart as it dropped through the
air. Streams of gray-skinned furies poured from the cage's openings.
Perhaps half of a hundred had been inside, anxious to follow the
scent of creatures they had been specially bred to kill. I pinned back
my wings and stretched my neck. Dayne's panicked thoughts
pounded inside my skull.

"What in the Abyss are you doing?"

I blocked him out, extending my claws, the wind pushing through
my nostrils. I was too late to stop the furies from escaping the cage,
but the creatures were still clustered when I finally reached them.
Dayne screamed as I plunged into the fury stream, swiping with my
claws, biting with my teeth, and thrashing with my tail.

My tactic seemed insane to a human, but I had a plan (sort of).
Furies were deadly, bred with a poison that paralyzed and killed
dragons, but even their stingers couldn't penetrate dragon armor.
They needed to lock onto us with their jagged, hooked claws to give
their mandibles time to burrow a hole in our soft flesh before their

stingers could be jabbed into us. Usually, furies came at us like arc-bolts or arrows, while we defended ourselves by maneuvering to avoid them until they exhausted themselves, or they were killed by bathing them with fire. The price of furies' speed was a severe shortage of endurance. The creatures picked a target, a path, and mostly had to keep on that trajectory or they would exhaust their fleeting burst of strength. They were the mayflies of aerial combat. I took this group of furies by surprise, exploiting these weaknesses.

I crushed, skewered, and tore a dozen of the buzzing creatures, twisting through their midst into a furious plunge. Despite my evasions, several clattered against my scales, but I didn't have time to worry if they'd locked on. I wanted to kill as many furies as I could, but disrupting their intended flight path would be almost as worth-while. I needed only to give my kin a chance. When I emerged from the deadly stream of furies, half their number were dead, and at least a dozen others flew erratically in directions away from my fellow dragons. The rest continued onward, but at least the dragons and their ryders would be aware. Even Dayne managed to survive my maneuver—furies craved only dragon blood. Although he seemed to have passed out. At least it kept him quiet and my mind clear.

I glided for a long moment, my wing aching, but it was the arrival of another sensation that I feared: the distinctive gnawing of fury mandibles on my scales. I had picked up two furies, one on my belly, another on the side of my neck. They had locked onto me. I smacked at my underside with my tail. I missed on the first hit but managed to snare the creature with a hind claw on my next attempt. The fury fell from my body, but its stinger was still attached. The other creature on my neck was out of easy reach for me but would've been an easy target for a competent ryder. Unfortunately, I had Dayne on my back, and he was still unconscious anyway. I twisted my neck awkwardly, trying to reach the second fury. I could almost get at it, but not quite.

I was about to try again when eight sharp talons raked across my back.

TWENTY-FOUR

Distraction had consequences.

In this case, the fiery pain spreading across my back was the price for ignoring the griffins while I dealt with the fury attached to my neck.

I reacted quickly to the attack, dropping into a free-fall dive just as a second giant bird sliced through the airspace I had occupied a moment earlier. Two more griffins came at me. I could've tried to evade them as well, but griffins did have their uses. Instead of veering off, I gave a hard flap of my wings, diving directly at the onslaught. Birds squawked with ire as we closed. At the last possible moment, I dipped a wing and twisted my neck, shoving myself directly into a griffin's feathered torso. It cried out in shocked pain, flapping its wings to escape. I plunged a foreclaw into its body, yanking the griffin toward me. When I was near enough, I grabbed the stricken bird with my other foreclaw and pulled the mangled creature's corpse along the length of my neck, using it as a bloody washcloth to wipe the fury off my body.

The stink of the carnage aroused Dayne from his stupor. "By Haven, Bayloo, the blood!"

I didn't enjoy soaking myself in griffin innards, but it worked. The fury was gone.

"It's just a dead griffin, my prince." I sensed his disgust, so I diverted his attention. "Your bravery was admirable in your first engagement. No other ryder handled themselves in such a manner."

It was true—Dayne was the only one of my ryders to pass out the first time he entered combat. The prince didn't get the insult, instead reacting with predictable pride. I didn't have to see him to know his chest was pumping outward on my back. With my ryder mollified, I flew at speed, circling back toward the valley of Hartspass and the rest of my brethren.

Chaos reigned in the skies as the other dragons flew about in a swirling maelstrom of griffin, fury, and fire. I neared the conflagration warily, reminding myself that I had a task to accomplish back in Eladrell. But I could not abandon my fellow dragons, either. Each one that fell would be one less I could save. I counted them, finding all but two accounted for of those who flew with us, but two among such a dwindling population was a grievous wound. I held out hope for the missing until my eyes caught sight of a bloodied corpse sprawled out over a jagged outcropping of rock just above the valley floor. The size and scales of the dead dragon told me that it was Apex. A second of my kin—one of my horned cousins—lay beneath the walls of the keep, her neck cracked. In the sky, most of the furies were gone, and those that remained barely had the strength to fly. Several griffins stubbornly continued to engage, but they were no match for the ash dragons. Still, there was no true victory to be had in this place. It was a trap that we had only partially evaded.

"We should return to Eladrell," I advised Dayne.

Prince Dayne was appalled. "Retreat before victory? They still hold the keep."

I'd forgotten his ego, but it could also serve me. "I fear you were correct about Joren-El and your brother, my prince. He may have led us into this trap. Perhaps he even killed Apex. The keep is nothing. We must get back to Eladrell to report this treachery."

Only a fool like Dayne—with some help from my own will twisting him—would've believed such a thing, but he did. I was deep in Dayne's mind now. I sensed his perception of the situation change as I desired. Suddenly, a disastrous engagement in which two dragons had died was an opportunity for him.

"Back to Eladrell!" Dayne screamed loud enough to make my head ache. "By order of your prince, we return to Eladrell!"

I swept in among my brothers and sisters, sinking my claws into the backside of a griffin as I did so. I roared to gather their attention as Dayne again shouted his commands to the other ryders. In the absence of a man like Joren-El with a clear mandate from the king to command, the rest followed us, setting a course back to the west.

I led my fellow dragons, and I enjoyed it. I had that in common with my ryder. As a slave dragon, I'd often been relegated to lesser roles due to my inability to belch fire, but being at the forefront seemed my natural place. I kept a close watch on the formation that followed me. There were plenty of injuries, but none seemed fatal for a dragon. Three ryders had been lost during the melee, which didn't bother me at all. They were slave drivers.

The first sign of trouble came when Lothar fell out of formation. He was among the ryderless dragons, and my brother had several torn, bloody wounds from his engagement with the Osteran griffins. Lothar hadn't communicated any distress, but that wasn't surprising from an ash dragon.

Cornethius, my gray-scaled brother with wings of mismatched sizes, moved with his ryder to investigate even before I asked it. A roar of distress from my brother followed. I turned immediately to tend to Lothar even though I sensed Dayne's disapproval of my course change. He hungered to accuse Joren-El of conspiring with his elder brother in some treason—everything else was secondary. I ignored his clamoring in my head. Lothar's flight had become erratic. He was in serious trouble.

"The scent of poison is on him," Cornethius told us.

The sour stink detected by my brother filled my nostrils as I neared. Lothar's eyes seeped with the pale milkiness of sickness. He could manage only to glide now, his wing shaking.

"There must be a fury on him," Cornethius' ryder called out, sounding like he actually cared. His name was Gathus. "He took several griffin strikes—the blood and injuries may have cloaked the greater danger."

"Another damn fool," Dayne muttered, although it was unclear if he spoke of Lothar or Gathus.

Cornethius nimbly adjusted his course, positioning himself under Lothar before unleashing a controlled burst of fire onto the injured dragon's belly, just beneath his foreleg. Dragon fire would destroy the fury stinger, but the poison's damage had been done.

Lothar's strength failed. One wing dipped precipitously as he fell into a tumbling spin. Cornethius and I dove after him. I reached Lothar first, wrapping my digits around his foreleg. My strength alone wasn't enough to stop his fall, but Cornethius joined me a moment later. Together, we stabilized Lothar enough, bringing him to the ground in the midst of some hapless farmer's field. I sniffed the air. It was a potato field, which I took as an ill omen.

Gathus slid down off his dragon to examine Lothar. The injured dragon's eyes drifted open, but they showed only confusion. It didn't take Gathus long to find the wound, a gap in a single scale. "The fury dug through, sure enough," Gathus announced. "But the opening is far narrower than others I've seen. Perhaps the fury that did this was weakened or injured. I think the gap isn't wide enough for the stinger, which is why he was able to fly for as long as he did. He must not have gotten a full dose of poison."

"The death of this brave dragon is on Joren-El's hands," Prince Dayne declared haughtily. "He and those who put him up to this must face punishment."

Gathus kept his face blank. "Lothar isn't dead."

Dayne seemed disappointed. "Well then, he shall be safe enough in this field. I will have a healer flown out to him. If we stay here, the others will reach the Fist before us. We must go now so I may speak with my father."

Gathus frowned. I could tell he didn't like the idea of leaving a dragon alone and untended in some farmer's dirt in the middle of nowhere. I agreed, for those reasons and more. If my suspicions about the Osteran plan were correct, I couldn't be sure when a healer would be able to return here. But even more, Lothar's injury provided me with an opportunity. I wanted Lothar with us, even if it meant carrying him, but Dayne would need a push to agree with that.

I passed images of Dayne being hailed as the Hero of the Battle of Hartspass and Savior of the Last Dragons through the link. Nothing too strong at first, but enough that I hoped to plant a seed. Cheering crowds were good. I added young human women throwing roses to the image. Dayne's mind stirred, but it wasn't enough. I added a scene of King Mendakas bestowing upon his younger son the king's own sword as a token for saving a precious ash dragon from the battle. To top it off, I imagined Dayne's brother Horace alone in a cell crying as the adoring masses cheered his younger half-brother. A thin crown of gold encircled Dayne's head in that one. Finally, he got it.

"Cornethius and Bayloo can carry him back to DragonPeak," Dayne declared. "We aren't far now."

I looked away, pretending to focus on the horizon as my eyes flashed a bright smile. The little prince was becoming easier to manipulate as I better understood how his mind functioned.

"Can Bayloo handle the weight?" Gathus asked, as if Dayne had any idea what I could and couldn't do. "His wing was badly injured."

"Bayloo can outfly any dragon in the sky," Dayne proclaimed without hesitation or consideration. "It is Cornethius' lame, deformed wing you should worry about."

I felt the shame that my brother dragon would never display openly. Cornethius' modestly undersized left wing probably bothered him the way not breathing fire had once irked me. Gathus' jaw tensed, but he only said, "Let us make for the DragonPeak."

Lothar was heavy. I couldn't have lifted him on my own, and it wasn't easy even with Cornethius' assistance. We flew low, stopping to rest no less than five times, with each break bringing a rebuke from Dayne. "The other ryders will speak to my father before me," he complained as we rested.

It took everything I had to keep the prince's impatience in check, subtly reminding him of the importance of returning with a wounded dragon that others may have thought lost. Surely, there could be no greater gift to his father, and no more obvious evidence of the prince's grandness. I might've slipped in a new potential title for him to salivate over: Prince of Dragons.

"Let the others speak of what you have done. It will merely make your father even more anxious for your triumphant return."

That seemed to please him. "Legends are made swiftly, but spread slowly," he muttered to himself.

Whatever. Fools are made slowly but die swiftly.

It was the longest, hardest flight I ever made, but together with Cornethius, I did it. We reached the city. But when Eladrell finally came into sight, it did not offer the welcome Dayne expected. Instead, fires burned in the city, but not in celebration. Dragons flew in the sky, their fiery breaths blazing, but not in greeting. The explanation for the scarcity of griffins at Hartspass was now apparent: they had been waiting for the departure of as many dragons as possible before attacking Eladrell and the Fist.

If Dayne was going to pee himself again, this would've been the moment.

He stayed dry. Until the first griffin came at us.

TWENTY-FIVE

I counted nearly seventy vicious birds dancing in the sky.

It could well be that the bulk of the Osteran griffins had been committed to this battle.

Dayne hissed at the scene. "Devious scoundrels."

I had to agree. The Osteran trap had been well executed—consistent with King Galt's cunning. They'd lured out not only the vanguard dragons of which I'd been a part, but most of Rolm's horned dragons had already flown east along the coast as well, its best soldiers on their back. Even though they weren't fire breathers, half of Rolm's dragons were absent, along with a good number of her best soldiers.

Surveying the scene, I guessed that the Osterans had used the absence of any dragon patrol to land their ships on the coast under cover of darkness, sending their griffins and war wolves against the Fist, along with at least three hundred soldiers. While that number might seem paltry against the defenders of the Fist, the wolves were all the difference. When fighting in a pack, those vicious beasts were worth ten men in a melee. The Osteran force had reached the citadel's walls, although they didn't yet appear to be attacking. A night attack could be perilous for humans, who couldn't see much in the night. The city of Eladrell itself didn't seem to be under direct assault—the mayhem there appeared to be a reaction to the fighting going on in the air in and around the Fist.

About ten dragons were being sorely pressed trying to fend off the horde of griffins. I recognized King Mendakas and mighty Triton in the heart of the fray, supported by the dragons who had returned ahead of me from Hartspass. A huge flock of griffins surrounded Mendakas, kept at bay by Triton's blue-tinged fire. Elsewhere, Organa and her ryder Del Quickblade roasted a pair of griffins flying beneath them, even as three other birds swept across her backside. Proteus and Bilig circled closer to the citadel, killing anything with feathers that came too close to the inner courtyard. Torches lit the top of the Fist's walls, revealing the presence of Rolman archers, most of whom were understandably hesitant to fire blindly into the night. I studied the battle, the arrangement of the forces. The dragons seemed to be holding their own, if barely. My presence would make a difference in the fight, but not a decisive one. At least that's what I told myself, because there were other things for a scheming dragon to do.

This attack was at least partly a gift in disguise—a far better distraction than anything I could've mustered. A wise dragon once said that only a fool walks away from ale or opportunity (actually, that was me). Now, I needed to seize my chance. I'd already succeeded in planting ideas in Dayne's head to manipulate him, strengthening his own paranoid inclinations. Just as I hoped when I'd encouraged his attention, Dayne's twisted thoughts made him more malleable than any true ryder, but I needed to go further. For my plan to succeed, to free my people, I had to get the prince to do something that benefited only me. He wouldn't want that. Which meant I needed to make Dayne my slave.

Before whipping the little prince, I had to get Lothar to safety. The logical course would've been to take him to DragonPeak, where there would be healers to tend to his wounds, but I didn't do that because I had need of Lothar for my plan. After what had happened in my cave earlier, I wasn't sure what the Keepers would do to me if I approached DragonPeak. Lisaam Payne probably knew full well what I was by now.

"They need you, brother," I said to Cornethius as the desperation of the battle became apparent. "Let us set him down here. It is too dangerous to fly to DragonPeak. I will get Lothar to safety."

Gathus hesitated, doubting my ability to carry a dragon alone. Yet, he wanted to be fighting. The other dragons were sorely pressed. Cornethius' instinct, too, was to fight. The pair fed on each other.

We don't want them with us, I told Dayne through our link. *We will have our own glory.*

"Go, Gathus," Dayne ordered like an obedient puppy. "Aid my father."

That push was enough. Cornethius and I lowered Lothar to the ground in a field beside the main road leading to Eladrell. His eyes opened as his claws touched the grass, which I took to be a good sign. He hadn't gotten a full dose of fury poison or he'd be dead already. The fact that he wasn't gave me hope that he would recover. Cornethius released his grip, soaring immediately toward the fray.

"We leave him here?" Dayne wondered. At night, the road was empty, the field desolate.

"For now," was all I said.

I sniffed at my wounded brother's injury. I was no healer, but I could smell the foul odor of fury poison mixed with his blood. He'd taken some of the stinger's venom, but not a lethal dose. I trilled at Lothar. "Can you hear me, brother?"

Lothar's eyes brightened momentarily in acknowledgement, which was enough to give me hope. He wasn't going to die. Indeed, I intended that he should live, and live well.

"Hold on, brother. I must leave you for a time, but I shall return. For now, rest and heal as best you can."

I took off, but flew a circuitous route, not toward the battle but toward the northern side of Eladrell, where I once again landed. I didn't want to attempt my next attack while trying to fly. I hoped this spot was far enough from the battle over the Fist that I wouldn't attract a griffin.

"You should dismount, my prince," I pushed at him. I wanted to see him for this part, to match my stare with his. "It is important."

Dayne obliged my request, suspicions brimming. With his feet on the ground he glared at me. "What in the Abyss are you doing?"

Rather than answer with words, I turned the full force of my will against my ryder. Dayne was agitated, which made him harder to control, but with the prince, a conspiracy was the best way to engage his faithless mind.

"The Sculptors are part of this devious plot against you, my prince."

Dayne already hated the masked men. In his twisted mind, they had conspired to keep him from attaining a dragon of his own for most of his life. This gave me an opening.

"What do you mean?" he asked through our link.

Digging through the recesses of Dayne's mind, I encouraged the perceived injustices he suffered from the Sculptors. Within him, I found dark memories, strengthened them, manipulated them, then turned them back to him. Whatever task he completed, the Sculptors always said it wasn't enough. Many times, they had dared to claim he lacked the stamina to climb Arrow Peak. A masked Sculptor had said he wanted to witness Dayne consuming a dragon bone. There were dozens of nights where the Sculptors had crept into the Fist to conspire with his brother. They whispered plots against Dayne. Oh, such injustice. Such jealousy against him!

I fed Dayne suspicion like he was a greedy pig. His mind swallowed it eagerly. When I thought he was near full, I laid on the biggest plot of them all: *the Sculptors seek to sever the link between the ryders and their dragons.*

Dayne's mind recoiled as if I placed his consciousness on a fire. I had gone too far, too fast. Dayne was paranoid, but not stupid. "That ... how could the Sculptors do such a thing as that?" His will strengthened, pushing back at me, aided by the rune-link's amplification. "How could you—a mere dragon—possibly know that?"

I only would have one chance to do this. I shot my demands at him as if they were arrows, hoping to plant more seeds in his ripe mind. "You saw the confusion over Hartspass. Dragons hesitating, confused, vulnerable to furies." I shoved the modified memories at Dayne. I showed him dragons flying erratically. "It was a trap. The Sculptors intended to lure the dragons from Eladrell to their doom! They want to get rid of you, because they fear you."

Suspicion still inundated the jungle of Dayne's mind. "Why would they do this?"

"Your brother." I knew those words had magic for Dayne. I coaxed all the latent childhood slights to the surface of Dayne's perception, a lifetime of injustice flooding his mind. "Horace fears what you are becoming. He cannot ride, so he seeks to replace all the ryders with his own loyalists. Horace has made a treacherous bargain with Oster."

Dayne wanted to believe me. He ached to find flaw in his half-sibling. Somehow, over the years, his elder brother had become a fount from which all terrible events flowed. It appealed to Dayne that every setback in his life was because of the jealousy of another, a belief nurtured by his domineering mother. I sensed Dayne's vulnerability, but surprisingly, a rational bulwark of his mind resisted me.

How could you know this? he demanded.

"My fellow dragons told me." Lying came so naturally to me now. "The others fear losing their links. We dragons love our ryders. They believe only you can help them."

Dayne ached to be a savior. A hundred dark evenings had been spent in his bed within the Fist, dreaming of winning the adoration of others when they finally saw his heroic acts. Within him swirled the pulling vortex of righteousness and revenge. It would all be his. I pushed my will onto his—fueling the thoughts that were already rooted within him. It was like pushing a boulder uphill with my snout. My head ached as I fought against the very nature of the rune-link that should've functioned in the opposite direction that I desired. Visions flashed within my mind as I concentrated, glimpses of another place, a reality of power just beyond my grasp. I heard my mother.

You are an ember dragon.

I slammed my will into Dayne's mind as if it were a sword. The prince's hands clutched either side of his head. "It's all..." He shook, but something within him continued to fight me. Or was the rune magic itself trying to protect him? "You're my dragon. You can't ..."

I intensified my assault on his free will. "We were meant to be joined. Our destinies are linked. Only the Sculptors seek to keep us apart. We must go there now—to their grand temple in the city. Within it is the secret to their magic, and its undoing." I stabbed at him again, sending him images of dragons bowing their heads as he strode before them, a crown of gold perched atop his head.

Dayne sucked in a breath at seeing my illusions in his mind. He gazed toward the city. I thought I had him, but when he turned back toward me, his eyes were ablaze with anger. His voice trembled. "You lie. You ... you are in my head."

Oh, chicken piss.

Dayne's will came at me in a violent spasm, its power intensified by the rune-link that joined us. His mind was different from any of my other ryders; they had been men of self-control, who commanded themselves and others with discipline and will. Dayne, however, was raw emotion, his untethered desires striking like the tip of a rapier. He finally realized I had tricked him. I had betrayed him. And worst of all, I had humiliated him. His wrath came at me, hot and powerful. I reeled, momentarily giving ground in this contest of wills. As I did, the fog of images and fake memories I'd inundated him with burned away, and Dayne realized the full extent of my deception.

"What are you?" He seethed.

I took pleasure in my reply. "I am not your slave. I am a dragon, the First of the Free."

With that, the lying was done. This would be a duel of wills.

Dayne had the rune. I had the desperation of a freed slave, and what-ever my heritage as an ember dragon bestowed upon me. I'd resisted Brindisi, I had manipulated Dayne, but I'd never tried to actually control a human mind, as I did now. If I failed, everything I had done would be for nothing.

The link created by the Sculptors' runes was a funnel, with the big side for the human. It took all of their will and concentrated it, making it far more potent when it came out the far end—allowing it to flow into a dragon's mind like a knife, sharper and stronger than anything a person could've managed without the magical enhance-ment. I needed to make the rune-link do the opposite of what its creators intended. I needed to be a needle of power, concentrating my will through the link. I was that, and more.

I poured my desperation to be free, to think for myself, to restore the pride of my race, into my assault. I rammed it through the link between us like I was jamming a claw up Dayne's ass. Dragons would fly free. This human would help make it happen. Rage and despera-tion blended to enhance my will. It wasn't enough.

Dayne screamed. He fell to his knees. But he didn't break. The architects of the runes were clever. It was one thing to resist will, it was quite another to impose it on another sentient being. My raw desire wasn't enough. I didn't quit. I suspected there was another way.

This magic was stolen.

The more I understood the runes, the more I thought about the magic my mother had used, and the more I realized I could reclaim part of my kind's legacy. I was trying to act like a human—trying to direct the desire inside me with my mind, the way the Sculptors intended the ryders to act. But I wasn't a ryder or a human. I could be more. I was of the race that had created this magic. I could manipu-late it in ways no human could.

In that moment, I perceived the link itself. I sensed the tunnel of magic, I glimpsed its structure—a strange weaving of glowing chords and threads glittering against a backdrop of the wider, unimaginable world. This was the reality of magic. I thought I heard an echo of my mother:

The Latticework, she whispered.

I didn't understand what I was seeing. I couldn't conceive of the power of the mind that had forged this weaving of magic. But I didn't need to. I needed only to change it, and something within me instinctively knew how. I was an ember dragon!

In an instant, I did what I must. The conduit that joined the control-runes between slave and master stretched, distorted, and evened. The magic that a moment before had protected Dayne became a level battleground in our battle for power. I poured in the same will and passion with which I almost broke Dayne. It was a glorious thing; as I let go of the false chains of human communication, I found power inside me. Even as I directed my will, I felt stronger, as if I was finally whole. I was a creature of power. I wanted my heritage, and I was going to crush anyone who tried to stop me.

Dayne toppled from his knees onto the ground, wriggling in mindless pain like a snake that had been cut in half. His eyes leaked their human tears. He cried in agony. One of my hearts might have tugged at me. I'd thought I'd be glad to lord over a person who wouldn't have hesitated to use me or any of my kind as a tool, but that wasn't the case. To turn someone who had been free into a slave wasn't pleasant. With the ghastrays, I'd sworn never to do it. But I had no choice. He'd done it to me first. I didn't stop until I had control.

That didn't take very long. Dayne was mine to command, so I did.

"Take me to the Sculptors."

TWENTY-SIX

I flew low over the walls of Eladrell.

Dayne rode on my back, appearing just like any other ryder in command of their dragon. Indeed, he thought this had been his idea; he hungered for the revenge he now thought was owed against the Sculptors. Dayne's mind had become his prison, just as his kind had done to mine. I felt no guilt; I'd been around humans long enough to know that they were happiest living in their fantasies.

Ordinarily, a dragon flying low over the buildings and plazas of the city would've raised an alarm, but pandemonium already reigned in the streets. The people on Eladrell's streets were either men of the city watch trying to maintain control or citizens intent on fleeing. The rest of the populace hid indoors. Only the most intrepid or the most foolish ventured outside for the purpose of viewing the fearsome battle unfolding nearby at the Fist. For a renegade dragon, it was a perfect moment to fly into the city. People, including the city watch, would likely assume my presence was part of the battle, or have more important things to occupy themselves with.

Eladrell was a sprawling mélange of structures, bridges, parks, and monuments, but I had eyes for only one edifice: the great

Temple of the Sculptors. The redoubt of the mysterious order was a magnificent construction of perfect squares stacked upon each other, each level slightly smaller than the one beneath, and topped with a golden spire on which an eternal flame blazed. Nestled into the far end of the city, within the shadow of the Fist above, it was separated from the rest of Eladrell by manicured gardens that included a quaint man-dug lake intersected by arching bridges, under which swam little golden fish. I landed on a trimmed grassy space beside the water. The fish glittered near the surface, their scales reflecting in the starlight. It was a strangely peaceful oasis in the storm of torment around me. Since no one was looking (or if they were, there was nothing they could do about it), I plunged my head into the lake, snatching two naïve fish who'd spent their entire lives in the safety of that watery playpen. I don't know what I was expecting, but it wasn't what I got. They tasted bitter—worse than chicken feathers. I swallowed anyway, because I didn't want to be wasteful. My hunger would have to wait to be satiated. I walked toward the temple.

"Get what you need from these false prophets, my prince," I said to Dayne as he climbed down from my back. "This will soon be your kingdom. Let us take from the Sculptors their instruments of magic so that the power can be wielded by your wise hand alone."

Dayne was long past resisting, but his mind was still conscious. "They will resist."

"If they are foolish enough to refuse, then these Sculptors shall face our wrath."

Prince Dayne approached the golden gates of the Sculptors' temple with his self-important strides. I kept pace close behind, looking fearsome as only a dragon can. For the first time, this prince carried out my mission. I intended for him to succeed.

None challenged us as we walked the tree-lined path to the temple. I heard the griffins squawk and saw the fire of my fellow dragons, but that battle was not mine—not yet. Dayne wrapped a fist against the grand metal doors. The sound echoed within the halls of the temple. I heard movement in the passage behind the portal, but no one answered Dayne's knock.

I fed the prince outrage. "Open up in the name of Prince Dayne," he bellowed. No human projected self-entitled fury better than my dear ryder. Still, no one opened the door. I had no more patience. Time was too precious.

I moved closer, smashing the twin doors inward with a single shove of my forelegs. They fell easily—the portals hadn't been built to withstand the stress of an attack. I heard the cries of a man struggling out from underneath. He really should've just opened the doors instead of lurking behind in the passageway.

I peered inside the torchlit corridor beyond the shattered doorway. The passage leading inside the temple stretched as wide as three dragons, but entering would've made me too vulnerable. I considered destroying the roof of the temple, but it was a rather large structure of sturdy stone construction, so that would take more time than we had available. Ever helpful, I used my digits to pull away the door that had fallen upon the Sculptor attendant. The man still drew breath, but he didn't move even when I prodded him with the tip of one of my claws.

"This one will not be a useful messenger," I said to Dayne.

Fortunately, the noise of our entrance hastened other occupants of the temple to come to greet us.

Sculptors pretty much look alike in their big ugly masks and matching robes, but the limping gait of the figure running toward Dayne and I told me that this was Aylin, the Sculptor who'd been present at my interrogation earlier with Del Quickblade. He wasn't likely to be helpful. I decided to kill him quickly if things didn't go well.

A bigger, fatter Sculptor trailed behind Aylin. He wore an amulet of gold over his neck. There were several acolytes coming as well. I thrashed my tail back and forth as I waited for these two-legged creatures to reach me.

"What's the meaning of this?" the fat Sculptor demanded, his mask hanging slightly askew, revealing the edges of a round, pudgy face that resembled a pale hog.

Dayne dedicated himself to my purpose, as if it had been his own. His voice was harsh and commanding. "Where is the Flux?"

The fat Sculptor panted for several long moments before he spoke. "How do you even know about the Flux?"

Aylin maneuvered beside his hefty companion, his wary eyes staring more at me than Dayne from behind his mask. This one had heard Quickblade's accusations. He didn't want to believe I was somehow free, but deep down, I was sure he knew.

"Honored Abbot," Aylin said to the fat Sculptor. "This is Prince Dayne and his bonded dragon, Bayloo."

The hefty Sculptor's eyes widened. "My prince, it is an honor, of course, but I do not understand why you are here."

I wasn't mollified by honorifics or manners, so neither was my prince. "Did you not hear me? Where. Is. The. Flux?"

I couldn't have said it better myself, at least not in human speech.

Humans often develop a slight tremor in their knees and voices when they become scared. The greater the fear, the greater the tremor. The grand Abbot was shaking—legs and voice—like a crystal wine glass in a winter squall, and doing a poor job of hiding it.

"I'm unsure what you are speaking about." He was a terrible liar.

Dayne yanked out his blade, pointing it at the Sculptor's neck. Aylin leaned toward the fat Sculptor's ear. The prince couldn't hear his words, but I could.

"The bond between these two may be corrupt," was the secret he shared.

The fat Abbot's eyes widened so much it appeared as if someone were trying to push them out of his skull from behind. The smell of fear coming off the men grew stronger, but it mingled with something else: determination. Four beady human eyes regarded me. Maybe some of the acolytes behind the two Sculptors stared as well, but I was concerned with the eyes attached to humans who truly under-stood power. These two did.

"*Kaza!*" the Abbot screamed as he reached into his robe and withdrew a fisted hand. He held a dragon-claw stylus like the one that had carved Brindisi.

Pain ripped through me, inside to out. In that way, the agony was unique from other wounds I had suffered. Even the magic of the Mizu wizard had been an external force, its torture an attack like others, albeit far more powerful. The Sculptor's assault ripped at something within me, tearing at cords that bound me with the rune. My scale armor provided no protection. That magical carving that had been a part of me since I was a hatchling blazed like a hot furnace of pain. Nor was I the only victim. Dayne joined me in misery, judging by his screams. He fell, wriggling about on the floor. The rune-link burned on both ends. But that wasn't enough to stop me. Pain couldn't deter me anymore.

I rumbled into the corridor, taking the fool Abbot into my jaws, squeezing only tight enough to let the silly creature know that if he tried to escape, I was going to bite him in half. I swept Aylin's legs out from under him with my tail. The Abbot dropped his stylus. The pain ceased. Dayne scrambled to his feet, his face hot with anger. He spoke my demands on my behalf.

"The Flux, now. Or I shall feed your heart to the dragon."

The last flourish hadn't been my idea. I doubted human hearts tasted any better than the rest of them, but I went with it. I pressed a tooth into the Abbot's ample tummy. Perhaps fat humans tasted better than the others?

He got my message. "The Flux is stored deep underground. In the ancient catacombs, a sacred pool, established by our ancestors."

Oh, ancestors my painted ass. I knew what that sacred pool contained. I'd seen enough of the liquid when they'd carved Brindisi; I'd felt the pain inflicted by their stylus. My mother had told me the source of the rune magic. It wasn't a big leap to know that the Flux was dragon blood. It was all part of the magic they had stolen from my kind. I wondered how long they'd had it and what magic they used to keep the ancient blood in liquid form and potent. I wanted to know how they obtained it, how they learned to use it in such a manner. But I had time for none of those things.

I sent my command for Dayne to deliver. "Bring it forth or be consumed."

"I—it cannot just be moved so easily. It is a great pool, and it can only be moved in special containers, enchanted—"

I'd feared that. "Four pots like those used by the acolytes will be sufficient for now," I told him through Dayne.

Aylin's bulging eyes transitioned from fear to sheer terror. His head shook. "Abbot, you mustn't. The dragon—"

I smacked the mouthy Sculptor with my tail again. I didn't need him blabbing some crazy theory about out-of-control dragons to the rest of the masked crowd. They thought their magic flawless, their carvings irreversible. Perhaps they were correct, perhaps not. But I was much more likely to get what I wanted if no one was considering if the impossible was indeed possible.

I couldn't really see the Abbot's face given the placement of my jaw around his torso, but I felt him wiggle his neck a bit. "Hosrick, fetch the Flux pots for Prince Dayne. Be quick about it."

"Very quick," Dayne confirmed. "Bayloo is a hungry beast. And ill-tempered with those who defy me."

I couldn't fault the prince's delivery. A white-masked acolyte scurried off, leaving a tense assembly of just under a dozen Sculptors and underlings standing about in appalled horror at the scene in the main corridor of their temple. I imagined the Abbot was the least pleased of the whole lot. I worried a bit that another of the Sculptors would attempt an attack, but the imminent peril of their Abbot stayed their hand.

The apprentice-messenger didn't dally. Quicker than I dared to hope, Prince Dayne had two containers of dragon blood in each of his greedy hands. I released the Abbot from my mouth, letting him crumple to the ground, his body soaked from my saliva. Lucky him. I tapped a claw on his chest and told Dayne what to say.

"Your life has been spared, this time. But I will brook no further interference of my orders, no further failures or defiance from this temple."

With that pronouncement, we departed, the prizes cradled in Dayne's arms like a newborn babe.

I took to the air, anxious to free the first of my brothers.

TWENTY-SEVEN

Lothar waited where I'd left him.

The battle over the Fist continued, with the sky scorched by dragon fire and the screeching of griffins. An ominous crackle of something that resembled thunder, but definitely wasn't, rolled off the battlefield as I came to the field where Lothar lay. He still lived. He even lifted his neck slightly as I approached—an encouraging sign.

My hearts beat against my chest as I moved beside him. Something ominous was afoot, but I was so close to my own goal, I couldn't afford to pay mind to anything else. My fellow dragons came first.

Dayne climbed off my back after I landed. I told him to place one of the Flux pots on the ground between Lothar and me. The rest he left in the dragon saddle that I wore. I prodded the pot Dayne had laid on the ground with my claw. It was small, made for human hands, not the far larger digits of a dragon. I fumbled about; perhaps I even shook it a bit. This pot was precious, laden with a desperate hope, but I didn't want human hands on it anymore. I wanted to be done with Dayne and all other humans. Awkwardly, I managed to grab the Flux pot between two digits of my foreleg.

Prince Dayne had fulfilled his purpose, as I needed. I had the Flux. My old, ruthless ryder, Karthus, echoed in my memory, urging me to give this useless prince the mercy of death.

"Dayne, stand before me," I ordered through the link.

The boy prince went rigid. For a moment something within him struggled, but not for long. My will had been tested and triumphed. I was the blade that had already won the battle. Dayne did as I commanded. I enjoyed the power. It was far better to be master than slave.

"Dayne, to heel."

My command surged through the link into his mind and this so-called prince obeyed as countless dragons had before this day. He fell to his knees.

A notion slithered into my mind like a serpent with a devious message. I could punish Mendakas for what he had done to me and mine. I looked down anew at my former ryder, the Prince of Rolm. I remembered my encounter with the king and queen in my cave. This near-boy was the most precious thing in this world to his mother. To slay her son would kill a part of her and wound her husband as well. For however long Mendakas lived, he would bear the agony of the loss of his child, a prince who died a slave. Oh, that would be a cold vengeance for the servitude we dragons had been forced to endure.

It would be easy. The prince just stood there, mine to command. My mouth grew hot and my hearts cold. I imagined myself ripping Dayne's head from his body. I pictured the anguish of his mother. Karthus would've done it, had he been in my position. Brindisi was the same. Only gentle Jona would've stayed the hand of vengeance. There was also the future to consider. I didn't need any more blood enemies. I decided to be better than my former human masters.

"Take shelter within the city, my prince. You are too valuable to your people to be lost in battle today."

Prince Dayne blinked several times at me, confused. He turned his head toward the Fist, at the griffins, and the battle raging above before coming back to regard me. He expected to join that battle. He opened his mouth as if to speak but closed it before any words came out.

He was an unworthy creature, pathetic with an inside full of hate. But to slay him only to bring pain to another would make me worse than that. I chose to be worthy of the sky. I was First of the Free, and I would use my newly won will to be better than the race that had enslaved me.

"Go now!"

This time, Prince Dayne ran. Toward the city, preserving his life. I hoped some good would come from that life one day. He quickly disappeared into the night and my attention shifted to the cause that mattered. The time had finally come to free the dragons. Lothar would be the first.

Like with all slave dragons, the Sculptors' runes disfigured my brother's chest just below his neck. The pattern of the magical carvings differed from my own, but only slightly. Their effect was the same: they made him a slave in mind and body.

The Sculptors believed their magical bonds unbreakable, but they were wrong. I was proof enough of that. I hoped I wasn't unique. I had some cause for hope: Jaxis' torment at the hand of Oster had been evidence that the link was not all powerful. The other stories of so-called mad dragons were cause for some scant hope. I didn't want to drive Lothar mad, though. I wanted to save him. When the other dragons had lost control, it had been in times of great stress. Their minds had been broken by the trauma that damaged the rune-link. I hoped for a better result with my brother, Lothar. This would be a clean break without harm to Lothar's mind. The Flux, the stylus, and even the runes themselves had all been taken from dragons. These instruments created the bond that held us. I hoped that same magic could free one of us.

I approached my brother Lothar slowly, my eyes urging him to be calm, that all would be well. I came closer than I ordinarily would have to another dragon, but he didn't seem alarmed. He was already exhausted and we all served a common cause, or so he thought.

"What I do, I do for our kind. Please know that I love you, brother."

These were strange words for one dragon to speak to another. Lothar's eyes dimmed in confusion. The venom made him weak. That provided me with an opportunity. I ripped my claws across his chest, the tips digging deep into his scales, scraping across the runes that had been carved there since Lothar's days as a hatchling. I'd only have this one chance to take him with complete surprise at such close quarters and I made the most of it. My blow mangled his chest scales, and blood seeped out of the gouges I'd made in Lothar's armor. My brother bellowed in a rage of betrayal. I couldn't blame him, but I couldn't quit either. I hurled a Flux pot at him as he lay on his side. The Sculptors' concoction spattered over the wounds I'd inflicted, over the desecrated runes. Inside my head, pain flashed, like a knife's blade cutting within my skull. In that precious moment when the hurt subsided, I glimpsed again that which I'd felt when I'd bested Dayne's mind—the vast magic of my kind that my mother had mentioned. *The Latticework.* In that moment, I saw the world for the first time, but it vanished with my brother's roar.

Lothar let loose a sound laced with a heartiness that belied his injuries. He struggled onto his feet, his eyes seething with anger. I held my ground, neither attacking nor retreating from my bloody brother. I peered at his eyes, searching for a sign he'd changed, that the pain I'd inflicted upon him hadn't been in vain. Instead, rage greeted me. Despite his injuries, I'd awakened some hidden reservoir of strength within Lothar. He attacked, snapping his neck toward me, his jaws wide. I danced backward, readying my wings for a quick launch in case he resorted to fire. He did. A tight spit of flame came at me, clawing for my chest as I beat my wings. I hovered, hoping Lothar would calm himself, hoping he'd come to his senses. Instead, he sent a second, larger breath of fire at me. The burst spread wide and high. I flew higher, but not quick enough to escape entirely. The flames bit at my scales; the pain was a mere trifle, and fire wasn't much of a threat to me as long as my scales were intact. Still, this wasn't going the way I'd hoped.

"Lothar, my brother, I seek not to harm you, but rather to wake you."

He replied with still more fire. I rose in the air, completing a low circuit around my fellow dragon. What had I done wrong? I'd been so certain I had the key to it all. I'd damaged the runes; I'd used the blood of dragons to cleanse his flesh. His ryder was already dead. Yet it still hadn't been enough. Worse, from the direction of the Fist, I saw a group of ugly dots flying toward me—griffins. I stared back down at Lothar, snarling below me, barely able to move but his eyes fixed upon me. In those eyes there was nothing but madness. My hearts were lead, but I came at him yet again, knowing that I'd face his fire. But I had to try. This might be the last chance I ever would have at this.

I roared with desperation at him. I needed Lothar's mind to break the chains that held it. The sound tore through the air, and it said: *Let us not be a race of slaves.*

I was certain Lothar heard me. He froze—or at least he stopped breathing fire at me. I came closer, roaring my urgent need yet again. Within my brother, something changed. A pallor I hadn't realized existed lifted from his eyes. For a fleeting moment, I dared to hope. Had I done it?

Then my brother's gaze shifted again. I felt the presence of an immeasurable force of magic—countless interconnected links in an impossible web that surrounded me and my brother. It connected us, I realized, with invisible bonds of unknown origin and purpose. I saw Lothar as part of the pulsing web of energy as he turned his head about, staring at the sky, the battle around the Fist, then finally at me. Lothar seemed like a puppet within the vastness of the Latticework. His eyes seethed in an unquenchable rage, a look without thought or reason. Within Lothar's gaze, my hope for my kind fell away.

My brother's stare hurt more than his fire. He leaped at me. I moved just a bit too slow. My hearts were heavy with disappointment, my reflexes numbed by the slow ache of despair. Lothar's claws caught my flank. I spun away, but he came at me with a speedy anger. His jaws locked on my foreleg. I howled, but not really from the pain. His bite hurt, but it was the realization of what I had to do that really crushed me. I'd been wrong about the Sculptors' runes. I was wrong about my brother. The bonds of slavery went deeper than the magic that had been carved into him. I should've thought about that. I realized he was held by something deeper. Now, I had to pay the price for my failure. The Flux pots in the saddle on my back shattered as we struggled, as did my hope for freeing more of my kind, at least on this night.

I whipped my tail into Lothar's wounded right wing and kicked at his damaged scales. Lothar's body shuddered in pain, but he didn't unlock his jaws. I hit my brother again, harder this time, but with the same result. Again, I misjudged mighty Lothar. He was a fighter. That was in his blood. The protective armor of my legs cracked as Lothar's jaw tightened, even as I continued to dig my claws into his exposed flesh, even as my tail beat at his side. I had no choice. I snapped at his neck. There was already a chink in his scales from the battle with griffins. I made that the focus of my attack. As I expected, the scales were weakened there. My teeth drew blood. His airflow became erratic. I didn't stop squeezing. Finally, the pressure on my leg relented. I thought he'd had enough. That he'd realized he couldn't win this. I didn't want to kill my brother. I too released my jaw. I was a fool.

A gaze of mad hate came at me. There was no quit within Lothar. Whatever drove him could not be silenced while he lived. A lifetime of slavery could not be easily unraveled. Something about the magic of the runes made its victims unable to win their freedom. The magic leash was both carved onto our bodies and connected to something far greater.

Lothar shot his fire at my wounded wing. It was my most vulnerable surface. If he could ground me, I was dead. Sooner or later, one way or another, the griffins or the slave dragons would find me. This had gone on too long. The griffins I'd seen were almost upon us. I had to finish the fight. So, I did.

I attacked, straight at Lothar's fire. Eyes closed, I surged into his flame, my wings tucked as close to my body as I could pull them. The heat of his breath surged over my face, spilling onto my neck and torso. My scales handled it well enough. Much of Lothar's strength had left him and I didn't let his assault persist. My jaw found my brother's neck. This time I didn't hesitate, I didn't offer mercy. I bit, sinking my teeth into his shattered scales. Lothar wriggled about, trying to dislodge me. He couldn't. I was stronger. My teeth passed into his flesh, the top and bottom of my jaw meeting each other within Lothar's neck. With a single anguished yank, I tore most of the center of my brother's throat away from the rest of his body. Lothar's blood gushed from my mouth as I watched him fall to the ground. His tail shook in a final frenzy, then crashed down with the rest of him.

Finally, Lothar was free. For the second time in my life, I leaked water from my eyes.

"Your death shall not be for nothing, brother," I vowed. "I do not have the answer today, but I now know I must look deeper. What my mother knew, I shall know as well. What was stolen from our kind, will be ours again. And you will have made it possible."

My words were desperate and laced with grief, but they were also born of an ember of knowledge growing within me. I had sensed the great magic that held my kind in slavery. I knew there was a way I could free my kind. I had hope.

It didn't last.

TWENTY-EIGHT

Griffins swarmed me.

The trauma of knowing that I'd killed Lothar momentarily dulled my self-preservation instincts. I wanted that bloody corpse to open his eyes again. I wanted him to be alive again, even as a slave. But that wasn't going to happen. I tried to remind myself that there was still hope. I just needed time to understand, but if I stayed where I was, I would end up as dead as Lothar.

The griffins had caught me still on the ground, where I lost the advantage of my maneuverability. There were three and they dove at me, talons twitching. I snapped at the lead beast, causing it to break off its dive at the last moment, my jaws closing around the empty air where it had flown a moment before. Two of its companions followed closely. I dodged one, but the other raked its talon across my neck. The sensational pain that followed shocked me—I've been scratched by many griffins in past battles, but the strength of this attack was different. My scales should've been better able to resist griffin claws. The beast's talons plunged into me, slicing three parallel tracks through a portion of the armor on my back, just below my neck. The wound stung like fire on a tongue. I roared, as much in surprise as pain, though. *That shouldn't happen.* Yet my damaged scales weren't the worst of it. The sheer force of the blow had rattled my bones as if I'd been struck by a mountain. What kind of griffin had the Pale Wrights of Oster wrought from their breeding pits this time?

I watched the trio circle in a tight formation barely above me. The next attack was inevitable. I heard Narsis cry out in pain from somewhere in the distance, but there was nothing I could do for my fellow dragons for now.

Dark griffin eyes peered at me with hate. The three killers dipped their wings and I braced for more pain. I might even have died in that spot beside my brother, Lothar, but for the return of my kin. The high-pitched roar of a horned dragon cracked the air, followed by another, and these were among the most welcome sounds I'd ever heard. From the east came my cousins. I could make out the outlines of the flock returning from the far coast, where they had been lured by the Osteran deceit. Bethy Rann and Crema would be with them. The horned dragons swept through the sky at speed despite the load of useless humans on their backs. Horns sounded from around the Fist—a deep, rumbling claxon made by the signal masters within the army of Oster. They too recognized the danger that approached. The griffins who hunted me broke off their attack, obeying the call of their imperiled masters. I took to the sky, climbing quickly into the crisp night.

Once I regained the clouds, I craned my neck to watch as my kin engaged Oster's mighty horde of beasts above and around King Mendakas' fortress. Smoke polluted the sky, but it didn't hide the desperation of the battle. While I had been occupied with freeing my brethren, the battle had turned against Rolm. The high tower of the Fist had been toppled and a portion of the outer wall battlements had collapsed into the courtyard. Griffins swarmed about the keep like bees around their hive. One gripped the hind leg of Narsis in its beak as she desperately fought—ryderless—to keep four more beasts at bay with erratic sprays of fire. The weight of the griffin attached to her leg dragged her ever lower in the sky even as she beat her wings. My remaining kin fared little better. Triton had been driven northward away from the primary melee by a dozen griffins. One of his hind legs hung at an unnatural angle. On Triton's back, King Mendakas had an arrow notched in his bow, but held his fire, his quiver nearly empty. Cornethius and his larger companion, Organa, flew in formation above the Fist, pursued by more griffins. When they paused to fight, they did so in tight formation, with each enabling the other to concentrate on a smaller area, without concern for enemies coming from behind. I saw no furies left in the air, but even against the griffins alone, my brethren struggled.

I had no love for Rolm, nor its king, but I could not help but count my fellow dragons who remained in the sky—there were but six ash dragons. It shouldn't have been this way. There should have been more than sufficient dragons to fight off the assault, even with the surprise Oster had achieved. But the new griffins' strangely sharpened talons that pierced our armor made the difference. The tension around my hearts lessened only slightly as the horned dragons entered the fray. One group of my kin kept to the air, their ryders launching a fusillade of arrows at the feathered attackers, while other dragons landed to offload the soldiers they carried against Oster's ground forces. I ached to be with them. I consoled myself that the tide was already turning. While the battle had swayed on the tip of a claw before the horned dragons' return, now it was Rolm with the clear advantage. Still, I wanted to be among my own kind. I flew closer to the melee, grinding my jaw, looking for an opportunity to strike. I shouldn't have been so sentimental.

The putrid smell of griffin assaulted my nostrils just before I saw it—a griffin had hidden itself in a patch of dark clouds above, hoping to strike me unaware again. It probably feared my fire—which I didn't have. I watched it cut the air, hungry for my death. I could discern no physical difference between this beast and any other griffin, yet it came far quicker than the rest of its kind.

There was no point in running from this strange griffin. It was too fast, and it was alone. I could beat any bird. I turned upward to meet it in the air. That was when I saw what made this griffin different: something was attached to the left side of the giant bird's neck. It wasn't feathery, and it didn't resemble anything a human could've made. Indeed, the attached passenger was no bigger than a human hand, slimy, with shiny, moss-colored skin—like a giant leech had somehow secured itself to the griffin.

Not somehow. Deliberately, I realized. The Osteran healers had symbiotic creatures they laid onto their soldiers and beasts to help mend their wounds. I wondered if this thing was something similar—except instead of healing a wound it granted greater strength and stamina. Or something like that.

The griffin's beak shot at my face. It wanted to ram me—fast and suicidal. I yanked my neck away at the last moment, getting one of my foreclaws in the griffin's path. Its beak tore into my digits, puncturing my claw. That hurt, but it also slowed the griffin. I saw the leech-like creature thumping like an attached heart on the griffin's neck. I tried to swipe the bird with my tail, but the griffin twisted away, back into higher airspace, before I struck.

I dove, picking up speed. Below, I saw that the Osteran force beneath its walls seemed to be withdrawing. Yet the carnage was not concluded for my kind. The griffins covered the escape of the Osteran army. I saw Narsis' left wing had a hole in it, and blood leaked out from Cornethius' underside as if it were piss. I unleashed a sound of fury. It had the desired effect of drawing the attention of several symbiont-enhanced griffins who had been harrying my brethren. I flew toward them and they at me. It then occurred to me that I had no idea how I was going to fight off three of these things. Could I tire them out like a fury? Whatever that leech on their necks was doing to them, it couldn't last forever. I suspected that the beasts' great stamina came at a price.

The griffins were on me before I thought of anything cleverer than to bite them before they bit me. The leading griffin came right at my face, expecting to gouge my eyes, blind me, pick my nose, whatever. A snap of my jaws forced a course correction, leaving me with a gash on the top of my head and a single griffin feather in my mouth. The other beasts flew close behind. I twisted, thrashing my tail. I got a cut near my hind leg without anything to show for it. This wasn't a fight I would win. I twisted down, flying fast toward the ground, heading for the sprawl of Eladrell. Ordinarily, drawing a bunch of griffins toward the most densely populated area in Rolm wouldn't have been compatible with my slave dragon mission, but I figured it was time for some payback for all I'd done for these humans.

The three griffins followed me, of course. Like dogs, if you run, they chase. This lot was fast. I pushed my wings as hard as I could. I passed over the outer wall of Eladrell, the eyes of every guardsman fixed upon me. I hoped the open-mouthed humans had the sense to take note of the creatures behind me. They did. I heard the sound of bows and ballistae from the city's defenders open fire in my wake, aimed at the low-flying griffins pursuing me. I craned my head back to assess the damage the humans managed to inflict. It was pathetic. Of the dozens of projectiles hurled, I saw only two arrows sticking out of one of the three pursuers. The injured beast didn't slow. Out of a corner of my eye I saw even more griffins coming. The Osterans weren't done.

My fellow dragon saved me, and a human too. The human archers on the walls of Eladrell might not be able to aim, but Bethy Rann could. She swooped in on Crema and put an arrow through the eye of one of the griffins. Its companion squawked at the new threat: three horned dragons coming at her, with Crema in the lead, and Rann standing up in the saddle with a bow in her hand. A second arrow took a griffin in the wing. That slowed the beast enough for me to skewer it with a claw.

They came after Crema and Rann, of course. Two griffins, then two more that seemed to appear from nowhere. A hidden reserve of several more griffins had arisen from within the Osteran army ranks to attack the other arriving dragons. I couldn't tell if these had leeches or not. The fight got bloody, quickly. Horned dragons' scales aren't nearly as tough as those of their greater kin; the griffins' beaks and claws didn't just tear into my smaller brethren—they sliced them apart. I did my best to help. I flew, bit, and clawed. I killed more than half a dozen griffins more quickly than I dared hope. Unfortunately, the easiest kills came against vicious birds gouging on dragon blood. The screams of falling ryders mixed with the agonizing calls of my battling kin.

Crema wasn't spared in the carnage. Rann did her best to keep the griffins at bay, the course of battle pulling her way from the city into the hinterlands beyond. Seeing the peril, I followed them, but there were griffins in my path. Bethy Rann put an arrow in one giant bird and shoved her blade through the eye of another that got a hold of Crema's wing. It wasn't enough. Crema's cry rang in my head as I chomped a griffin head. I turned toward the sound in time to see the dragon falling in a downward spiral, Rann still on her back, firing arrows as they went down. Crema vainly flapped her remaining intact wing and the bloody shreds of the other as I dove for them. The effort only drew the attention of another griffin. It rammed its beak into Crema's throat before I could do a thing about it. The beautiful dragon's neck slumped, and her body went deathly still. Rann's anguished gaze locked with mine. I put everything I had left into my dive, my pain and damaged wings be damned.

Rann called to me over the wind. "Get closer."

As much as it pained me, I couldn't save Crema. As I drew beside her, I was sure that there was nothing left to save except a broken shell. I let loose the anguished song as I had when my mother passed even as I matched Crema's fatal dive, although this rendition was neither as long nor as sorrowful as she deserved given the circumstances. Rann leapt from Crema onto me. Once she secured herself, I broke out of my dive, my roar still ringing through the sky. The other dragons noticed. They stared at me. Something about the song had touched them even through the haze of their bonds. At least, that is what I hoped. It lasted only a moment. For the other dragons, there was still a battle to win. I lost sight of Crema in the melee. I hoped she somehow survived her wounds—she was a dragon, after all—but I doubted it. The wound in her neck was deep.

Even with their reserve griffins, Oster's forces could only hope to save themselves from total annihilation. Despite being smaller and fireless, the horned dragons were agile and their ryders' bows were deadly. Only a handful of griffins remained, and a few strength-giving leeches couldn't change the numbers. A sorrowful horn blast sounded from amidst the Osteran army. Every griffin in the sky turned to the sound. The battle was done—almost.

The Osterans continued retreating. Narsis, Cornethius, and Triton offered no mercy. A snaking line of soldiers hurried back toward the sea. Only when one of my brethren came close enough to attack the fleeing invaders did the few remaining griffins attack.

I was content to let the Osterans leave. There was no telling what else the Pale Wrights had bred in their pits to send against us. I hoped the human ryders who commanded my remaining brethren would have the good sense to feel the same way, but of course my hope didn't last for even ten beats of my wings. King Mendakas had not reigned as long as he had by letting enemy armies escape from his grasp. He had already (with my considerable assistance) devastated most of Oster's griffins. Of course, he would look to finish them and their fleet. The more Oster lost here, the weaker she would be when King Mendakas led the armies of Rolm against the Shard once again. He ordered his remaining dragons to attack.

A wave of Triton's fire sent the remains of the Osteran army to flight in every direction. Their spirit broke along with their lines. Men ran all about, wolves howled in pain, but these posed no real threat. They had nothing left to offer. Galt's gambit had failed terribly.

I sped through the sky, banking west once I'd reached my desired altitude. I soared around DragonPeak to investigate the Osteran fleet. I saw most of their ships had already sailed, with only a pair of intrepid vessels daring to remain to pick up any stragglers.

There was enough starlight reflecting off the waves for Rann to see the ships fleeing as well. "Should we go after them?"

I didn't need to think on that question. "There's been enough death. Let them go their way. I shall go mine."

"Where is that?"

"To the Mizu, to find my lost sister, if I can. To find the secrets my mother didn't have time to share." Or die trying. I'd failed my brethren here in Rolm; if I failed my sister as well, what use was I to anyone? But I wouldn't fail.

"What about the Wall of Fire?"

I thought of the ghastray, Vengeance. Dare I trust such a creature? "I know the way through."

I sensed Rann's surprise, but she didn't question me. She took a hard swallow. "I understand, you must care for your blood. I must do the same."

Her words sent a surge of guilt through me. Rann and her brother had risked their lives to try to free me and my fellow dragons, although I still didn't completely understand why. I spoke impulsively. "Come with me."

I could hardly believe what I had said. Rann was handy with a bow and sword, but I wasn't sure if I wanted her or any human with me.

"Why?"

"You seem to know about that land across the Wall of Fire."

"My destiny is here," Rann said firmly. "I have someone to kill, and much else to do, besides."

"I intend to come back," I assured her. "This is not over. There is hope for my fellow dragons still. We shall be free. My sister shall be flying beside me when I return to liberate my race. Come fly with us. You are worthy."

Before Rann could give me an answer, an ominous shadow crossed the sky: Triton and King Mendakas.

TWENTY-NINE

I didn't change my course.

I flew toward the horizon, away from Rolm, and away from the fleeing Osteran fleet. For a brief moment I still hoped that perhaps the King of Rolm would leave me to my own journey and focus on seeking his prey in the distant sea. Stupid hope—he did not. Triton turned toward me, coming fast. He was old, but still swift. In my current condition, I didn't think I could outfly him.

When the king and his slave dragon were close enough, Mendakas called out, "Bayloo, who is riding you?"

"Bethy Rann, Your Majesty." She said the title with bitterness. Surely, the king had guessed what I was by now.

"Where is my son, Bayloo?"

I beat my wings harder, but Triton kept pace. "I don't know."

The giant dragon's shadow passed over me. He was so close I could feel the wind coming off his wings. "Bayloo, what happened to my son?"

It made no sense to fight Triton if I could avoid it. I told the best story I could muster. "He is in Eladrell. He is unharmed." I could've told him I'd spared his son's life when I could have easily taken it, but I knew that wouldn't help me here.

If the king had more questions, he didn't bother with them at that moment. He was fixed on this battle, this victory. "Bayloo, we must fly to destroy the Osteran ships. When we finish them, Oster will fall to its knees before our dragons even arrive."

I stole a glance at Triton, at his muscled chest, his massive teeth. He had some broken scales but I'd fared worse than he in the battle. I wasn't going to be able to fly away fast enough.

I probably should've said nothing. I should have just pushed myself for more speed to try to escape. Instead, I gave in to my longing to speak to this king of humans. "I'm not yours to command."

I don't know if Mendakas replied. After I spoke, I dove toward the sea, picking up speed from the descent. Then I beat my wings as hard as I could, trying to separate from Triton. The sound of the wind and the beating of my hearts surrounded me. The distance between Triton and I grew for a brief time. I'd given Mendakas a choice: go after me or the Osteran fleet.

I knew that the king salivated for victory over Oster. They had invaded his kingdom, killed so many of his dragons, and besieged his fortress. A man like Mendakas should pursue the enemies of his kingdom.

Instead, he came for me. So much for his final victory. Perhaps he figured he could do both—that the other dragons would destroy the Osterans. More likely he knew a free dragon was a far greater threat than an already weakened Oster.

Triton flew at me. I could've pressed myself for more speed, truly testing my endurance against his, but that would've just delayed the inevitable. I was already tired and in pain. The longer this went on, the worse for me. I needed to conserve some strength to fight Triton.

I spoke to Rann since we had no link. "I do not want to kill my brother dragon, which means you need to kill Mendakas."

"I shall do so with pleasure. I've been waiting most of my life for this."

I didn't understand Rann's hunger for this human's death, but I wasn't going to question it now. Rann wasn't finished talking, though —humans never were. "I want something in return, before you go. You must return me to Rolm, to one particular spot of my choosing."

"Where?"

"First, your promise. Anyplace I ask."

I growled in annoyance. "Is this the time to bargain?"

Rann wasn't intimidated. "Isn't it?"

I grunted my agreement. I'd made too many promises, but this couldn't be avoided. Triton closed in. Mendakas would die.

"Aim true and I shall carry you where you wish, so long as it is not beyond the known lands of Rolm. I make no promises beyond that."

"Done." I heard Rann notch an arrow. "Word has it that his armor is dragon scale. Impenetrable. Only the gap between the neck and helm is vulnerable. A tough target, but I can make it if you can get me a clear, steady shot."

My answer was to bank as sharply as I could. Triton and I came toward each other, nose to nose. But I didn't attempt a direct pass. I didn't want Rann to get roasted by his fire; also, passing a bit high on either side would give Rann the best angle for a shot. Of course, I had to hide the game I played, so I had to pretend that I was actually willing to engage in a straight-on engagement with Triton. Since I wasn't a fire breather, that's what he'd think I wanted—to get close enough for us to tear each other to pieces with claws and teeth.

My brother's jaw drooled saliva as we flew at each other. I knew he'd be anxious to use his flames. Fire breathers think they're so superior. I held my course, giving Triton what he thought he wanted. Of course, Mendakas was no fool, nor was he one to wait for his enemy to take the initiative. He unleashed Triton's breath earlier than I expected—at too distant a range to do any real damage, but in as wide an arc as the dragon could manage. The flames couldn't harm me, particularly at that distance, but they would've roasted Rann. I couldn't let that happen. I banked left, maneuvering sooner than I'd intended. As I changed my direction, Triton's fire stopped. He dipped his neck, giving Mendakas a clear shot at me. The king knew how to use a bow as well as any of his ryders. His arrow punched right through my wing, with a speed and force I didn't expect. I wondered if Mendakas had enchanted magic arrows of some kind—spoils of the war with Ulibon that he'd kept for himself.

He and Triton probably expected me to dive or try to change my course again, but I didn't. The ferocity of the arrow actually saved me. The puncture was a clean one, the hole only the size of the arrow tip. I could still fly, and I did. I had to give Rann her shot. Triton realized what I planned a moment before Rann fired her own arrow. It was a good shot, straight and true. It might even have been lethal if Triton hadn't swerved at the very last moment. The arrow struck Mendakas in the center of his chest, just below his neck. It would've killed most men, but his dragon scale armor saved him. Rann might as well have hit him with a pebble for all the impact it had.

Triton came after me again, positioned for another blast of flame. I tried to keep above him, keeping only my underside exposed and Rann safe on my back. He unleashed his breath; it hurt where I'd been cut and gashed by the griffins. I just didn't have the maneuverability to out-dance Triton in the sky anymore. Eventually, he'd get a shot at my backside and Rann would die. I risked a desperate strike. As Triton's fire faded, I dove back toward him, spinning as I did it. I hoped Rann had the sense to hold on tight instead of trying to use her bow while upside down.

I intended to take a bite of Triton's wing, to maim him so badly he'd have to return to land or risk the death of his ryder. My injuries slowed me. Or maybe Triton was faster than I anticipated. In any case, instead of getting his wing, Triton's tail smacked me in my face —hard. Nothing hits with the force of a dragon tail. My head shook. For a moment I lost all sense of direction. A sharp pain indicated that Mendakas had put another hole in the scales of my hind leg. He was trying to cripple me. Likely he sought to understand what had happened and to make me a slave again. I didn't know how bad the new wound was, but it hurt, and I knew this fight wasn't going my way. I tucked in my wings and grabbed Triton, trying to sink my claws into my larger kin. He wriggled and spun, but I managed to get a front and rear claw on him. With my extra weight attached, we sank in the air. He grunted and snarled, and I did the same. Triton scraped my belly with his claws, yanking several scales off my body. A blast of nearly blinding pain shot through me.

Triton's huge jaws closed on my neck. I thrashed, but he had me. His teeth sank through my armor. I'd be dead in another few moments. I could've ripped his wings with my own claws, but that just would've meant two dead dragons instead of one. I stopped struggling and waited for my brother to finish me.

"Triton, release him." It was Bethy Rann. "Release him or your ryder dies."

My brother's teeth relaxed but didn't leave my neck. We continued to fall from the sky, and it took several precious heartbeats for me to realize that Rann had leapt from my back during the melee and taken King Mendakas by surprise. With the king strapped in his dragon saddle, Rann had been able to outmaneuver him, despite his armor. At the moment, she had a dagger to his throat. Triton didn't crane his neck to look at the situation, but he didn't need to. The link would enable him to sense Mendakas' peril.

We slowed our fall. Rann pressed her advantage. "Last chance, Triton."

Mendakas reeked of venom. "You'll burn slowly for this, girl."

"But my death will mean yours as well, a fate you are so deserving of. Do as I say, or we all die in the sea."

The runes that bound my brother meant that Mendakas would decide his own fate and mine. The king decided to live. The command came through their link. Triton's jaws opened, releasing me. I shoved away into the sky. My injured wing hurt and balked. I managed to keep myself aloft, but not much more than that. There was no way I could outrun Triton, and Rann knew it.

Without my weight dragging him, Triton quickly steadied himself in the air.

Rann spoke loud enough that I could hear. "Triton, take us back to Rolm. Let Bayloo go on his way. Then I'll release your precious king."

No, I screamed inside. *I can't allow another sacrifice.*

Jona had already died for me. Now Rann would as well. Mendakas and Triton would never let her live after this. Because of me. Yet I also didn't see any other way out. I needed to save my sister and I was selfish of my own life.

I let out a roar of frustration. Rann understood me.

"Make this count, Bayloo. Fulfill the quest Great Dawn set you upon. Afterwards return, for a debt is still owed, and this land still has need of you."

I was to go on alone. Something gnawed at my hearts. Did I fear to be alone? I had never been without a ryder, not truly. I had never had my own desires or controlled my own destiny. It was harder than I expected.

Perhaps Rann sensed my hesitation. "You carry hope with you, Bayloo. Now fly, noble dragon. With courage. Find your sister. Then return to us. I too believe there is hope."

I didn't want this gift or this burden, but I took it.

"You have my promise to return. I will not forget you, Bethy Rann."

She laughed. "You have much to learn, Bayloo. I'm sorry I've not the time to teach it all to you. Fly true." Rann kicked Triton's flank. The dragon understood her message even without a rune-link.

I craned my neck to watch Triton fly toward Rolm, leaving me in a lonely sky.

Alone, I flew west, to the Wall of Fire and the lands of the Mizu beyond. There I would find my sister. There I would find the source of the magic that enslaved my race.

I flew to my destiny.

Here concludes Book 1 of The Remembered War.

THANK you for beginning this journey. Writing is my dream, one which becomes reality only through readers like you. If you enjoyed this book, I would be deeply grateful if you could leave a review on Amazon. A few words from you to your fellow readers brings more joy than a barrel of fine ale to a free dragon.

Bayloo's journey continues in **A Dragon's War**, available on Amazon. Get in HERE.

Here is a brief summary: Across the Wall of Fire, in the vast land of Ni-Yota, a civil war rages. It is to this war-torn land that Bayloo's sister has been taken. As he searches, Bayloo is engulfed by the dark machinations of the opposing sides, but more than his sister's life is at stake. To survive the dangers of Ni-Yota, Bayloo must confront the true reason for his mother's desperate plan and his own enslavement. CONTINUE YOUR JOURNEY IN BOOK 2, A DRAGON'S WAR.

You can also get a **free** prequel novella of The Remembered War, A Dragons Doom by joining my mailing list at www. robertvanenovels.com. In those pages you will learn the story of how rune magic was stolen from the dragons and of the beginning of the rise of the Kingdom of Rolm. Signing up also will let me inform you of new releases and other whimsical musings of mine.

These adventures of dragons and magic, of tragedy and triumph, are just beginning. A fantastic adventure awaits, I promise.

--Robert Vane

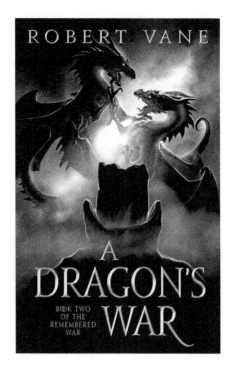

Order a Dragon's War on Amazon.

Printed in Great Britain
by Amazon

73102870R00149